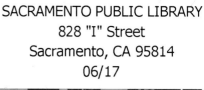

NO GOOD DEED

NO GOOD DEED

GOLDY MOLDAVSKY

Point

Library of Congress Cataloging-in-Publication Data available

ISBN 978-0-545-86751-1

10 9 8 7 6 5 4 3 2 1   17 18 19 20 21

Printed in the U.S.A.   23
First edition, June 2017

Book design by Yaffa Jaskoll

For Alex. This is all your fault.

1

I was sitting in my family's Honda Odyssey, heading toward my destiny, but the GPS kept rerouting. Maybe I should've taken it as a sign. Was a higher power trying to tell me something? That I should turn back? That my fate was not, in fact, to be found in the Catskills of Upstate New York? Even if a higher power wasn't trying to dissuade me from going to summer camp, the higher power in this minivan definitely was.

"Gregor, I just do not understand why you are going to a camp for at-risk teens," my mother said. She was in the driver's seat and sneaking glances at me through the rearview mirror.

"It's a camp for *activist* teens," I said. "And I'm going because this might be the most important thing to ever happen to me."

Even as I said it I knew it sounded melodramatic, but I really did believe that. And not only because it was going to look amazing on my college applications. Camp Save the

World was a brand-new summer camp started by Robert Drill, creator of DrillTech. Not only was he one of the richest people alive, he was also one of the most philanthropic, donating nearly 90 percent of his billions to worthy causes. I'd read his autobiography nine times, and each time the message was clear: Life was about doing good. Robert Drill didn't want to be remembered for the way he changed the tech world, he wanted to be remembered for making the world a better place. He was a personal hero of mine.

So when he started Camp Save the World this year, a summer program for teenagers who wanted to utilize their strengths and talents to make a lasting impression on the world, I had to sign up.

"What will you kids even be doing there?" Mom said. "Are you all going to sit around and make protest signs?"

Honestly, that sounded pretty awesome. "I'm sure there'll be normal camp activities. Swimming. Canoeing."

"So you're just going to sit in a canoe, holding a protest sign? Shouting at people? You could drown!" my mother said. "Did you pack extra underwear?"

"I won't drown, and yes, I did," I said. "Did Dad not explain any of this to you?"

"I tried, son," Dad said. He was in the passenger seat, and while he may have been talking to me, all of his attention was taken up by the enormous, crinkly map in his hands. Dad was sure we'd get there just fine with the paper map, even though Mom already had a GPS mounted on the dashboard. Not to mention the backup GPS app I kept sneaking glances at on my phone. Dad's eyes volleyed from the map to the view out his window, squinting at the unfamiliar country terrain. My father had always lived in a city, first in Mexico as a kid, and then in New York. Upstate was a totally different world than he was used to. "I think we need to take the next right."

I checked my GPS. "Actually, stay on this road," I told my mom. She listened to me, and my father did not protest.

"I told your mother: If this camp is good enough for Ashley Woodstone, then it is good enough for our son. Do you have a crush on Ashley Woodstone, Gregor? Is that why you wanted to come to this camp?"

I hated rolling my eyes in front of my parents. I hated giving them any ammunition to brand me a petulant teen, but my eyes were legitimately in pain from the strain it took not to roll them right now. Thousands of civic-minded kids ages fourteen to eighteen had applied to be campers at Camp Save the World, and I, Gregor Maravilla—a thus far admittedly unremarkable sixteen-year-old from Sunset Park, Brooklyn—had been one of the lucky one hundred to win a spot. So of course all anybody wanted to talk about was Ashley Woodstone.

"I don't have a crush on Ashley Woodstone."

"Are you sure?" Dad said. "She's quite the actress. Katrina's a big fan."

In an effort to get in touch with the mysterious dealings inside my little sister's brain, my father had taken up watching TV and movies with her. My dad, as creepy as it sounded, was probably an expert on all things Ashley Woodstone. Even though there was no way Katrina was a big Ashley Woodstone fan.

"There's no way Katrina is a big Ashley Woodstone fan," I said. "I don't think she started liking Ashley Woodstone until she found out that I'd be going to the same camp as her."

"That is totally not true," Katrina said. She was sitting to my right, and now she elbowed me in the side. "I have always been a huge fan of Ashley Woodstone."

"Fine," I said, deflecting her jabs. "Good for you. Can we stop talking about Ashley Woodstone now?"

Katrina pulled out her phone and held it up to my face. The screen was a frozen still from the video I'd gotten in my welcome email from the camp. I'd seen the video once. I did not need to see it again.

Katrina pressed play.

"Hi there, I'm actress, activist, and altruist Ashley Woodstone," came the voice on the video. "I just want to congratulate all those who won a spot at Camp Save the World. Ever since I heard about Robert Drill's new idea for a camp, I knew I wanted to be a part of it. As you probably already know, when I'm not making movies and winning awards for those movies, I'm out there in the real world, trying to better the lives of others."

The screen transitioned to images of Ashley Woodstone in destitute locations, surrounded by tearstained children.

"I'm there," Ashley said in voice-over, "wiping tears from children's faces, and offering them all of my old belongings." More footage, this time of Ashley Woodstone handing a little girl a pair of pink sequined boots, and a little boy an iPhone. "And I said to myself, 'Hey, I'm a teen, and I've got a campaign to help Save the World too!' That's why I contacted Robert Drill, and I'm happy to announce that the lucky teens who have won spots to the camp will get to join me there. I'll be a camper too!"

Thankfully, Katrina stopped the video and put down her phone. There were a million reasons why I was excited to go to Camp Save the World. The fact that megastar Ashley Woodstone would be there was not one of them. I may have only seen her in one movie, but for reasons that I really did not want to dwell on, I did not like Ashley Woodstone.

"You get to go to camp with Ashley Woodstone and you're being a jerk about it," Katrina said. "Do you have any idea how totally lucky you are?"

"Not that I'm going to try to meet her or anything, but

what if she turns out to be awful?" I said. "Would you like me to tell you if I meet her and she's a total snob?"

"If she's mean it's probably because you deserve it, because you're an idiot who hates everything."

"Mom!" I didn't want to resort to asking my mom to intervene, but seriously, what the hell was this? My twelve-year-old sister didn't get to call me an idiot in front of my parents and get away with it.

"Gregor, be nice to your sister."

I needed to get out of this car. I needed to get to camp already, even if Ashley Woodstone was there.

"If I do meet Ashley Woodstone," I whispered to Katrina, "I'm not going to mention you at all."

"If you do meet Ashley, she'll hate you just as much as I do," Katrina said. "You wanna know why, Gregor? Because you're a loser. You're a bigger loser than Anton."

"She's not wrong," Anton said. My older brother sat to my left, taking up way too much space, as usual. "I'm pretty weird, but you're definitely weirder."

"Who asked you!" I said. "What the hell are you even doing here? You're nineteen! You're in college!"

Anton shrugged and watched the passing foliage out the window. Technically he was on summer break, but that still did not explain his interest in seeing me off to camp. "I thought you could use some brotherly advice. Instructions on being cool."

Anton was greasy, pasty, and inconvienent. Easily mistaken for a human-sized zit. I seriously doubted he would have anything helpful to say on that front.

"Look, this camp is a big deal," I announced to the car. I clicked through my phone until I found the article I was looking for. "Buzzfeed even wrote about it. 'Five Reasons Why We Wish We Were Young Enough to Attend Camp Save the World.'"

Anton whipped out his own phone. "Funny. I found another article on that site, only this one's called 'Five Ways Robert Drill Could've Spent His Money That Would've Been More Productive Than Spending It on a Camp for Entitled Teenagers.'"

"It does not say that." I looked over at Anton's phone. I was sure he was joking. He wasn't.

"An entire camp for social justice warriors."

"'Social justice warrior' is a derogatory term," I said.

"Which is why I used it in a derogatory manner."

"It's a camp for young humanitarians."

"You're a sixteen-year-old going to camp as a *camper*," Anton said. "Most people your age go to camp as counselors. How does that make you feel?"

I didn't need Anton to tell me that going to summer camp as a teenager wasn't something one would necessarily deem "cool." But spending the summer with a community of people who thought like me—who were passionate at a young age about using their skill sets to make the world a better place—was better than how I usually spent every summer: stocking the shelves at Mom's grocery store and going home to watch old episodes of *The Golden Girls*.

"Don't tease your brother about camp," Dad said. "Anton has his YouTube videos and Katrina is the best speller in her grade, but Gregor doesn't have anything like that in his life yet. And he's obviously looking to this camp to find himself and make us proud. This camp and Ashley are obviously very important to him." It was always impossible to tell if my dad was being sarcastic through his accent, but then again, I was pretty sure my dad didn't know what sarcasm was.

"Okay, I'm just going to state this openly right now so that everyone can hear me," I said, my voice appropriately raised and hopefully authoritative. "I do not care about Ashley Woodstone. I've barely seen any of her movies. I think her being at Camp Save the World is weird and probably the result of nepotism and it distracts from what we're really there to do. I will be avoiding her."

Dad smiled at me and then at Mom. "He has a crush on Ashley Woodstone."

"Oh, honey, you have a crush on a movie star?" Mom said. "Just make sure not to get your heart broken if she ignores you. Did you pack the Band-Aids?"

I slumped down in my seat.

8

"Rule number one for not being a total ass in front of Ashley Woodstone," Anton said. "Now listen carefully, because this advice will alter your existence and open up entire worlds for you."

I had given up on protesting, which I guess Anton mistook as me listening.

"Don't. Be. Weird."

"Great advice," Dad and I said at the same time, though our tones were totally different.

"If I know you at all, I know that you packed your Superman poster," Anton continued. "Don't put it up."

My Superman poster was in fact at the bottom of my trunk, carefully folded in half. Putting it up was the first thing I planned to do when I got to camp. "What's wrong with my Superman poster?"

"What's *not* wrong with your Superman poster? First off, you're not seven years old."

"Superman has gotten really dark in the past few years," I muttered.

"It's bad enough that you chose to wear a Superman shirt on your first day of camp," Anton said.

"There's a boy in my class who likes Superman too," Katrina said. "He eats his own snot."

"How much longer until we get to camp?" I asked my parents.

"According to this map we're about one hour away, son," Dad said.

I looked at my GPS. We were only ten minutes away. Good.

"I don't know why you have to go all the way to the wilderness to learn how to help people," my mom said. She would not let this go. "Why can't you do something like your brother? His YouTube videos help so many people, and he doesn't even have to leave the basement to do that."

"Anton isn't helping anyone with his YouTube videos. They're just him playing Minecraft."

"And he makes so much money from the ads," Mom said.

"Face it, Gregor," Anton said. "I'm something you will never be: famous."

"You're famous *on the internet*."

"So you admit it."

I'd officially had enough. I tried to make my mind go blank, tried to picture green pastures and kickball and people coming together to save the world. Because there was more to life than being famous. "There are children in the world who are starving!"

The car erupted in groans. It was the worst possible response to that statement. And exactly the sort of mind-set I needed to change. I needed to make people care about hungry children. This—right here—was the reason I was going to Camp Save the World.

"Gregor, please don't talk about such things right now," Dad said. "You'll upset your grandfather."

"¿Qué?" Grandpa Maravilla said from the back. The minivan was big enough that my entire family had crammed into it to see me off. Including my grandfather.

"Nada, Papa, los niños te quieren mucho," Dad said. "Isn't that right, kids?"

"Sí," we all said.

"You'd be smart to take my advice," Anton whispered. "Out of the two of us I'm the only one with a girlfriend."

Darcy. Anton's girlfriend. She was premed, so she was more ambitious than Anton was about anything. I didn't know much about Darcy because she wasn't much of a talker. It was impossible to see her without a stack of notebooks in her hands, furiously flipping pages or taking notes, making more crinkly paper noise than actual verbal noise. Her ponytail was forever coming undone, no matter how many pencils she stuck into her hair. "There's just the minor issue of your girlfriend paying more attention to her studies than to you," I said.

"She's here, isn't she!" Anton barked back.

I turned in my seat and looked over the back of it. Darcy had been so quiet this entire ride that I'd almost forgotten she was there. Her face was, naturally, obscured by a book. It should've surprised me that my brother's girlfriend would want to see me off to camp even though she'd hardly ever said a word to me, but the truth was, it didn't. My family did things together, despite how I felt about it.

"Okay, forget Ashley Woodstone for a second," Anton said. "This camp is going to be full of other girls. Girls who might actually talk to you about hungry kids or dying antelope or whatever if you play your cards right."

I was listening.

"For five weeks you're going to be bunking with these girls in a sleepaway camp, away from parental supervision. Have you even given any thought to that?"

Weirdly, no. I'd only been thinking of how great camp was going to be. I'd thought of the camaraderie between people with similar interests and life goals, the friendships that would inevitably form, the great "meeting of minds" between me and the other campers. But I'd not given any thought to one of the things that would undoubtedly contribute to that greatness.

"Girls," Anton said, lowering his voice so our parents couldn't hear. "You know what camp is good for? Firsts. First kisses. First times. First bases, if you catch my drift."

I stared at Anton, and not because he was being weird, but because he was probably right.

"Dude," Anton said, his voice so low I was basically just reading his lips at this point. "Everybody gets laid at summer camp."

I didn't like talking to my brother about getting laid, but still, my mind lingered on what he'd just said. On girls. Specifically on girls in summertime, which presented them in a hazy, rosy glow. But the idea of "firsts" was just as appealing as the idea of girls. There were so many "first times" of things I'd yet to experience. Camp could change all that.

The road was narrowing, the woods getting fuller, so I knew we were getting close to the camp. I looked out the window. I still couldn't see the camp, but up ahead, there was a kid standing on the side of the dirt road, clad in all black and holding a picket sign. I couldn't make out what the sign said until we got much closer, only a few feet from him. And then I read it.

DOWN WITH CAMP!

"Turn back!" the kid shouted at us. "Camp is for fascist conformists!"

"What was that?" Mom said. "Why was that boy yelling at us? I don't know if I like this camp, Gregor."

But before I could tell her again that this was likely going to be the best place on earth, we were driving under the big archway with huge letters spelling out my destiny.

CAMP SAVE THE WORLD

There was an excitement bubbling up in me—butterflies and swelling music and all that. The car hadn't even fully stopped before I was reaching across Katrina to open the door. "Come on, come on," I said. When the car did stop, I practically pushed my way out. I grabbed my duffel and trunk from the back and looked around.

"Have a good time at camp, son," Dad said.

"Try and stay away from the canoes," Mom said.

"Get me Ashley Woodstone's autograph," Katrina said.

"Remember: Resist the urge to be weird," Anton said.

Darcy smiled, but really she was just opening her mouth to pull out the pencil she was chewing on.

I went to Grandpa to say my final goodbyes. "I'm gonna make you proud, Grandpa Maravilla. I'm going to save the world."

"¿Qué?"

I smiled and gave him a hug. Then I turned to face the camp again. And I didn't look back.

2

I did actually have to look back one last time. One of the rules at Camp Save the World was that campers were not allowed to have any electronic devices. "We don't have that many rules at this camp," said a man whose name tag read JIMMY! HEAD COUNSELOR! "Rule number one is to save the world. Rule number two is to have fun. And rule number three is no cell phones allowed." He then handed me a piece of paper with rules four through twenty-three and sent me chasing after my parents to leave my cell phone with them.

But after that, I was on my way to my new home for the next five weeks: Cabin 8.

Cabin 8 looked mostly like the summer camp cabins I'd seen in movies and TV: bare wood walls, some dressers, and a pair of bunk beds. And sitting on one of the top bunks was a guy stuffing paintbrushes into a satchel.

"Hi," I said. "I'm Gregor."

The guy—shaggy, shoulder-length blond hair pulled back

beneath a red bandana—looked down at me, a crease between his eyebrows.

I tried again. "What's up?"

He continued to stare. I attempted to dispel the awkwardness by chuckling, but to my surprise, forced laughter in a quiet cabin with a confused person watching was in fact the textbook definition of awkward. I hauled my stuff toward the bottom bunk but stopped when I noticed a photograph taped to the wall right next to it. In it, a perfect-looking African American guy was standing with his golden retriever on what looked to be the top of a mountain.

"I'm guessing this isn't you," I said. Almost as soon as I said it I wanted to kick myself. Was that supposed to be a joke? I wasn't even sure, and by the looks of it, Paintbrush Dude wasn't sure either. I swallowed and scratched an imaginary itch on my forehead. "Sorry, did I say something, or . . . ?"

"He doesn't speak English."

I spun around at the sound of the voice. The perfect-looking guy from the photograph was standing in the doorway, looking even more perfect in person. I was tall, but he was taller and much less gawky. His face was all strong angles and confidence. He walked over to shake my hand. "I'm Win Cassidy."

"Great name," I said. "I mean, I'm Gregor Maravilla."

We both turned back to Paintbrush Dude, who was still watching us, a dubious expression on his face.

"I think he's from Italy or Albania or Croatia or something," Win said. "All he knows how to say is 'I like paint.'"

That couldn't be right. "What's your name?" I asked him.

In a heavy, indiscriminate accent, Paintbrush Dude cleared his throat and very deliberately answered, "I like. Paint."

"I'm calling him I Like Paint," Win said. "ILP for short."

An immigrant kid who didn't speak English being called I Like Paint? This was not okay on so many levels. I felt disgusted and outraged on his behalf. And although this unnamed kid looked kind of angry at me for some reason, I wasn't about to let this go unaddressed. "Isn't that kind of problematic?"

"Oh, definitely," Win said. I was surprised he agreed with me. He stood with his legs akimbo and folded his arms over his chest, regarding our bunkmate seriously. "But he's really not giving us much to work with. Plus, I think it could be potentially more damaging if we gave him a totally new 'Americanized' name, like Brian or Todd, you know? But don't worry, it's absolutely a priority of mine to find out ILP's real name as soon as possible and set things straight."

ILP—he was already ILP in my mind, despite how wrong I felt about calling him that—didn't seem to care. He gathered up his paintbrushes and hopped off the top bunk, shooting us one last confused look before he left.

Win rummaged through the top drawer of one of the

dressers. He had the air of someone who'd been at this camp forever and already had a set routine and knew where everything was and had to rush off to meet his already large group of friends. "I gotta go, but I'll catch you at orientation?"

"Sure!" I said.

It was already starting to feel like this camp was a new beginning for me. Like my life was finally about to start. And like Anton was wrong about everything.

I went over to the other bunk bed and dumped my things over the bottom bunk. I took out my Superman poster. Everybody else in the world was obsessed with the latest Superman movie, which had just come out two months ago. I was not. And in my own small protest against the shitshow that was that movie, my poster represented Superman from the comics. I pinned it on the wall, just over my pillow.

This was going to be a good summer. I could feel it.

When I was thirteen years old I stood in line for an hour to get Robert Drill's autograph. He was signing copies of his autobiography at one of the big bookstores in Manhattan. It was a Sunday and it was the first time I'd ever taken the subway by myself.

Robert Drill was barely forty then, and he'd already done so much with his life. He'd started in game programming as a wunderkind at fifteen, and then he'd moved on from gaming to coding to create one of the biggest social media applications in the world. And then he'd started DrillTech, the foremost corporation in the advancement of modern technology. But instead of just sitting on all his billions, Drill had started the Robert Drill Foundation, donating the majority of his money to worthy causes all over the world. More than the tech stuff or the billionaire status, *that's* what he was known for. Helping people. To me, he was a real-life hero. He may not have had the super strength or special gadgets or spandex suit or whatever, but he was still a hero: blessed with power and using it for good. Obviously, I wanted to be just like him.

I told him so when I gave him my book to sign that day in the bookstore. And I'll never forget what he said to me. He said: "You have the potential for greatness. You could feed the children of the world one day."

I never forgot those words. They shaped my Feed the Children campaign. They shaped my entire life.

Orientation didn't start for another hour, so I had time to take a tour of the camp grounds. Even though I hadn't left New York, this part of it—the country—felt totally different. It even smelled different, like earth and rain and sunlight weren't just things that I could see and feel but things I could breathe in with every deep inhale. Coming from Brooklyn, I wasn't used to seeing this much green all around me, or this much sky.

The camp was flanked by a lake and the woods. The girls' cabins were spread out along the water, while a row of boys' cabins was on the other side, next to the playing fields. Between the two sections of cabins was the Counselors' House, a place big enough to have a wraparound porch. The office was on the first floor, while the sleeping quarters were on the second and third floors. I thought maybe the Counselors' House was set up between the boys' and girls' cabins as a sort of buffer to make sure girls and boys did not intermingle late-night (rule number seven: no after-hours fraternization between campers). If that was the case, the layout was archaically heteronormative.

The clubhouse and the mess hall were both on the west side of the camp, and tucked away in the east was the recreational room. A brief stop inside showed me that there was a large flat-screen TV hooked up to a DVD player hanging on a wall and a couple of couches and beanbags facing it. At the other side of the room was a Ping-Pong table, and along the other walls were shelves, sparsely filled with books. I picked up a few to get a taste for the selection. *The Hunger Games* and Robert Drill's autobiography.

Outside the rec room, there was a group of campers I hadn't noticed before, painting the back wall. It looked like they were painting a mural. ILP was among them, the only one on a stepladder. He was drawing a picture of the earth and other kids were already filling in some of the countries, each painting in a different color.

It was heartening to see campers working together and supporting each other with their causes—and camp hadn't even officially started yet. This was exactly the sort of thing I'd never see at school. Kids helping each other out. I hadn't even met most of these people, but I already respected my fellow campers.

The great thing about this camp was that everyone here was passionate about something. It was easy to be cynical about stuff. Most everyone I knew was cynical about something. Like my family, for example. They were all cynical about what this camp—or I—could accomplish. It was hard being an idealist in that kind of environment. But here, everyone was an idealist. To get into Camp Save the World you couldn't just have a general desire to do good; you had to have a documented record of all the good you'd been doing thus far, with a focus on a specific cause that was close to your heart.

At this camp, you weren't what you'd always been. You weren't the guy in the band, or the kid with the deadbeat dad, the pastor's daughter, the dweeb who sits in the corner. Here, you were—to put it mildly—the champion of the most worthy cause, the foremost expert in your field. Here, you were amazing. I was surrounded by campers who were bound to become interesting people at college parties.

I knew that together we could make a difference. And for

once I didn't feel like a total nerd for having such a corny, optimistic point of view.

A girl with short hair and bangs that fell above her eyebrows half skipped, half jogged toward me with a pink bakery box in her hands. "Have a cupcake," she said, out of breath but exuberant. "It's vegan. My campaign is Go Vegan."

I bit into my surprisingly delicious vegan cupcake as she took off. I loved it here already.

The playing fields were the last part of the camp grounds I had yet to explore. It was called the playing fields, but it was really just one vast blanket of grass, flanked by the woods, a basketball court, and a rink. Knowing nothing about sports, I had no idea if the field was ideal for baseball or football, but for the first time in my life I was excited to try out either of those games. That was another part about camp that I was happy about. There was an innocence to it. Playing ball and running barefoot through the grass, and girls wearing awesomely small breathable fabrics and . . . people getting it on in public?

The couple I spotted caught me off guard. I'd nearly stumbled over them on my way to the rink. A guy and a girl, on the ground, wedged up against the waist-high rink wall, fervently making out.

They hadn't seen me yet, so I ducked into the rink before

they could. The camp was basically made up of uneven terrain—dirt, gravel, hills, roots, stumps. But the rink was smooth concrete, so of course that was where I tripped. At least there was no one to see me land on my shoulder.

Then I heard the unmistakable scraping sounds of skateboard wheels, thunderous as they barreled toward me. I was face-to-face with the board, sure it was about to crash into me, when it stopped abruptly, a hunter-green Toms shoe stepping off it.

The shoe belonged to a foot, which itself belonged to an ankle. I followed it up to a pair of drawstring pants, cinched at the cuffs. I followed the pants up till they came to rest lazily on slender hips, exposing a sliver of skin. White tee. And then there was her face.

Rosy. Glowing. Apple-cheeked. She was East Asian with long black hair split down the middle. It was probably time to stop staring, to break up this unbearable awkwardness with a few words. Any combination would do, but I could not let go of that face yet. She had a beauty mark on her mouth, right where top lip met skin. There was another speck on the top of her cheek, like it'd fallen there, delicate as a tiny snowflake. Like she'd been sprinkled with the stuff and tried to shake it off. Two beautiful specks, turned dark by the sun.

"You okay?"

I blinked, reconfigured myself. "Walking is . . . harder than it looks."

She smirked around a piece of gum in her mouth. As she chewed I had weird thoughts that involved me wanting very badly to be gum.

"I didn't think anyone was here."

"I was sitting against the wall," she said. "This is the only good place to skate around here. And smoke."

Now that she mentioned it I could detect the remnants of cigarette smoke on her. Before this moment smoking was never something that I wanted to do, but now all I wanted was to sit against the rink wall and share a cigarette with her. I could imagine passing it back and forth between our fingers, talking about the meaning of life and falling in love or whatever.

"What's your name?"

"Gregor Maravilla."

"I'm Poe."

"Like Edgar Allan?"

"Like Nicolas Cage's character in *Con Air*: Cameron Poe. My parents were huge fans."

"Oh! Did you know Tim Burton wanted Nic Cage to play Superman in a movie? It didn't work out but there are pictures of him in the costume and—"

"It's after Edgar Allan."

Had I just gone into the Nic Cage *Superman* story again? I was never dumber than when talking to a hot girl. My mouth's first response to beauty was always word vomit. A long moment stretched between us, and in its awkward silence, so much was confirmed. Mostly, that Poe was obviously the smarter and more sophisticated of the two of us. And I was a childish idiot who believed everything he heard and couldn't go five minutes without talking about Superman. I had to save this moment before it killed me.

"There are people about to have sex right outside the rink."

I was so useless. Poe's eyes went wide, and she skated to the wall, not stopping until she was leaning over the side. I caught up to her and pointed the pair out. They hadn't graduated to anything more than sloppy kissing yet. Except for face licking. There was aggressive face licking now. Poe watched them with bare curiosity. I tried not to watch Poe with bare curiosity myself.

"Wow," she said. "They're really going at it."

"They obviously don't know about rule number seven."

"You a stickler for rules?"

"No," I said too quickly. "I hate rules." *Stop talking.*

"Nothing like watching two people going at it to put you in the mood . . ."

I loved this camp. I loved it so much.

". . . or totally turn you off," Poe continued. She pushed off the wall and was now rolling away. "Nice meeting you, Gregor."

And I was left to watch her go, wondering what flavor her gum was with only the lingering fantasy of my lips on hers.

3

Orientation was at the clubhouse. Rows of folding chairs had been set to face a small stage just a foot above the floor at the head of the room. The stage setting was complete with a red theater curtain covering the wall. By the time I got there, most of the seats were already filled with campers. The requisite panic of choosing the right seat—the same one that I'd always felt at the start of every new class on the first day of every new school year—set in, but then I spotted my bunkmate Win. He was waving me over and patting the empty seat next to him.

The room buzzed with excited chatter. People were whispering, animated, huddled together and trading stories. I was sure everyone was talking about their campaigns and the things they'd done to merit a spot at this camp, but as I made my way to Win I realized that they weren't talking about that at all. In fact, they were talking about one specific thing.

"Is anyone here her bunkmate?" one girl said. "That would be so cool."

"I hear her cause has roots in feminism."

"There's no way she's here with a feminism campaign, 'cause that's what I'm here for."

"Whatever. I just want to see Ashley Woodstone in person. She's so pretty."

The myth of Ashley Woodstone had followed me from my family's car into the camp and she hadn't even made an appearance yet. Awesome.

"She's probably just looking for some good PR now that the world knows her boyfriend was a psychopath."

This made me stop for a moment. I had to admit, I was curious despite myself. But the word "psychopath" got thrown around all the time (which was really insensitive to people with mental health issues), so I didn't think much of it. Everyone here may have been obsessed with Ashley Woodstone, but nobody seemed to be asking the question that I thought was most pertinent: *Why the hell was a movie star even at this camp?*

I got to Win. "Thanks for saving me a seat."

"No problem. I know how stressful it can be finding a suitable seat partner."

Somehow I doubted that about him. "Yeah, especially when all anyone wants to talk about is Ashley Woodstone."

Win nodded. "I know, right? People are all antsy, waiting for her to show up. But I get it, she's famous." He was playing aloof, but I caught him discreetly surveying the crowd, probably checking to see if Ashley had shown up yet.

I didn't want to talk about Ashley. But. "I heard somebody say something about her having an . . . unstable boyfriend."

"You don't know?"

I shook my head.

Win stared at me, eyebrows raised. "You been livin' under a rock, buddy? He's one of The Ruperts." Win was about to say more when our head counselor stepped onto the stage.

"Hello there, everyone!" Jimmy said, taking a deep breath and smiling wide at the crowd. He was the same guy who'd given me the list of rules earlier. Jimmy looked to be in his late twenties, over six feet tall and broad-shouldered, with dirty-blond hair that fell around his ears in overgrown curls. He had the physique of a jock but the geeky nervous excitement that I recognized in myself. I could see it in the smile on his face. I could even see it in the way he clutched the clipboard in his hands. "I'm Jimmy, your head counselor, and I want to personally welcome you to Camp Save the World!"

All thoughts of Ashley Woodstone left me and I got caught up in cheering along with everyone else.

"That's what I'm talking about!" Jimmy said. "You're all very special campers, and you'll be getting to know each other throughout the day, but before we get to that, I have a special surprise for you."

28

His hand was on the curtain. Suddenly I was convinced Robert Drill was behind there. He had to be here somewhere. I knew he had a business to run, but this was his camp. There was no way he was going to miss the first day without making an appearance.

"Did somebody say Ashley Woodstone?"

Literally no one had said Ashley Woodstone, and yet I'd never seen a crowd grow suddenly so alert so quickly before. Everybody turned toward the door at the sound of her voice, and there she stood. Movie star Ashley Woodstone, in the flesh. The first thing I noticed about her—and there was a lot to notice—was her smile. It was the biggest thing she was wearing.

And then I noticed what she was actually wearing. It was a ridiculous outfit. By my count she was offending at least three different people in the audience. She wore a gigantic fur coat, lederhosen, and a Tupac Shakur T-shirt. I wasn't sure how the Tupac shirt was offensive, but since she was a white girl born way after his death, surely it had to be.

She walked down the center aisle, trailed by an entourage of three people: a gawky man sweating in a three-piece suit, a woman with big hair, and a huge man who looked like he was maybe chiseled out of stone.

Ashley stood before the curtain, her three companions standing aside. Jimmy stepped off the stage like he didn't want

29

to get in the way. This was definitely not the surprise he had in mind for us.

"Hello, new friends!" Ashley said. "I know what you all must be thinking. 'How does she get her hair like that?' Well, that would be the work of my fabulous hairstylist, Angela, over there."

Angela, the woman with the big hair, waved, and Ashley clapped. "Give it up for Angela!" The campers followed her instruction and clapped. "Standing next to her is Harold Barbowitz, lawyer extraordinaire." More scattered applause. "And there's Pika, my bodyguard. Unfortunately, Harold and Angela can't be here all summer long, but they have graciously agreed to help me demonstrate just what my cause is all about."

"This should be interesting," Win whispered.

"My campaign is called Eat Dirt. I know what you're asking yourselves. 'Does Ashley Woodstone actually want us to eat dirt? Is that what she's saying? That sounds kinda kooky.' Well, friends . . . that's exactly what I'm saying!"

Ashley paused here, clearly for effect, which was good because I needed a moment to wrap my mind around what she'd just said. Ashley Woodstone wanted us to eat dirt. She was not joking. I looked around to see if the rest of the campers were just as dumbfounded as I was, but everyone stared at Ashley with rapt attention. Even Win, who clearly wasn't expecting Ashley's presentation to be *this* interesting.

"Not only is dirt kind of secretly delicious, it's also incredibly good for you," Ashley said. "Studies conducted by independent researchers have concluded that the kind of dirt on which this very camp stands is rich with organic minerals and life-sustaining properties that are good for your skin, hair, and nails, not to mention it's a great way to cleanse your arteries. I truly believe that the only reason eating dirt—or any naturally growing thing in nature—isn't as popular as it should be is because people are just uninformed on the matter. That's why I'm ready to be a spokesperson for dirt. Think of all the hungry people we could serve if they only knew the benefits of eating dirt."

If I was hearing Ashley correctly, my campaign was completely useless, apparently.

"And now," Ashley went on, "my assistants will demonstrate how easy and delicious eating dirt can be. Harold, Angela . . ."

The big bodyguard took two earthenware pots out of a bag and handed them to Harold and Angela. They looked into their pots warily. Because of course they would. Because they were about to eat dirt. Was anyone else seeing this? Was this actually happening? I looked around, searching for hidden cameras. Surely this was all part of a movie she was filming. At the very least, this had to be a kind of performance art. I scooted closer to the edge of my seat. Harold and Angela each dug their hands into their pots and came back with a handful of loose soil. Angela went first. She brought the dirt to her mouth, made some closed-mouth munching noises and movements, and let the dirt fall back into the pot. "Mmmm," she said. "So good." She was pretending to eat the dirt. Like when a toddler makes you a special dish from his play kitchen using plastic food and you have to pretend to eat and love it for his benefit.

"No, Angela, eat it for real," Ashley said. "The campers are ready to see it. They need to see regular people eating it. You too, Harold."

Harold and Angela looked at each other and seemed to speak telepathically. Then they looked at Ashley. Her grin never wavered, clearly trying to reassure them. They both brought a handful of dirt to their mouths and munched at the same time. All any of us could do was watch and wait as two adults dutifully and painfully slowly ate dirt at the request of their teenage boss.

"Holy shit," Win said.

We waited for them to swallow. Neither of them had made the requisite gulping motion yet. But then Harold gagged and ran to stage right to bend over and cough out all of the mud clogging his throat. Angela spit it out.

For the first time since I'd seen it, the smile on Ashley's face began to fade. But as soon as it did, her bodyguard took the stage, grabbed the pot out of Harold the lawyer's hands, craned his neck back, opened his mouth wide, and poured the dirt into it. He munched and swallowed and never took his eyes off of us. I can honestly say I've never been more frightened of someone in my life.

32

Ashley's smile was back in place as she turned to us again. "See? Easy. Thanks for your time!"

Was she kidding with this? Was this some sort of—

All of the campers jumped to their feet, cheering and hollering and clapping so loud I wasn't sure we'd seen the same presentation. Even Win was clapping. "Are you serious?" I said.

"It was a little strange, but she was earnest. And if the science is sound, then how bad could it be?"

Ashley left the stage and was replaced by Jimmy once again, who clapped and smiled, seemingly awed by her display.

"Well, wasn't that something?" he said. "A wonderful surprise. And I've got another one for you. A lot of you have been asking me about him . . ."

A few people in the audience gasped. I was one of them. Was I right? Was Robert Drill himself going to come out from behind those curtains?

"Yes," Jimmy said. "Mr. Robert Drill himself would like to tell you all something . . ." He grabbed the cord to pull the curtain back. I leaned closer in my seat. ". . . via prerecorded video!"

Jimmy pulled back the curtain to reveal a huge screen with Robert Drill's smiling face on it.

Oh. I slumped back in my seat.

"Hello there, campers," Drill said, "and welcome . . . to Camp Save the World!" The music that started playing must've been straight out of a Spielberg movie, it was so epic. And even though I was disappointed that we were only seeing Robert Drill via video instead of in real life, the music was already lifting my spirits. It was the perfect soundtrack for kids ready to save the world. "When I created this camp I had these founding principles in mind: All ideas are valid. All campers are to be respected. And have fun! Speaking of fun, I've got a surprise for you. I was so astounded by the projects that you kids are working on that I thought to myself, well, camp just isn't enough. You need a prize."

If he didn't have our attention before, he definitely had it now.

"Yes, a prize. At the end of your five weeks here, I will award a special prize to the camper who shows the most enterprise in getting their cause off the ground, be it through action, example, or just sheer devotion. A special point system will be implemented, awarding points to the campers who demonstrate quantifiable growth in their activism duties. At the end of the summer, the camper with the most points will win an internship with the Robert Drill Foundation, where they will spend next summer in our Florida offices, side by side with me, making a real change in the world. So good luck, campers. Get creative! Start saving the world! And may the best man—or person!—win."

Like Win had said. Holy shit.

4

I don't want to say that Robert Drill's announcement of the internship irrevocably changed things at camp, but there was no denying that things were different now. A few people were still talking about Ashley Woodstone's bizarre Eat Dirt presentation: "I think it's symbolic for the mistreatment of women throughout history," one girl within earshot said. "I think it's a protest against a capitalist society," another guy said. (Was I the only one paying attention? The girl was advocating *eating dirt*.) But mostly people were talking about what had already come to be known as "The Prize."

An internship with Robert Drill himself—in the paradise land that was Florida—helping to change people's lives. Truth is, it was all I could think about too. Working closely together with my hero? I had come to this camp for a reason, but now I had a purpose. All thoughts of the innocence of camp and working together with new friends were now totally eclipsed by the promise of The Prize. Winning

35

the internship could change my life. But I had no idea how to do it.

We knew very little about The Prize or how to win it. Robert Drill's video had been vague: Show your true activism spirit and you'll get points. All any of us could do was guess how.

I think the bonfire dinner was meant to be a sort of mixer for us to get to know one another. Instead, it turned into a platform for us to show off how good we were at protesting. Since there were no instructions on how to win points for The Prize, it was up to every camper to be creative. We had to prove that we weren't only great activists but the best activist here. To that end, people were already starting to flex their activism muscles.

There was a girl circling the fire with a picket sign that read SAVE THE TREES. She was trailed on her march by a girl with a picket sign that read SMOKE KILLS! (It originally read SMOKING KILLS, but she'd crossed out the NG and turned the I into an E.) And behind them was yet another protester. His sign said JUST SAY NO TO DRUGS. I wasn't entirely sure what his protest had to do with the bonfire.

Meanwhile, the only thing I was showing off was how good I was at eating. I sat on a log, balancing a plate of potato salad on my knees. I could probably figure out a way to make this whole bonfire play into my Feed the Children campaign somehow. I could stand up and make a speech to anyone who'd listen about all the food that would probably go to waste tonight. But any efforts at all to form a coherent string of words on the subject were squashed anytime I caught a glimpse of Poe.

She sat on a log on the other side of the fire, the orange firelight dancing across her smiling face, making her look otherworldly. Well, more otherworldly than she already was. She was talking to some people, Win among them. They were laughing. Sharing jokes. Too comfortable to bother with protesting, and knowing that one of them would probably win the internship anyway. I could be one of those people. I could just get up, walk over there, and start a conversation. Pick up where we left off, tell her how much I enjoy the works of Edgar Allan Poe.

"Are you reciting 'The Raven' to yourself?"

I turned to my left. Sitting on the other end of the log was a girl I hadn't noticed before.

"Nope." *Was I?*

"Are you sure? Because it sounded like you were. And it also sounded like you didn't know it very well."

"I'm absolutely sure I wasn't reciting poetry to myself," I lied. "Thanks for asking."

She scooted over until she was right next to me and stuck out her hand. "Feminism," she said.

"Excuse me?"

"My campaign is Feminism. What's yours?"

"Oh. Feed the Children."

"Hi, Feed the Children."

"Uh, that's not my na—"

"I'm glad to see I'm not the only one not protesting right now."

I nodded. "People are really getting into it."

"It's like, I get it, we've all got a mission, but we should be using this time to network."

Another reminder that I should have been mingling instead of sitting by myself and stuffing my face with potato salad. I suddenly wondered if I was late to the game, if I should have been forming strategies or alliances or something weird like that. "For the record, I consider myself a feminist," I said.

Someone snickered beside me and then said, "But do you consider yourself a masculist?" He was wearing a sleeveless shirt, so I could tell that he was ripped. Every time he plucked a baby carrot off his plate the muscles beneath his olive-toned skin seemed to pop in exclamation.

"What?" I said.

"I couldn't help overhearing your discussion," he said. "It's a simple question, Feed the Children. Do you support the masculism movement like you support the feminism one?"

"You're gross," Feminism told him.

"Not surprised you feel that way about a man," he said.

"I don't see a man here," she said.

The guy turned to me and smirked. "Women, am I right?"

This whole conversation was increasingly weird, but more than anything I was just confused. "Who are you?"

"Men's Rights," he said.

"That's a cause?"

"Not only is it a cause, it's the cause that's going to win me a trip to Florida next summer. But good luck winning The Prize, Feed the Children. That is, unless Win Cassidy manages to beat you to it."

"Win?" I said, looking over to see my bunkmate still talking to Poe. "What's his campaign?"

"End Hunger," Win said. I'd left Men's Rights behind to interrupt Win and Poe's little party, curiosity getting the better of me.

"End H-hunger?" I stammered. My efforts to feed children had never felt so useless.

"Hey, G," Poe said. *G*. Nobody had ever called me G before. I kind of liked it. "Aren't you gonna ask what my campaign is?"

"Of course, yeah."

"My cause is QUILTBAG."

Quiltbag. I wasn't sure of the details, but it sounded like a sweet campaign. My mind automatically went to Poe knitting a quilt, warm and cozy under the weight of it. Did she deliver the quilts to homeless people? In bags, perhaps?

I was about to ask her when Win leaned over to say, "QUILTBAG stands for Queer or Questioning, Undecided, Intersex, Lesbian, Transgender, Bisexual, Asexual, and Gay."

The quilt disappeared from my daydream, and all that was left was the pointy knitting needle. "Gay?"

"Or genderqueer," Poe said. "I'm the head of the Gay-Straight Alliance at my school. I also started a support group and hotline outside of school."

"Cool!" I said. I nodded and smiled. "Really cool."

I don't know why I kept saying "cool." I was a broken record, and my mind kept skipping on the possibility that this meant that Poe was probably gay. I know I'd only been crushing on her for a few hours, but still, the crushing was all-consuming. And now I was just crushed. But then I immediately kicked myself for dwelling on that, because I seriously should not have been thinking of Poe's sexuality in terms of my crush on her. Poe's sexuality was absolutely none of my business.

"I consider myself an ally," I said.

Poe smirked and seemed to share a subtle look with Win. "Cool."

Her "cool" was punctuated by a speeding football that

came out of nowhere and soared right onto my plate. It splattered potato salad on my shirt. Yes, I was still holding my plate of potatoes. I jumped up, dropping my plate to the ground, while a few people around me moved away, laughing. Why was someone at this camp even playing football?

"Damn," Poe said. "You better go change."

"Yeah!" I said, trying to laugh it off. I needed to disappear. The closest exit seemed to be the woods.

All the socializing and protesting and networking from the bonfire was a distant noise as I stood in the dark woods, but the humiliation of what had just happened had followed me here. My favorite shirt was ruined. I'd worn this Superman shirt so much that the red of the *S* was faded, but it made it look gritty, which I appreciated. I flicked some of the potato salad off. And then an index finger that didn't belong to me appeared out of nowhere to swipe at the potatoes too.

I shrieked and jumped back, tripping over my feet and falling on my ass. I looked up and saw that the finger belonged to none other than Ashley Woodstone. It was now in her mouth, sampling the potato grease off my shirt as if she'd just snuck chocolate frosting off a birthday cake.

"Not GMO-free," she said. "You did the right thing, smearing it on your shirt like that."

41

"You can taste GMOs?"

"Can't *you*?"

I was still breathing hard from the shock, my mouth hanging open, my eyes squinting up at her, trying to adjust to the dark and make out her silhouette. She blended into the woods seamlessly, even with the giant fur coat. Or maybe because of it. The fur seemed to snag any leaf it came into contact with, so that Ashley Woodstone resembled a small, leafy hill on two legs. The full camouflage was probably why I hadn't seen her before. There were even leaves in her hair, a light-brown cape of tangled, twiggy tendrils. And the side of her forehead was dirty and smeared with what I could only assume was mud. The whole look gave off the impression that Ashley Woodstone's favorite pastime was very possibly gathering leaves into a pile and diving headfirst into them. Not how I envisioned most celebrities.

"What are you doing here?" I meant in the woods, but I guess I also meant here, at camp, with the rest of us. I worked hard to win a spot at this camp, and all Ashley Woodstone seemed to do was come up with a ridiculous campaign and flex her Hollywood connections to get here. She was just a distraction for what this camp was really about.

"I live here."

Much like with her Eat Dirt presentation, I was having trouble comprehending her.

42

"Did you do it in protest?" she said.

"Excuse me?"

"Smear the potatoes on your shirt. Was it a protest? Is your campaign Eat Organic?"

"No," I said. "Feed the Children."

"Oh, cool!" She was smiling at me. It was a good smile too—white teeth, identical pinprick dimples at the corners of her mouth—but then a good smile was kind of a movie star prerequisite. She wasn't unlike the popular girls at school, and yet she had something that those girls didn't have, something I couldn't explain but that was instantly clear. No matter how much dirt you threw on her, Ashley Woodstone was clearly a star.

A twig snapped and I nearly sprained my neck looking for the noise. Twenty feet behind me stood a huge man with his arms crossed in front of his chest, his biceps so enormous it looked like he was cradling a couple of basketballs. "Who the hell is that?"

"Oh, that's just my bodyguard, Pika," Ashley said, not even looking at him. Now that I'd had a better look I recognized him as the man who'd eaten the dirt at Ashley's presentation. He was scary-looking in daylight, to say nothing of him standing silently in the woods, watching me.

"Why's he just standing there?"

"Don't mind him. He's just bodyguarding," Ashley said. "Is that a Superman shirt?"

43

I wiped the remaining potatoes off my front and flicked them onto the ground, using some leaves to wipe my hands. I knew what was coming. "I love Superman!" Ashley said, plopping down beside me. If I thought her smile was big before, it was impossibly bigger now, aided by sparkling eyes that inexplicably caught whatever light there was in the dark woods. "I was actually in the Superman movie that just came out a couple months ago—*Superman: Dusk of Ascension*. I played Lo—"

"I know," I said. I didn't want to hear her say it. But there it was, the reason why I inherently did not like Ashley Woodstone.

Two months ago I'd gone to the theater at midnight, handed in the ticket I'd bought a month in advance, and sat in my seat like someone sitting in a warm bath after a long winter. By the time the end credits rolled, that warm bath had turned into an ice one, and I sat frozen and dumbfounded in the flickering lights of the worst Superman movie ever made.

And that wasn't just a matter of opinion. *Superman: Dusk of Ascension* had turned the *Daily Planet* into a gym where Clark Kent worked. A *gym*! Their official tagline was "Lifting planets—daily!" Superman's costume was an Under Armour compression shirt with the *S* logo on it. One of the movie's villains was a gymrat. Not a gymrat like the type of person who spends all day at the gym but a gymrat like an actual rat scurrying between the actors' feet in key scenes. The rat was voiced by Morgan Freeman. Suffice to say, *Dusk of Ascension* not only stomped all over my Superman-loving heart, it ripped it out, right there in the theater, while I sat petrified in horror, my bag of untouched popcorn growing colder as it greased my knees.

Of course, it wasn't Ashley Woodstone's fault that she was in the worst Superman movie of all time, but she was a part of it. She was completely miscast as Lois Lane. In my opinion, she'd taken part in ruining the character.

Maybe it was a stupid thing to dislike someone for, but it was my reason and to me it was valid. Superman meant a lot to me.

"Are you a big Superman fan?" Ashley asked. Her smile was clueless. "Of course you are, you're wearing a Superman shirt. I'd be happy to talk to you about the movie if you want."

After all the time I'd spent trying to wipe it from my memory? "No, thanks."

"Oh. Are you one of the Superman fans who didn't like it?"

The number of "Superman fans who didn't like it" were legion, but we must have been just as numerous as fans who did like it, because *Superman: Dusk of Ascension* made a crapload at the box office. Though I did know of a few people from online forums who saw the movie multiple times just so they could become experts in the many things wrong with it. "A lot of the reviews were pretty harsh," Ashley said. "But I remember one review specifically because it said I had no chemistry with Superman."

That was seriously the least of that movie's problems. But also true.

"I've been thinking about that review nonstop since I read it," Ashley continued. "And I think I figured out why they were so right. It's because I couldn't understand Superman's appeal. And if I couldn't understand Superman's appeal, then how could I make Lois understand it? You know?"

"Not really."

"I need to understand the essence of Superman. You can help me understand him."

"Me?"

"Yeah!" Ashley said, her eyes ablaze with what looked like an exciting new idea. "Do you think you could help me develop my character for the sequel? The new movie focuses heavily on Lois's romance with Clark. I brought the script to camp with me."

A Superman script? For a sequel? I was repulsed by the thought of another movie in this awful franchise continuing to ruin the most important figure in pop culture, and yet . . . I was intrigued. Getting a look at the new Superman script would be something that everyone on every Kal-Elchan would swallow kryptonite over.

But no. I was firmly against this new Superman era. And Ashley Woodstone. "I can't help you."

"Why?"

"Because the best thing about your version of Superman is that Jimmy Olsen is an instructor at SoulCycle. It's too far gone for my help."

"How 'bout this," Ashley said. "You think about it and get back to me. It'll be so fun." She dug her fingers into the ground and scooped out some earth. "Hungry?"

I laughed but she didn't, so I stopped. Was "No freaking way" a strong enough response? "I already ate."

She shrugged and sprinkled her snack back onto the ground from whence it came. I wondered if there was a five-second rule when it came to dirt. Probably not. "So you actually . . . eat dirt."

Ashley smiled at me like I'd just complimented her hair or something. "Dirt's my favorite."

I was in Bizarro World. "Can I ask you something?" I said.

"You can ask me anything."

"Why dirt?"

"Why is this night different from all other nights?"

"I don't follow."

Ashley took a deep breath and wiped her hands together, smattering the rest of her dinner over her lap. "I was in the Tanami in Australia this past spring, stranded in the desert with a shaman and a one-hundred-and-five-year-old monk. The circumstances were dire, as you can imagine, but then the monk began to eat dirt. She invited the rest of us to join her. I will admit, dirt down a dry throat for the first time can be a little uncomfortable, to say the least, but you know what they say when you're in Australia with a monk."

I really didn't.

"Do as she does. So we ate dirt. And here I am today. I realized then the sustaining power of mother earth's bounty. After that, I went on a full six-day journey around the world, studying the startling benefits of dirt, and I came to a very powerful conclusion: The world has already given us the nutrients our bodies are so desperately yearning for. We just have to open our eyes. And our mouths. And devour it."

I nodded like I understood, but I did not understand. "Do you think maybe the monk began eating the dirt because she'd gone mad with hunger or the sun was frying her brain or something?"

"Oh, no way. I had a team with me carrying a caravan full of food and drink. One thing didn't have to do with the other."

"Oh."

"Yeah."

As per usual when talking to girls, I was so lost. "Do you really think you're going to get people to go for that? The whole eating dirt thing?"

"Absolutely. People tend to listen to you when you're a celebrity." Of course. "Think of all the hunger we could eradicate if we just turned people on to eating dirt?" Ashley continued. "We could *feed the children*." She winked, but I was starting to get ticked off. She didn't seem to take my campaign seriously at all. Actually, it sounded like she was trying to make my campaign obsolete.

I stared at her and she stared at me and I got the distinct feeling we were both thinking radically different things about each other. But I couldn't begin to guess what was going through her mind. I had only spoken to her for a few minutes, but already it was clear that her brain worked in ways that I couldn't even imagine. We sat like that for so long, so still that it was only the sight of a bright orange thing slithering across her shoulder that snapped me out of my stare. "Um. You've got a bit of . . . salamander on you."

"Oh, wow," Ashley said. "But maybe there isn't a sala-mander on me; *maybe* there's an Ashley Woodstone on this salamander."

I stared at her a bit longer.

What? How was I here? How was I at a sleepaway camp talking to a movie star about a salamander on her shoulder? No—a movie star on a salamander. The moment was so sur-real I couldn't even be sure it was happening. The longer this whole conversation went, the more it felt like Ashley Woodstone's main purpose at this camp was to serve as a dis-traction. I stood. "I have to go."

"Wait, what's your name?"

"Gregor Maravilla."

"I'm Ashley Woodstone."

"I know."

"Hi."

"Bye," I said.

I began walking back toward the light of the bonfire and nearly bumped into Ashley's bodyguard. He was a couple of inches taller than me, which afforded him the opportunity to stare me down. He grunted at me and I took off faster.

I heard Anton's voice in my head, telling me what to do when I met Ashley Woodstone. *Don't be weird*, he'd said.

He had no idea.

5

My bizarre encounter with Ashley was all I could think about as I made my way back to the cabin. The bonfire was still going, though by the sounds of things it was winding down. But I wasn't interested in going back there with my potato-soiled shirt and my mind full of dirt. Even though I hadn't seen Ashley eat any, and even though I hadn't indulged in it myself, I felt the dirt all over me. In me. Around me. I kept wiping down my shorts, feeling like I was covered in the stuff.

When I got to Cabin 8, Men's Rights was dumping his bag onto my bed.

"What are you doing?"

He turned around, a none-too-pleased expression on his face. "We're bunkmates? But I'm already so sick of you."

The feeling was mutual. "That's my bed."

Men's Rights looked at my shirt and then at the Superman

poster I'd pinned up. "Should've known this was your bed. I mean, how many people above the age of eight still like Superman?"

I ignored that last part. "Why is your stuff on my bed?"

"I'm not sleeping on a top bunk. My muscle mass? I'll crush whoever's under me by day two."

"Yeah, but . . . I got here first." Solid argument.

"Look, I don't want any trouble," Rights said.

Good.

"So I'm just going to leave my stuff next to the bed, go take a shower, and by the time I come back I want all your stuff off my bed."

"That's not fair." Also solid, I thought.

"'That's not fair'? This is going to be too easy." Even though he was shorter than me, the closer Men's Rights came to me, the more I seemed to shrink away. "You know what else is going to be easy? Winning The Prize."

Is that what this was about? "We're all trying to win The Prize, dude."

"Yeah, and I'm going to be the one to actually do it, *dude*. There is no one that's going to get between me and a vacation in Florida."

"It's an internship, not a vacation."

"Give me a break," Rights said. "Going to Florida is all anyone cares about."

"Not me. Do you know how many children are starving around the world? Did you know that in Latin America alone, there are—"

"Hold up, why are you bringing up Latin America to me? What, you think everyone in Latin America is hungry or something, Feed the Children?"

"Of course not. And my name is Gregor."

"I'm Colombian. Do you want to feed me?"

"No, obviou—"

"The last thing the people of Latin America need is some white kid with a savior complex."

"Actually, I'm Mexican," I muttered. "Part Mexican. My father's Mexican."

Rights laughed, which was exactly the reaction I was always afraid of anytime I told anyone I was part Mexican. "Wow, you're white," he said to me. "But say Mexican one more time." He grabbed a Costco-sized vat of moisturizer out of his bag, and a towel. "I'm going to shower. But make no mistake, Superman. The Prize is mine. And so's the bed."

I watched him leave, frozen in my incredulity and alone in the cabin. I couldn't just let this guy bully me into giving up my bed. As far I was concerned, there was only one thing I could do about it.

*   *   *

I couldn't find a single counselor anywhere. Maybe it was immature of me, looking for a grown-up to tattle to, but Men's Rights's muscles were huge and mine were comparatively deflated. I didn't really have any other choice. An authority figure would be the best way to solve the problem.

But there was no one around. The bonfire was still going, but the only person in charge there was Jimmy, and he was busy with everybody else. I went to the counselors' office, but the place was dead silent.

I wandered the camp, looking for someone until I stopped by the rec room. ILP was still there, painting his mural, only this time instead of a crew of campers helping him, he was alone. Maybe it was my current mood, but suddenly, nothing seemed sadder than watching somebody paint a mural about unity all by themselves.

"Hey," I said. ILP stopped painting for a moment to look at me, his dubious eyes scanning me from head to toe. "Can I help?"

His eyes lingered on me for a moment longer before ignoring me altogether and focusing on his task again.

"Hey, I just want to let you know that I'm not going to call you I Like Paint. It's not right. We'll figure out your name soon enough, okay, buddy?"

He shook his head and his paintbrush at me. "Not Buddy," he said. Then he pointed at himself. "I Like. Paint."

Okay. So much for that. There was a large overturned

bucket on the ground a few feet from the wall, and I decided to sit and watch him. It'd only been a day, but ILP had gotten pretty far with his painting. Half the world was colored in. ILP was in the middle of drawing a star in the general area of the Mediterranean.

"Is that where you're from?" I asked.

This seemed to animate him, and suddenly ILP was pointing emphatically to the star on the map and talking rapidly in a language I did not understand. He jabbed the star on the map with his paintbrush and then another spot all the way on the other side of the globe.

"That's California," I said. "We're in New York." I pointed to the map. "It's on the East Coast. *EAST COAST*."

ILP's eyes, open so wide a moment ago, shrunk back to their beady size as he stilled again, back to his quiet self. He continued to paint, and I continued to watch.

"You homesick? You ever been to camp? I haven't. It's kind of different than I thought it would be." I don't know why I was still talking to him since he couldn't understand a word I was saying, but it felt nice talking to somebody. Maybe *because* he couldn't understand a word I was saying. "Don't get me wrong, I was excited at first, but then, I don't know, things started getting weird. There's Ashley. She eats dirt. And then there's this other girl, Poe. I really like her. And it's none of our business what her sexuality is."

ILP continued to paint, and I was hypnotized by the wide brushstrokes of his paintbrush and the sounds of crickets all around us. "And then there's Men's Rights. He's our bunkmate, by the way. He's an asshole. And there's the contest now too. I hope that doesn't change anything, but I'm afraid that it will. It probably already has. What do you think I should do?"

ILP muttered something that I obviously wouldn't have been able to make out even if I could hear him.

"Maybe I should just wait until tomorrow. Tomorrow's the real first day of camp. We'll get to work on saving the world finally. Right?" ILP ignored me. But I was fine with that. "Good talk."

It started to rain on my way back to the cabin. By the time I got to it I was soaked, and so were all of the clothes that I'd packed for camp, which were dumped in a pile outside the door. On top of it all was my Superman poster, so drenched it was nearly pulp.

6

I was starting anew with a crick in my neck. Though I couldn't blame it all on the uncomfortable top bunk that Men's Rights had effectively forced me to sleep on. (I'd gathered my pile of stuff outside the cabin and come in from the rain to find Rights snuggled up in my former bed.) No, I could probably blame the crick in my neck on the fact that I was spending most of this morning's calisthenics with my head turned away from my body at a ninety-degree angle so that I could get a better look at Poe. She was standing four rows away from me. Actually, she was jumping four rows away from me. Everyone was. Morning calisthenics included running in place. Poe was very good at running in place. I should not have been staring at her jumping figure. Actually, I hated myself for objectifying her. Not enough to look away, though.

"Excellent work, Camp Save the World!" Jimmy said. He stood in front of us in a camp T-shirt and khaki shorts. "Now everybody . . . jumping jacks!"

Poe looked awesome doing jumping jacks too. I wondered if I looked awesome doing jumping jacks. I wondered what Poe would make of me if she glanced in my direction. Would she be just as impressed with my jumping jack ability as I was with hers? Or would her attention be drawn away to Win, bouncing beside me with the grace of a gazelle, the smile on his face radiating warmth and confident awesomeness. I tried to keep up with him, though I ran out of breath at a much faster rate.

"Check out Ashley," he said, gesturing with his chin.

In the back corner of the group I spotted Ashley Woodstone between the jumping campers. She sat on the ground, cross-legged, playing with a blade of grass.

"Is she exempt from calisthenics?" I asked.

Win shrugged mid–jumping jack without disturbing his rhythm. "I guess you don't have to do the exercises when you've got someone else to do them for you."

I looked at Ashley again, and then I looked at her enormous bodyguard, practically shaking the ground with the force of his jumping jacks. The way his arms sliced through the air, you had to wonder if his method of exercising wasn't also a windmill attack technique, should anyone dare come too close to Ashley. You were definitely taking your life into your own hands if you went anywhere near his flapping wingspan.

"Great workout, everyone!" Jimmy said. We all stopped

jumping while he looked down at his watch. I thought he was checking his pulse, but after a moment it was clear that all he was doing was checking the time. He looked up into the sky just as the sound of a helicopter became clear. "I have a surprise for you all before we head out for our first day of camp activities. A special appearance by a very special person . . ."

Win and I looked at each other, our eyes going big as the same thought crossed our minds.

"Robert Drill!" we both said at the same time.

"Robert Drill!" Jimmy announced.

A buzz filled the air, the sound of our excitement nearly matching the growing roar of the approaching helicopter. It made sense: Robert Drill wouldn't let camp officially start without making an appearance here first. I wondered if he would rappel down from the helicopter, right into the middle of the playing fields.

"Yes," Jimmy said. "Look up and you'll see him!"

We all watched the sky. A lone black helicopter hovered above us. Then the helicopter sped away.

"And there he goes!" Jimmy said. Win and I looked at each other again, only this time with much less excited expressions. "I'm sure if you wave he'll be able to see it." Jimmy waved dramatically at the helicopter, which only got smaller as it sped away. None of us waved. "Fun fact about Mr. Drill: He's got an estate in Upstate New York which is only forty-five minutes away from the city via helicopter and about ten minutes away from here via car. Pretty neat, huh?"

We stared at Jimmy.

"Well," he said. "Off to your activities!"

Camp Save the World did things a little differently than other camps. Instead of an individual counselor for every cabin, each bunk was on their own. I guess they thought we were old enough to look after ourselves. Or they wanted us to cultivate our independence. Or something. Instead of bunk counselors, we got activity counselors. So now, the kids of Cabins 7 through 9 stood at the edge of the lake, waiting on instructions from our water sports counselor.

Hakim was a tall guy with a seemingly perpetual bored expression on his face. "Today we're canoeing." Exactly what my mother was afraid of. "But first things first," Hakim said. "Ashley Woodstone will be joining us for this activity!" The bored expression on his face instantly disappeared and was replaced with something more radiant. Ashley strolled up to Hakim and waved as though she were perched atop a parade float, which didn't seem so out of place since everyone clapped. My hands stayed limp at my sides.

"Thanks for that introduction, Hakim," Ashley said. "But

don't mind me. I'm not here as a celebrity. I'm just a camper, like everyone else."

Just like everyone else, except with the type of rabbit-fur hat that old Russian men wore in the dead of winter. Who wore fur to go canoeing? Ashley Woodstone did.

"Let's have fun out there, guys!" Ashley continued.

Hakim nodded. "Yes, let's all listen to Ashley. I loved you in *Apples to Cantaloupes*, by the way. Wasn't that a great film?" Everyone clapped again. "Now," Hakim said, "if Ashley doesn't have any more questions, why don't we get—"

A girl from Cabin 7 raised her hand and didn't wait to be called on to speak. "Just a few questions before we begin." She wore a yellow T-shirt with S.P.E.W. on the front in block letters. It must've been an abbreviation for her cause. "Are you proficient in water sports? And do you know CPR?"

"To answer your first question, no, I am not," Hakim said. "I was the leader of the Minneapolis chapter of Occupy Wall Street. I applied for a job here to help young activists, and I got assigned water sports. So anytime you swim, snorkel, or canoe, you'll be reporting to me. I know very little about water sports, so don't ask me about them. I do have a hunch, though, that for canoeing, *rowing* is likely to propel you along, so my best guess is that you should do that. And to answer your second question: also no."

It seemed my mother had good reason to worry.

"If anyone else decides that they want to sass me—"

"I wasn't sassing you," S.P.E.W. muttered.

"—I will dock you points."

"Points?" I said. "You can dock points for the internship?"

"I can dock and award points at my discretion," Hakim said. "We counselors have that power."

"How are we supposed to get the canoes into the water?" S.P.E.W. asked. The canoes were lying facedown by the water's edge.

"I don't know," Hakim said. "Push them?"

"We carry them," Rights said. "Two men per canoe."

"Men?" Feminism said. "You don't think the women can carry our own canoes?"

"No, I don't," Rights said. "But don't let that stop you from trying."

Feminism wore a baby-blue T-shirt with the words FEMINISM NOW stretched across her chest. So stretched the letters were warped.

"What are you staring at?" she snapped, and when I looked up I realized she was talking to me.

"Uh. Feminism?"

"Okay, everyone, we don't want to upset Ashley," Hakim said. Ashley was staring at the leaves of a tree. "Two people per canoe. Which means two of you will have to sit out."

S.P.E.W. raised her hand again. "I'd like to protest the

unfairness of having someone sit out of an activity just because the camp can't provide an adequate number of—"

"Great," Hakim said. "You'll sit out, then."

Another kid raised his hand. He was wearing a shirt that read DIABETES AWARENESS. I was beginning to wonder if maybe I should've made my own shirts before coming to camp. "Can I protest too?"

"What's your protest?" Hakim asked.

"I just don't like water."

"Fine. You sit out too. Everyone else, find a partner and get in a canoe and . . . do something. Again, don't ask me what."

Instead of immediately finding a partner, I picked out a canoe first. There was only one I wanted. It was red and blue. Superman colors. It practically had my name on it. I looked for Win, thinking we could partner up, but he was already in a canoe with ILP. Rights stood at the other end of my Superman canoe, lifting it up with one hand. "Are you just going to stand there, Superman, or you going to carry your weight around here?"

I wondered if there was room for any more sit-out protests.

It felt like we were lost at sea, shipwrecked, abandoned on a raft that was taking in water. We'd only been rowing for fifteen minutes, and we were in the middle of a rather small lake. But in an effort to one-up each other, Men's Rights and I had rowed as hard as we could, circling the lake three times.

I leaned over the side of the canoe, arms aching, the sun in my eyes, and every bit of my exposed skin already tinged pink thanks to the blazing sun.

"What's the matter, Superman, can't handle an oar?"

"I can handle an oar!" I panted. "And stop calling me Superman." My voice sounded foreign, probably because my throat tore to shreds every time I gulped in air. For his part, Rights sounded slightly out of breath but in obviously better shape than me.

"Nah, bruh," Rights exhaled. "I don't think you can handle an oar."

What did it even mean to handle an oar? I gripped mine again, feeling the weight of it, letting myself imagine me swinging the blunt end of it into Rights's jaw. Would he think I could handle it then?

I shut my eyes. I couldn't let the culture of toxic masculinity encourage violence as a means of solving problems. When I opened them, a lone guy on a canoe floated by in front of us. He wasn't even trying to row, and he'd turned his oar into a picket sign, the words CANOEING IS FOR FASCISTS written neatly on the paddle.

"You're the guy who's boycotting camp," I said. "Why?"

"You think I'm at this camp by choice?" Boycott Camp said. "My parents made me apply because they heard it was free and they've been saving for a monthlong summer trip to Italy for the last two years and this killed two birds with one stone."

"So you applied with a Boycott Camp campaign? Why did they let you in?"

"Your guess is as good as mine," he said. "I don't want to be here. But it was either this camp or a summer of forced volunteer work at my church after I had a minor arson incident."

"Arson?"

"Everyone always focuses on the 'arson' part of that sentence instead of the 'minor' part." He shook his head and dipped his oar/protest sign into the water, pushing away from us like he couldn't waste his time talking to someone who just wasn't woke enough to understand his plight. I hoped I hadn't offended him.

"Look on the bright side, Superman, you're not the biggest weirdo at this camp. Now what do you say we do another few laps?" Rights said. "We've still got . . . ah . . . forty-five minutes left to this activity."

Forty-five minutes? I could only lift my arm enough to bring my canteen to my lips. There were a few drops left in it. I was unequivocally doomed. "Absolutely," I said.

"Hello, Gregor Maravilla."

I looked up. Ashley Woodstone glided along in her canoe, smiling beneath that ridiculous fur cap. In one hand she held a glass filled with a frothy pink drink—with a red-and-white-striped paper straw poking out of it and a slice of pineapple balancing on the glass's rim. In her other hand she held a flower. One thing that wasn't in either hand? An oar. Behind her, her bodyguard gripped both oars in his fists. They may as well have been toothpicks for the lack of exertion on his face.

"You're not rowing," I said.

"Oh, I can't," Ashley answered. "For insurance purposes the contract for my next film stipulates that I not do any strenuous activity that may be detrimental to my health or cause me any harm."

"How convenient for you."

"Hello, Ashley," Rights said. "I don't believe I've had the pleasure of introducing myself yet. Men's Rights."

Who introduced themselves using only their campaign?

"Nice to meet you, Men's," Ashley said. "You boys look like you've been working hard. Can I offer you a virgin daiquiri? They're Pika's specialty."

"That sounds fantastic," Rights said.

Pika rested the oars across his lap and reached down to grab a pitcher. He poured Rights and me our drinks and handed a glass to each of us, looking none too pleased to be doing it.

The daiquiri wasn't that bad. Actually, it was pretty great. I swallowed mine in one gulp. Rights took a sip and winced, but quickly covered it with a smile. "My, that's sweet," he said. "Do you know the sugar content of this drink, by chance?"

"Hmm," Ashley said thoughtfully. "Pika?"

Pika shrugged and picked up a carton of sugar. It seemed he made all of his drinks on-site. Between the rowing. He turned over the carton of sugar to show us it was empty.

Rights promptly poured the rest of his drink into the lake, still grinning at Ashley. "Well, thanks anyway, Ashley, but it's important to watch one's calories, and I'm afraid I've reached my limit for the day. I'm sure you understand."

"Totally," Ashley said. "I'm from Los Angeles."

"Oh, I know," Rights said. "I'm actually a really big fan of yours. Most men wouldn't admit that they watched every single episode of *Smarty Pants*, but I'm not ashamed to say that I have."

"Thank you," Ashley said. She looked at me, a curious expression on her face, though I couldn't tell if it was because she was expecting me to say something similar or because she telepathically agreed with me that Men's Rights was a douchebag. "Have you seen all of the episodes too, Gregor?"

"Not a single one," I assured her.

Weirdly, Ashley's smile turned up to full brightness. The bodyguard started rowing again, apparently bored with

67

the conversation, though Ashley didn't seem to mind. "Well, it was nice seeing you boys!"

Yet another bizarre encounter with Ashley Woodstone. I was beginning to understand that all encounters with her would probably be strange. But stranger still was the way Rights had spoken to her. He'd smiled and used nice language. It was disconcerting.

"Do you have a thing for Ashley Woodstone or something?"

"Yes."

I didn't expect the candor. It was my experience that anytime anybody asked you if you liked someone, your immediate response should be to deny it. But Rights apparently had no qualms about crushing on a girl who wore fur hats on a canoe.

"I am Ashley Woodstone's type. And by the end of camp, she'll be mine."

"How do you know Ashley Woodstone's type?"

"Have you seen her last boyfriend? He was ripped and good-looking. And so am I."

"I heard her last boyfriend was unstable. Maybe you do have something in common with him."

Rights smiled, but there was no mirth behind it. "You're not still mad about me taking your bed, are you? You need to be a man and get over that."

"I take offense to your use of the outdated term 'be a man.'"

Rights looked at me sideways. "You would," he said. "Anyway, back to the matter at hand: Now that Ashley's boyfriend is in jail, it's up to me to make a move."

"Ashley's boyfriend's in jail?"

"What planet do you live on, Superman?"

Not only was I the only person at this camp who didn't care that Ashley Woodstone was here, I was the only person here who didn't know anything about her either.

"Well, if it isn't Feminism," Rights said.

She was alone in a canoe. It seemed a lot more people had opted out of canoeing today. I was impressed that she'd gotten this far without anyone's help. And then I wondered if I was only impressed because she was a girl and if I would've felt differently if it was a boy who'd been rowing alone.

"Sure you don't need anyone's help rowing?" Rights called to her. "I can pull double duty if you like."

Feminism dug her oar into the water and stopped right beside us. "Does it look like I need help? I got as far as you did, didn't I?"

"Let's see how much help you need now," Rights said. He grabbed hold of the edge of her canoe and moved his hand so sharply I didn't have time to realize what he was doing. Feminism's canoe tipped over completely. She was overboard. I jumped up, nearly toppling our canoe over too.

"What the hell's the matter with you?!" I yelled.

Rights shrugged. "If she really wants to prove that she doesn't need a man's help, then let her."

Feminism's head broke through the surface of the water and she gasped for air. "You bastard!" she shrieked.

I watched her paddling in the water, and there was only one thing for me to do. "I'm coming, Feminism!"

I dove into the water. I tried putting my arm around her, but as soon as I did she pushed me away. "I said I don't need anybody's help!"

"Stop being so stubborn. You'll drown! Also, me saving you is not the same as me implying that you need a man to save you. I'm saving you as a person, not a man."

"What the hell are you talking about?!" she snapped. "I can swim!"

At least, I thought that was what she said. I only got every other syllable, since she was dunking my head underwater every time I surfaced. I was swallowing more water than I was air, and it suddenly occurred to me that in my attempt to save Feminism from drowning I was drowning myself. No, I was being drowned.

Before I could dwell on it too long I felt a tug on my collar. There was an arm around my chest, pulling me up, and then: sweet air. I gulped it in and heard her voice.

"I've got you, Gregor Maravilla."

Ashley freaking Woodstone.

"I'm fine," I said, though my voice was ragged and waterlogged.

"Don't fight it," Ashley Woodstone said. "I played a lifeguard in a music video once. I know exactly what I'm doing."

There was no point in fighting her off. I held on to Ashley Woodstone, and after a moment I realized she was holding on to her bodyguard. She had an arm around his neck, and he pulled us toward shore at an amazingly quick pace. I'd never ridden on the back of a dolphin before (completely unethical) but it couldn't have been very different. Not that I was comparing Ashley's bodyguard to an animal, because that would be wrong too. I tried to avoid everyone's gaze as we passed by the other canoes on our way back to the dock, but I soon realized that no one was actually looking at me. They were looking at Ashley.

"Ashley's in the water!" someone shouted.

Others pointed at her.

"Ashley, are you okay?" someone else said.

Then people started to jump in.

Nearly all of the boys in the lake swam to the dock with us.

The bodyguard pulled Ashley up onto the dock first, and then me. I lay on the wood, and Hakim's head hovered above

71

mine, blocking the sun as he watched me with a horrified expression on his face. "I knew there was a reason for all these life vests!" he said, dumping a bundle of tangled orange floaties beside my head, uselessly. "Do you realize you almost drowned *Ashley Woodstone*?! Ashley, I'm awarding you ten points for saving a camper's life."

"Thank you." Ashley's face appeared next. "But are you okay, Gregor?" she said. "Do you need CPR? What year is it? Who's the president? Who won best actress at last year's Oscars?"

"I don't know," I said.

"It was Meryl Streep!" Ashley cried. "Someone send help!"

Hakim went running.

A few of the boys who'd gotten into the water climbed onto the dock and surrounded Ashley. They enclosed her in a tight circle of concern, effectively shutting me out.

"Ashley, do you need CPR?" one of the boys said.

"Step aside, I'll do it." Rights. That bastard.

"I'm fine, everybody," Ashley said.

I tried to sit up to show that I too was fine, but Ashley used her palm to press me firmly back down onto the dock. "Don't try to get up," she said. "I've played damsels in distress in romantic comedies before. Their first instinct is usually to show that they're perfectly capable of doing things on their own, but they are almost always wrong."

I breathed and stared up at Ashley Woodstone. "I'm not a damsel in distress."

She smiled down at me. "Shhhhhhhhh," she said.

Not for the first time, I wondered what the hell was happening at this camp.

7

Hakim forced me to go see the camp nurse, even after I assured him that I hadn't actually drowned and was, in fact, perfectly okay. Not that Nurse Patrosian could help me much anyway. I knew this because while I'd sat on the chair in her office, she'd lain on the cot, her fingertips pressed against her furrowed forehead, and said, "I can't help you."

"I don't need help," I'd assured her.

"I'm overwhelmed."

"It's only the first day of camp."

"And there's already been eleven near fatalities."

I left her office with a lollipop and the realization that visiting the camp nurse in the future would be an exercise in futility. And it appeared that dining at the mess hall was fast becoming an exercise in humiliation.

The broken telephone version of my rescue attempt earlier in the day had cast me as the asshole who'd aggressively tried to drown America's sweetheart, Ashley Woodstone. It was becoming increasingly clear that Ashley Woodstone was my kryptonite. Anytime she was in close proximity to me I turned into a disaster. I had to stay away from her.

It didn't look like Ashley was anywhere in the mess hall, but I wasn't going to take my chances. I sat at a scarcely occupied table in the corner of the large room. Just as I bit into my bread roll a piece of paper slid next to my tray. It read GLUTEN FREEDOM FOR ALL, and there was a list of reasons to go gluten-free.

"You really should consider a gluten-free lifestyle," said the girl standing in front of me. She stood stiffly with her stack of leaflets held close against her chest in her crossed arms, her squared shoulders reaching for her ears. She didn't make eye contact with me as she spoke, which made it easier for me to continue chewing my bread without guilt.

"I'll think about it," I told Gluten Freedom. She gave me a curt nod and walked away. I wasn't sure how campaigning for a gluten-free America was going to save the world, but I could understand the girl's reasoning behind this display.

Overnight, a scoreboard had appeared outside the mess hall, covering the entirety of its eastern wall. At the top, large letters spelled out INTERNSHIP SCOREBOARD, and below it were a list of the campers who had somehow managed to score themselves some points toward winning the internship. Five campers already had a point. Men's Rights, incredibly, had three. And at the top of the list, with an unprecedented ten points for "saving my life," was Ashley Woodstone. She didn't even need The Prize and she was already winning it. It made me dislike her even more than I already did. Anyway, my best guess was that Gluten Freedom was trying to get herself on that coveted scoreboard.

I looked over to the guy sitting next to me and held up the gluten-free leaflet. "People are getting serious trying to win some points, huh?"

He nodded. "Personally, I think leaflets are a pretty lame method of protest." He talked around a mouthful of macaroni, which he kept shoveling into his mouth with his right hand, not letting the fact that it was encased in a pristine slime-green cast slow him down. I stared at the cast, wondering if he was one of the eleven "near fatalities" Nurse Patrosian had told me about.

"You doing anything to win points yet?" I asked.

"I'm doing it right now."

I stared, waiting for him to continue, but he kept me hanging, taking another leisurely bite of his macaroni.

"I'm talking to you," he finally said.

I laughed. "What?"

"My cause is Unity Through Multiculturalism. By talking to you I am bringing multiculturalism into your life. Before I started talking to you, you were just a white dude having dinner, alone. Now you're a white dude having dinner with an Indian American acquaintance. I hope the counselors are taking notice."

"Actually, I'm half Latino."

"You look pretty white to me," he said. "You're wearing cargo shorts." He looked under the table and then popped back up. "And Pumas. Face it, man: You're white beyond belief."

Great.

"So who are you?"

"My name's Gregor Maravilla."

"I don't mean your name, man. Your cause. What are you here for?"

Right, I'd almost forgotten that no one here had names. "Feed the Children."

"So why are you sitting at this table?" he said.

I looked around, worried that there would be someone whose seat I had taken, but it was just the two of us. "You belong at the Hunger and Poverty Table," Unity said. "Or maybe the International Causes Table. Sometimes campaigns overlap."

"Wait, everyone has grouped up into categories? When did that happen?"

"Today at lunch."

Which I'd skipped for my useless visit with Nurse Patrosian. "What are the categories?"

"There's the Environmental Table, the Socioeconomic Table, Culture and Humanities, Education, Health and Disease, Human and Civil Rights, and Hunger and Poverty. Animals and International Causes got grouped together because there aren't enough people in each cause to fill up a table. Then there's the Miscellaneous Table, or as I like to call them, the weirdos."

"Weirdos?"

"They're the people who don't belong at any table or in any category because their campaigns are total jokes."

The Miscellaneous Table was only a couple of tables away from ours. I didn't know most of the kids at the table, but I was suddenly curious about what their campaigns could possibly be. There was the girl I'd seen earlier today with the s.p.e.w. T-shirt (ever a mystery) and the kid who was protesting the camp itself, and another kid taking bites of his dinner in between bouts of strumming the guitar balancing on his lap.

"And then there's the Cool Table." Unity pointed to the center of the room, at the table that every other table in the mess hall seemed to face. "The Cool Table defies categorization. If anyone at the Cool Table even has a campaign, I don't know what it is. They are not known by their campaign names. They are the few and blessed among us who can walk around and answer to their given birth names."

Poe and Win were sitting at the Cool Table. Unity was right—nobody called Win End Hunger or Poe QUILTBAG. For some reason even the thought of calling them by their campaign names seemed ridiculous. Even Balthazar-Adriano, who had the audacity of having two first names, wasn't called by his campaign. He was sitting right next to Poe, and I could almost read his full name on her lips as she talked to him. I mean, the guy couldn't even be bothered to have a nickname. I made a mental note to not introduce myself as Feed the Children and only introduce myself as Gregor.

"If you wanna switch tables I'd pick the International Table over the Hunger and Poverty Table," Unity said. "That way I have an excuse to go over there, since we know each other now."

"Why do you want to go to the International Table?"

"Because I want World Peace."

"We all want world peace."

"Yeah, well, I got dibs."

I was confused for a moment until he pointed out who he was talking about: a gorgeous girl with a big smile, big blonde hair, and even bigger—

"Boobs," Unity said, gulping down more macaroni. "World Peace has the biggest boobs at this camp."

I couldn't ignore the fact that World Peace did indeed have big boobs. I tried my best not to openly stare. "You shouldn't call 'dibs' on a girl," I said. "Women aren't property. And she's more than just her figure, man."

"She is so freaking hot," Unity said, ignoring me. I thought he was still talking about World Peace, but it seemed his attention had already been stolen by someone else who'd just come into the mess hall.

I was beginning to notice that Ashley Woodstone had a way of walking into places. The way she walked into rooms was the way people looked when they caught a train just in the nick of time: a bit frazzled but ultimately relieved. Behind her was Pika the bodyguard, of course.

"She eats dirt," I said.

"She can eat whatever she wants looking like that. I'd like to unite her with my multiculturalism."

I side-eyed Unity. Whatever that euphemism meant, it couldn't have been good. Ashley grabbed a tray and set out for the food line, but she kept being interrupted by people. Girls and guys alike came over one by one to introduce themselves. I couldn't hear what the campers were telling her, but whatever it was, it definitely had the air of animated gushing. Ashley asked her bodyguard for something, and he took a Sharpie out of his pocket like it'd been waiting in a holster. She then proceeded to sign the forehead of the guy she was talking to. He went back to his seat with a scribbled message covering the entirety of his face.

Ashley signed people all over the place while her body-guard got her dinner.

"Dude, do you think I could get her to sign my tongue?"

"Shouldn't you try for your cast first?"

"Everyone gets their casts signed. I want Ashley Woodstone to hold my tongue."

I was beginning to lose my appetite.

"Dude, she's waving at you! Why is Ashley Woodstone waving at you?"

Ashley was coming over to our table. Her bodyguard put down her tray first, and then Ashley sat before it. I guess her diet consisted of more than just dirt. She also seemed to like salad.

"Gregor Maravilla!" Ashley Woodstone said. "We meet again!"

"Unity," Unity said, nearly pushing me aside to shake Ashley's hand. "Pleasure to make your acquaintance."

"Pleased to make yours," Ashley responded. She did look honestly pleased. A few feet behind her, the bodyguard held back any more campers who threatened to interrupt Ashley's dinner.

"How are you feeling, Gregor?" she said. "Any PTSD from the drowning incident?"

"I wasn't drowning."

"Wait, *you're* the guy that Ashley Woodstone saved from

81

drowning today?" Unity said. He was looking at me like maybe mine was the more valuable friendship to have instead of the other way around. But my attention was pulled away from them as I watched the bodyguard shove a guy away from us by the face.

And then Poe rolled back into my life. I say rolled because she slid into view on her skateboard. She hopped off and was about to take the seat next to Ashley's when the bodyguard blocked her way.

"Let her through," I said. "She's with us."

Pika stepped aside and Poe came to sit down. "Hey, Gregor, thanks for that."

Unity's look had graduated from awe to love toward me. Someone from the Cool Table had actually referred to me by name.

"Hi, I'm Gregor's best friend, Unity."

"Hey, Unity." Poe turned toward Ashley. "I'm Poe. I just wanted to come say hi and tell you that I'm a huge fan and ask if I could get an autograph?"

"Sure!" Ashley said. She held her hand out behind her, and Pika handed her the Sharpie. Poe stood up and lifted her T-shirt high enough that I could see the bottom of her bra. It was lime green with yellow polka dots.

"Can you do it on my rib cage?" Poe asked.

My plate of chicken got colder. The macaroni in Unity's mouth went unchewed. As I stared at the intricacies of the fabric of Poe's beautiful bra I tried to be as PC about it as I could. I tried to turn off my male gaze. I assured myself that I was not turning Poe into an object, that she was not lifting up her shirt just for my benefit. But then, I was just a teenage guy seeing a real-life girl in a real-life bra up close for the first time—I wasn't about to turn away either. I thought about what Anton had said, about having new experiences at camp. He wasn't kidding.

When Ashley was done, Unity and I leaned in to read the message.

You are a beacon of sunshine. Love, Ashley Woodstone.

"Awesome," Poe said, letting her T-shirt fall. "Thank you." She glided off again on her board, but not before touching Ashley's arm.

Without breaking his stare, Unity leaned toward me and whispered, "I'm going to sit next to you for the rest of camp."

"So, Gregor," Ashley said. "Given any more thought to what we talked about?"

I was drawing a blank. "Hmm?"

"The Superman script. Whadayasay, do you want to help a girl out?"

"Uh . . ."

Unity jabbed me in the ribs. *"Dude,"* he whispered without moving his lips. "When Ashley Woodstone asks you for something, you do it."

His ventriloquist lip thing was really quite impressive, but before I could even attempt to respond in kind, Jimmy blew on his whistle to get all of our attention.

"Hello, Camp Save the World!" he began. He stood on a small stepladder at the entrance to the mess hall. "This first day of camp has been truly magical. Save for the near drowning of Ashley Woodstone. I'm glad to say that Ashley is perfectly okay, everybody. But I also want to emphasize that Ashley Woodstone is extremely precious to this camp, and we want to keep from drowning her in the future, okay?"

If I didn't know any better I'd say Jimmy was looking directly at me. I avoided his gaze.

"Now, for tonight's very important announcement. As I'm sure you've all noticed, there is now a scoreboard on the side of this mess hall. The rest of the counselors and I have been absolutely thrilled to see some campers taking initiative with their campaigns. Why, just today, I've already been given three different leaflets outlining some of your causes. Awesome work, guys! Finding creative ways to promote your campaigns is a great way to secure some points for the scoreboard. But the other counselors and I have come up with an additional way to distribute points. A more quantifiable way to map your progress. And that is . . . weekly competitions!"

My eyes darted back up to Jimmy.

"Every week until camp ends we will hold competitions to test who among you are real activists. Five competitions in all. And tomorrow will be the first one. Here's a hint: You'll be making picket signs for your campaigns! Okay, I've said too much! May the best man, or woman, or non-binary individual, win!"

8

Previously, none of us were sure how to get points up on the scoreboard. Now we had something we could work toward. None of us knew what to expect from the competitions, but we were all keenly aware of their importance. You could feel it in the stuffy air of the arts and crafts room. Every camper had packed inside, awaiting further instructions.

"You all got a placard and a stick at calisthenics," Judy, the arts and crafts counselor, said, standing at the head of the room. "Morning activities have been canceled so you can work on your picket signs, which you will picket with at lunchtime in front of the mess hall. I have been assigned as judge for this competition, so here's some tips on what I'll be looking for: My favorite color is plum. My least favorite color is maroon. And yes, my most hated band is Maroon 5, but that has nothing to do with my feelings for the color, I assure you. So you'd be wise to steer clear of any Maroon 5 song lyrics in your picket signs, okay?"

We'd only had a quick intro to arts and crafts yesterday. All I knew about Judy was that she was an undergrad at Oberlin with a vague history of activism (she'd posted flyers around campus protesting Imagine Dragons) and that she was only at Camp Save the World because it would provide credit toward her anthropology degree. She'd told us all this while leaning back in her chair with her feet up on her crafts table, right before announcing that arts and crafts couldn't be taught and that we should do "whatever the hell" we felt like. I wasn't sure any of this was relevant to the competition, but I kept it in mind anyway, being that she was a judge.

"That being said," Judy continued in a raised voice, "I *do* love Adam Levine. So if you can incorporate his likeness somewhere into your designs, you might just find yourself a few points richer this afternoon."

Hated Maroon 5, loved Adam Levine. Got it.

"Okay, begin. It's starting. GO."

Something broke open when Judy said go, and I don't just mean the packet of glitter that suddenly—and somehow maliciously—dusted everything in sight. The excited stillness of before had morphed into a frenetic energy as everyone turned into sharp elbows and knees, clambering for the front of the room. I could see there would be no equal distribution of supplies. It was every person for themselves, and already people were succumbing to the cutthroat crush. There was

Clean Air, who'd gotten pink acrylic paint squirted in her eye, and End Homelessness, who'd skidded backward on his ass after losing a battle of tug-of-war that involved a gallon jug of glue. And there was Save the Trees, who screamed and swung her coveted jug of glue over her head as a means to repel anyone who dared to take it (or maybe as a result of a breakdown from the thought of all the wooden sticks being used in this activity). And then there was me, lying on the floor, having been knocked in the head by that very gallon of glue.

"Gregor Maravilla!"

Of course it was her, standing above me. Ashley Woodstone crouched down, her face scrunched up as she scanned me. "You're resplendent!"

"Huh?"

She lifted my limp forearm, and I could see that my skin was sprinkled with purple glitter.

"This is upsetting and beautiful," Ashley said. "Are you okay? What year is it? Who's president? Who holds the record for most Oscar acting nominations?"

"I don't know."

"It's Meryl Streep! Somebody send help!"

I sat up quickly. "I'm fine." I looked around the room now that the glitter had settled. It was almost cartoonish how quickly all of the supplies had gone.

"You didn't get any supplies," Ashley said.

I walked over to the table. All that was left was a red marker and a loose pile of googly eyes. I pocketed it all. It would have to do.

"You don't have any supplies either." I turned to Pika to make sure he wasn't holding bundles of art stuff. He wasn't.

"Oh, I already finished my picket sign. When I heard what the competition would be last night, I called in a favor from a friend and she ca—"

I stopped listening when I saw Poe through the open doors. "Cool story good luck bye!"

I jogged out the door and sidled up next to Poe, walking in stride with her. "Looks like you scored some good supplies." She had a whole box full of paints in her arms. "How'd you manage that?"

"I just asked I Like Paint if he was willing to share from his personal stash. I mean, I asked him, and he couldn't answer, obviously, and he didn't seem to mind when I walked off with this stuff."

"That's nice of him."

"It's really a travesty that the camp hasn't managed to get him a translator yet. I'm thinking of staging a protest on his behalf."

"I totally agree. I can help if you want."

"Sure," she said. "Either way, I think he's set for this comp. I don't think he's threatened by any of us. He's obviously going to win this one."

I hadn't thought of it before, but Poe was right. ILP would probably submit his mural as his picket sign. And he'd had a head start, working on it all this time in lieu of partaking in any of the activities.

"You think you could help a guy out, share some of your supplies? All I got were some eyes." I fisted a few of the googly eyes in my pocket and swished them around in my palm to show her.

"Sure. But you'd have to do something for me in return."

"Like what?"

"I need a subject. Care to pose for me?"

"You going to paint me like one of your French girls?" *Titanic* was my mom's favorite movie. I mentally thanked her for indirectly helping to provide this perfect line.

"How do you know about my French girls?"

I'd only been at the camp a few days, but I'd already gotten a care package from home. My dad sent me a book, and in his letter he wrote, *Anton says this is what you might call a "gag gift." And while I do hope it makes you laugh a little bit, I also thought you might appreciate it, on a more serious level. I hope this helps with your crush on Ashley Woodstone.*

The book was called *How to Get a Girlfriend.*

It was definitive proof not only that I was a loser but that my own father was aware of it. I thought about burning the book immediately, lest anyone catch me with it. But then I tucked it under my pillow when I was sure no one was looking. Gag gift or not, it might prove helpful at this camp. And sitting here now, under the shade of a tree as I drew on my placard while Poe painted me, the book was finally coming in handy. Chapter two was all about the importance of listening. So all I did was listen as Poe told me about her life in Paramus, New Jersey. She was an only child. She was a second-generation American. Her grandparents were from Kaiping, a city that was about ninety miles from Hong Kong. Poe got to visit when she was eight, but she hadn't been back since. She couldn't wait to graduate so she could move to New York and attend the NYU Tisch School of the Arts, where she would major in fine arts. She already had a thesis project sorted out in which she'd paint the portrait of every LGBTQ person who came into her life. Watching her paint, it was easy to see she really was an amazing artist.

Listening was important, of course, but as chapter three of *How to Get a Girlfriend* said, I also needed to find some common ground for me and Poe to bond over. But that was proving difficult. I was not an amazing artist, I hated poetry, my favorite band was not Radiohead, and while I could understand it, I did not want to escape New Jersey. I threw out a lifeline, hoping she'd catch it. "Do you like superhero movies?"

"Superhero movies?"

"Yeah," I said. "They're kind of my fave brand of movie. I know everyone loves Marvel right now, but I'm much more of a DC fan. I prefer my superheroes gritty and kind of broody—the last Superman movie notwithstanding, of course. That movie was a joke."

"Superhero movies?" Poe said again, as if she hadn't heard anything I'd just said. "I don't really go to the movies unless there's a new Whit Stillman playing at the Angelika."

Poe from Paramus still managed to see cool movies in cool indie theaters in New York by cool indie directors I'd never heard of. The more she told me about herself, the more I realized just how different we were and how little hope I had of getting her to look at me the way that I looked at her.

"Isn't Ashley in that new Superman movie?" Poe asked. Something changed in her voice suddenly; something happy and light caught on the edges of Ashley's name.

"Yes."

"I might have to watch it, then."

I focused on my picket sign, trying to ignore the fact that Ashley Woodstone was infiltrating my time with Poe.

"You and Ashley are friends, right?" Poe asked.

"I wouldn't say that, no."

"She's always hanging around you."

"I don't understand it either," I said. "Doesn't it bother you that she's at this camp?"

"Why should it?" Poe said.

"Nepotism. Special treatment. We worked hard to get here, and she comes in with a bogus campaign and just expects everyone to listen to her because she's famous. She doesn't even need the internship. And what about her campaign?"

"What about it?"

"Eat Dirt? It's ridiculous."

"Dirt's not that bad. I tried some."

I put down the marker and looked at Poe. She was focused on her artwork, smiling serenely as she drew as though she hadn't just admitted that she'd eaten dirt. "You what?"

"Ashley says it's nutritious."

"Ashley says a lot of weird things."

"I really think you're being too hard on her, Gregor. Ashley's campaign may seem a little odd, but people just need to be more open-minded. Plus, dirt's supposed to be really good for your hair and nails."

I sat there dazed.

"I think Ashley's great," Poe said. There was that special tone of voice again, the one that seemed reserved only for people whom Poe deemed worthy. My own name on Poe's lips sounded like a hacking cough by comparison. Poe may have been painting my likeness, but it was clear by the look in her eyes that it wasn't me she was seeing in her mind anymore.

Count on Ashley Woodstone to ruin my day. And she didn't even have to be here to do it.

Lunchtime came and you'd think a war had broken out by the fervor of our protesting. One hundred campers shrouded in plum-colored poster board stormed the mess hall. We blocked the entrance as if we'd all silently agreed that lunch was our biggest foe and letting anyone into the building meant failure. Not that anybody wanted in.

Campers stomped, marched, punched fists into the air, and chanted their own made-up rhymes, drowning one another out. The flames of activism raged on. It was infectious. I pumped my own picket sign into the air and shouted, "FEED THE CHILDREN NOW!" at anyone who came near.

"Is that Bruce Willis?" Unity asked, breaking through the crowd to suddenly appear before me, his eyes narrowed as he looked at my protest sign.

"What? No," I said, looking over my sign again to check that nothing in it had radically changed. No, it was still the same sign, with the same drawing. "It's Adam Levine. The guy from Maroon 5."

"Oh, cool," Unity said. "I included him too." Unity's picket sign was just the words UNITY THROUGH MULTICUL-TURALISM surrounded by smiley face stickers in all different colors. Near the bottom left of the poster was a magazine cutout of Adam Levine's face. "I'm just letting you know that your Adam Levine looks like Bruce Willis. Is he eating a butt?"

"What? Dude! It's Adam Levine eating a plum! Because our arts and crafts counselor likes plums."

"She likes Adam Levine and the *color* plum. Not Bruce Willis eating ass."

"Hey, Gregor, hey, Unity!" Win strolled up with his picket sign, which may as well have been a professionally made national ad campaign for its beauty. It was just a blown-up black-and-white shot of a small child sitting alone in a village, eyes huge and all cried out. He was holding a small piece of bread. The picket sign didn't need any words on it for me to know what it was about.

"I thought the picture alone, without commentary, would be much more powerful," Win said. "I took this photo last year on a trip to India. It's started a lot of conversations with everyone I've shown it to. Hopefully, it can do the same today."

Unity put down his sign. "Powerful stuff," he said solemnly.

"Yeah," I said. Win's picket perfectly encapsulated the importance of ending hunger. Not like my sign, which apparently looked like Bruce Willis eating ass.

"Hey, is that Adrian Grenier?" Win said, brightening up as

he looked at my sign. "I love Adrian Grenier. Great actor, awesome activist."

"It's Adam Levine."

"Oh, I think the googly eyes were throwing me off."

I knew I shouldn't have given Adam Levine googly eyes.

"Well, good luck, guys." Win continued to protest, and all Unity and I could do was watch him go. This was probably part of Win's plan—show everyone that haunting photograph and leave them in the dust, crying, dejected, and without the ability to pick up their own signs.

"Win Cassidy is, like, the perfect guy," Unity said.

"I know."

"Well, what do we have here?" It was Men's Rights this time, fists casually in his pockets, biceps casually bursting from his short sleeves. Unity immediately ducked back into the crowd.

"Is that 1996 Olympic gold medalist Kerri Strug in your picket sign, Superman? And—wait a minute—is she *eating ass*?"

It took everything in me not to swing my picket sign at Rights, but the guy right next to me was chanting about ending violence and it would not have looked good.

"It's Adam Levine," I said. "Everyone else who's seen it clearly agrees."

"Oh, Adam Levine, really? How nice," Rights said. "I feel bad for you, Superman. Everyone else? They're going to get points just for participation, but you? I wouldn't count on it, man."

"You don't even have a picket sign, Rights."

"Oh, but I do." His shit-eating smirk turned into a full-fledged shit-eating grin. He took his hand out of his pocket like it was an act of charity, pointing up to the top of the mess hall. I turned around to see what amounted to a full billboard hanging from the roof of the building. It was a photograph of a shirtless Men's Rights standing beside a shirtless Adam Levine. Together, their smiles blessed the proceedings of the picketing below. There was only one word, in bold white letters, written over the picture: MEN.

"Adam Levine and I go to the same gym in LA," Rights said. He took his hand out of his other pocket. Wadded up inside it were crumpled dollar bills. He tossed them at my feet. "Here's a little something for ya. Go feed the children of Latin America with that, asshole."

I'd been humiliated a lot in my life. In school. Even by my own family. But there was nothing quite like standing with a couple of dollars at my feet, holding a picket sign of someone who looked like anyone but Adam Levine, as the real Adam Levine shirtlessly smiled down at me from above. I was clearly not winning this competition. The only thing I could rely on now was the hope that what Rights said was true: Maybe I could earn a measly participation point. This competition could not get any worse. And then Ashley Woodstone showed up.

You could tell when Ashley showed up because crowds silenced and then parted like this was the Red Sea or something. But this time it actually looked like Ashley had come from the depths of the Red Sea. She wore a tiny tank top and shorts and she was covered from head to toe in dirt. I stood watching her like the rest of the crowd: jaw unhinged. Of course, she came right toward me.

"Gregor Maravilla!"

"Ashley Woodstone." Her name was all I could say for the moment. Her hair looked to be encrusted in mud, her face streaked with it. I was pretty sure her tank top had been white once upon a time. "What . . . ?"

"I decided to turn my picketing into a sort of performance piece. Performing is what I know best, after all. Plus, this whole look coincides with the photo shoot I did yesterday."

It was then that I saw the enormous picket sign Pika was holding up. It was a photograph of Ashley looking a lot like she did now, except in the picture I was pretty sure she was not only covered in dirt but also stark naked. I say "pretty sure" because big block letters spelling out EAT DIRT covered her chest and then . . . the bottom half of her. The photo showed everything and nothing.

"I got my friend Annie to come in last night for the shoot," Ashley went on. "She's an amazing photographer. She's shot everyone before. Anyway, we're running it in the *New York Times* today as a full-page ad. Isn't it a wonderful protest, Gregor?"

I looked at the picket sign and then back at Ashley, her smile blindingly bright. Then I looked back at the picket sign.

"Hey! Is that Adam Levine?" Ashley said, pointing at my sign.

Judy walked up to us at the most perfectly worst time. "Ooh, it's your big moment of judgment," Ashley said. "I'll get out of your hair."

She stepped into the crowd and I thought fast, quickly finding my voice again. "It's Adam Levine. And that's a plum," I told Judy before she had the chance to think anything else.

She did not look very happy as she examined my sign. "Is your sign a protest of Adam Levine?" Judy said.

"I know the googly eyes were a bad idea, but I tr—"

"I know some people don't appreciate his talents, but it's a little uncalled for to cover him in crap, don't you think?"

What? I looked at my sign, and there it was. Right over Adam Levine's face, where Ashley must've pointed and touched my poster, was a smear of dirt that looked all too much like a skid mark. I closed my eyes tightly, not believing my luck. And not believing how royally Ashley Woodstone had screwed me, again.

"I can't give you any points for this," Judy said.

"Of course you can't." I nodded, defeated.

And then, out of nowhere, I Like Paint appeared on the scene. He'd thus far largely avoided all activities in order to focus on his mural. But now he was here. The guy was shuffling around, wearing only one shoe, sobbing, his bandana askew. And he was completely covered in red. He was dripping in it. At first I thought it was blood. The sight of a guy stumbling around covered in blood was startling enough, but as he got closer, I could see that the red was far too bright and thick to be blood. It was paint.

ILP collapsed onto the ground in a slippery heap. Though none of us could know what had happened, it was clear that ILP had been attacked.

Hello, Mother, hello, Father, here I am at Camp Save the World.

It's been a week and everything's going great. You guys were worried about sending me away for the summer, but you have nothing to be afraid of. I've made friends. My bunkmates are great. And I'm learning so much about how to save the world. Everyone has been getting along great and absolutely no one has tried to sabotage anyone else, especially not by destroying a beautiful unity mural.

I'll write again soon with more updates on my progress.

P.S. If Anton or Katrina are also reading this, I just want you to know that I've met Ashley Woodstone and she is weirder than I am. She eats dirt. I mean that literally.

9

The counselors' office was a lot bigger than I expected, and a lot messier. There were papers strewn on every surface—on top of filing cabinets, desks, the floor—but I ignored all of the disarray and stared at Jimmy, who sat behind his desk with his chin balancing on his knuckles, looking back at me.

"I didn't do it." I thought that much was obvious. After all, I'd been at the picket competition when ILP suddenly staggered into view, covered in red paint. It was hard to know exactly what had happened to I Like Paint since he couldn't communicate with us, but his mural told a lot of the story. It had been completely covered in a giant splash of red paint except for the center of it, where the negative space of ILP's silhouette remained. He'd apparently thrown himself against the wall, arms outstretched, fingers splayed, taking on his attacker's vicious paint assault. In the end, it was a futile attempt to protect his art. ILP's attack had everyone on edge, including Jimmy, who looked at me with a lot more skepticism than I was expecting.

But it turned out Jimmy's skepticism had less to do with my involvement in ILP's mural's destruction than with my presence in the office. "Children, what are you doing here exactly?"

I shrugged and fidgeted in my seat. "I just thought you might want to investigate what happened to ILP's mural. And I wanted to offer my help." I know it sounded decent and selfless, but I can't lie—a big reason for coming here was to try and get points. So far I was the only camper without any points on the scoreboard. Men's Rights's billboard had gotten him the attention he wanted and a spot in third place. Win's beautiful original portrait of a hungry child got him to second. And Ashley Woodstone's professionally photographed poster had catapulted her to the top of the scoreboard. Even ILP had gotten sympathy points, and not only had his entry been destroyed, it hadn't ever even been in contention. Maybe if I showed some initiative in trying to help my fellow camper, Jimmy would see that and spread the point wealth.

Plus, the whole thing with ILP's mural had ushered in a whole new dynamic at camp: the era of the prank. It had only been four days since the mural incident, but there'd been enough pranks in those four days to fill up a summer.

Water Conservation cut off the water to the girls' showers.

Abstinence and Sex Positivity had been locked in the sports shed together.

Someone put ground beef in PETA's vegetarian burger.

Seat Belt Safety spent hours tied to a tree before someone found him.

A counselor had to cut Plastic Kills out of her bed after someone came into her cabin in the middle of the night and burritoed her in plastic wrap while she was sleeping.

Most of the pranks occurred in the middle of the night, when you were less likely to be caught by counselors. Not that that really mattered. The counselors didn't seem to think any of this was troubling, deeming all the pranks acceptable since they fell under the umbrella of activism. If Down With Styrofoam knocked your coffee out of your hand during breakfast, it wasn't because she was trying to prank you, it was because she was protesting your criminal and outdated use of a Styrofoam cup. She even got points for it.

Which made the fact that I didn't have any points yet sting even more. "I want to help find whoever did this to ILP. I mean—I Like Paint. I mean, the Person Who We're Calling I Like Paint Until We Figure Out His Real Name."

Jimmy smiled at me and sat up, straightening a few things

on his desk. "That's very commendable, Children. But unfortunately, we don't have any leads."

"What about the security cameras? There's one right by the rec room. Have you checked the footage?"

"We have. Definitely. Thought about it. But, the thing is, I just don't know how to work a VCR." He gestured with his hand to the corner of the room, where an ancient analog television set as big as a microwave sat beneath a layer of dust. "Or is that a VHS? I keep getting those two confused."

Was he serious? Jimmy looked like he was post-college-aged. There was no way he didn't know how to use a VCR.

"Strictly DVD players in my house when I was growing up," Jimmy said. "Do you know how to work a VHS?"

"Well . . . not exactly," I admitted, feeling suddenly embarrassed for accusing Jimmy of not knowing about antique tech when I wasn't any better. "But it can't be that hard, right?"

"No, probably not that hard." We both looked over at the VCR, almost wistfully. Neither of us made a move to stand up and touch the thing.

"Children, what happened to I Like Paint's mural was sad, but have you considered the idea that maybe the attack was a protest? Maybe somebody didn't like ILP's message."

"His mural was about unity."

"And there are a lot of loners at this camp," Jimmy said. "Think about how triggering that mural could've been for them."

I didn't say anything because I needed a moment to process what he was saying. The longer camp went on, the more I'd begun to question Jimmy's ability as a head counselor. Just this morning at calisthenics he'd tried to surprise us all with a "very special visitor." It was then that I'd noticed that there were feet sticking out from behind the curtain that Jimmy stood in front of. My heart rate spiked. Was this it? Was today the day that Robert Drill finally visited the camp?

"It's none other than . . . Mr. Robert Drill . . . 's personal second assistant, Andrew Sealon!" Jimmy announced. "As I'm sure you noticed," Jimmy said, "he has quite an uncanny resemblance to Mr. Drill himself." They were both brunets. "And that's not nothing!"

Jimmy tried, but he wasn't a great head counselor. "It kind of sounds like finding ILP's attacker isn't a huge priority for you," I told him in his office.

"Oh, it absolutely is, Children. But it's also a priority for me to let campers express themselves in whatever way they need to. When Robert Drill gave me this camp, it was under very clear instructions: 'I don't care. Just do whatever you want.'"

I sat up straighter at the mention of Drill's name. "What do you mean 'gave' you this camp?"

Ever since Camp Save the World was announced, there'd been questions surrounding it. Even some controversy.

People wanted to know why Robert Drill, the savviest of businessmen—the scion of the tech world—would open up a camp for teenagers in the Catskills. Bloggers wrote think pieces about it, and strategists tried to determine Drill's endgame—if this was a purely charitable venture, if this was a PR ruse to clean up his image after that plan to open a school in Indonesia backfired when all the teachers went on strike, if this was some sort of financial investment.

"Well," Jimmy said, "you know that Robert Drill is my stepdad, right?"

I stared at Jimmy. "I didn't know Robert Drill was married."

"He married my mom in the fall. It was a beautiful private wedding. And obviously the happiest day of hers and my life. I idolize that man. His commitment to civic duty is an inspiration."

"Robert Drill is your father?" I couldn't move off that fact.

"I'd been pitching Robert ideas for his foundation—really great concepts for charities and organizations—but he didn't want to back any of them. Then I started asking if he needed any help around his office, but he told me that I was too over-qualified to work side by side with him and that if I could come up with an organization that could fit into the parameters of his Robert Drill Foundation that he would get behind it. And I thought: Robert Drill and I have something very important in common—we're great humanitarians! Have I told you that I drive a hybrid, Children?"

"No?"

"Well, I do. Anyway, I thought: Here are two great humanitarians—why not create a summer camp to find the country's next great humanitarian? And so Camp Save the World was born."

10

"You guys don't think that's kind of weird?"

A few of us had come to the rec room after dinner with the intention of checking out the damage to ILP's mural. The messy gash of red looked like something out of a Stephen King novel, and we quickly realized that we couldn't do much to help it. Also, Unity had brought Settlers of Catan and he insisted on playing, so any pretense of helping to repaint ILP's wall was forgotten. We sat in the rec room with the pieces of the game board laid out on the coffee table between the couches. I told the guys all about my meeting with Jimmy, but they were hardly as put off by it as I was.

"Is it weird that Robert Drill is Jimmy's dad?" Unity said. "Kind of. Is it weird Drill gave Jimmy a summer camp? Not really. Rich people give awesome gifts. Anybody wanna trade for sheep?"

"But doesn't it sound like Camp Save the World is just a

really elaborate way for Robert Drill to keep his annoying new stepson out of his hair?" I said.

"Robert Drill wouldn't put his name and money behind something if he didn't believe in it all the way," Win said, trading a card with Unity. "He made that video we saw on the first day. And there's the internship. I don't care if this camp is just a gift for his stepson if it means I get a great opportunity to intern with the Robert Drill Foundation."

"Yeah, who cares about the 'why' of it all?" Unity said. "I just want a trip to Florida. Miami, man!"

"The Robert Drill Foundation has offices in Tampa," I said.

Unity's brows furrowed, but only for a minute. Then his face lit up again. "Tampa! Alright!"

"Too bad for all of you that Superman already has The Prize in the bag," Men's Rights said. "Isn't that right, Superman?"

No one invited Rights, but there he was, at the other end of the room, playing an aggressive game of table tennis with Boycott Camp. "Nobody's talking to you, man," I said.

"Oh, so sorry to interrupt a bunch of losers spending their night playing a game in the rec room."

The irony was incredible. "*You're* spending your night playing a game in the rec room," I said.

"And I am dominating this Ping-Pong game!" Rights bellowed, slamming his paddle against the edge of the table.

"You're six points behind everyone else because you started with only three resources!" he said.

I looked down at the board. I only had two little orange settlements in play, compared to everyone else's towering cities. Rights was right. He was also probably right about all of us being losers, playing a board game when everyone else at camp was probably sneaking off, having debauchery. Was "having debauchery" the correct term? Of course I wouldn't know, having never had it.

We were probably the only guys not sneaking away to go be with girls. I wondered what the girls were doing right now. What did girls do at night, before lights-out? Were they braiding each other's hair? Telling each other secrets? That was probably a sexist thought. But were they making out with other guys? And was that a sexist thought too? Even if it was sexist, I couldn't stop thinking about it.

The biggest sign that we were a group of losers was that I was among them. Win was the anomaly. He sat across from me on the other couch, his left ankle resting on his right knee, his arm stretched across the top of the couch, totally casual. Win being here was charity. He could probably advance on the scoreboard just for hanging out with us. Sneaking off with girls at this time of night was probably too easy for him at this point. Maybe he was tired of it. "Why would anyone do that to

ILP's mural?" he said. "It was a good mural. ILP is a really talented artist."

"Isn't it obvious?" Rights said. Every time he swung his paddle the Ping-Pong ball shot across the room with enough force to take someone's eye out. "His mural was *too* good. He was getting a head start on winning The Prize. Someone at this camp understood that and decided to settle the score." The way Rights said it made it seem like the idea of "settling the score" was an exciting and justified one. Like he was upset he hadn't thought of it first.

I had been suspicious of Rights since the beginning of camp, but I was even more suspicious of him now. Vandalizing I Like Paint's mural for no good reason at all seemed like something Rights would do. The only thing poking holes in my theory was that Rights was practically standing right next to me when ILP appeared, dripping in paint.

"Whoever did it, I'm glad," Rights said. "Things have been too boring around here."

"Really?" Boycott Camp said. "Because at dinner I saw someone put sugar in Diabetes's sugar-free punch. Pretty unboring if you ask me."

"What?" Diabetes Awareness said. He was sitting next to me on the couch, and his head popped up just as he finished rolling the dice. He spun a seven.

"You have to get rid of half your cards," Unity told him.

Diabetes grimaced and started to count his stack of cards. "You guys, if you see someone messing with my sugar intake, please tell me."

"How can you call everything that's been happening boring?" Unity asked Rights. "The lake-throwings are dope!"

No one knew who had come up with the term "lake-throwings" (which I personally found kind of unimaginative), but the name had stuck. Aside from all the random new pranks, there was one thing we could all now rely on: For the last four nights, one camper had been thrown into the lake. It happened at different times every night, but always while everyone in camp slept. The unlucky camper would have their mouth duct-taped shut and would then be carried out to the lake, where they would be unceremoniously thrown in.

One kid a night for the last four nights.

There weren't many clues about who the attackers were, but one thing was sure: The campers they picked for the lake-throwings were unpopular. So far the victims had been Zombie Attack, S.P.E.W., Anti-Robotics, and Endangered Species.

"It's only dope because it hasn't happened to you yet," Win said. He was taking the diplomatic approach, but I didn't miss that "yet." I smirked.

"Endangered Species is my bunkmate," Diabetes said, his eyes twinkling with guilty excitement. "I didn't even know anyone had snuck into our cabin until he came back at sunrise, dripping wet."

"The internship is bullshit," Boycott Camp announced suddenly. He deflected Rights's shot by covering his face with his Ping-Pong paddle. "This camp is supposed to be about people coming together for the greater good? Please. Drill has us pitted against each other trying to win some stupid prize. It's completely fascist. Nobody deserves to get it. Least of all someone like Ashley Woodstone, who could just go to Florida anytime she wants."

"What's up with her Eat Dirt campaign?" Diabetes said, laughing. Though his laughter tapered off as he got lost in thought. "Is it healthy, though? Like, maybe we should be eating dirt?"

"That girl is a loon," Rights said. "But that's standard for Hollywood people."

I obviously wasn't Ashley Woodstone's biggest fan, but it bothered me that they were talking about her like this, laughing behind her back. "Aren't you, like, in love with her, Rights?" I said.

"Girl might be crazy, but she's hot," he said. "Especially when she dresses up in dirt and gets professional pictures taken and then puts those pictures in ads. I've never wanted to buy a newspaper so bad."

All the other guys nodded and made noises of agreement,

which made me feel left out again. Maybe Ashley was objectively good-looking, but I couldn't separate her outward appearance from her out-there philosophies. She may have been a megastar, but all I saw was a girl who liked to play in the mud. And then eat it.

"You guys think she's eating dirt right now?" Unity said, a far-off, disturbingly aroused look in his eye.

"Nah," Boycott Camp said. "I heard that when the moon's full, Ashley Woodstone likes to prance around naked in the *woods, stoned.*" He giggled to himself. "Get it? *Woods stoned?*"

But none of us were laughing. "Isn't the moon out tonight?" Unity asked.

The six of us hid behind a fallen log, just the tops of our heads peeking out as we watched Ashley Woodstone prance around in the woods, possibly stoned, but very much not naked.

Finding her had been easy. I didn't know this, but apparently Ashley wasn't staying in any of the cabins with the other girls. She had her own private place in the woods, which didn't surprise me. Of course the celebrity would get privacy. Another reason I thought Ashley didn't belong at this camp. Diabetes said he knew where it was, so we followed him. As we got deeper into the woods, we began to hear what sounded like singing. And then we saw her. Ashley Woodstone barefoot, hair loose and flowing as she danced in fluid circles with her face tilted toward the moon but her eyes closed to it.

The way the moonlight lit the woods, it was like I was watching a scene in a movie. Everything was tinged in sparkling pale blues. I wondered if somehow Ashley had arranged it all to look this way. Life tended to feel like a movie when Ashley was around—dramatic, unrealistic, large—and this was another example of that. She looked like a druid, a fairy from ancient fantasies. She was probably dancing to summon a moon goddess or something ridiculous like that. But I had to admit, it was kind of . . . transfixing.

She wore what looked like a Victorian-era nightshirt that could also have been a Coachella-ready dress. Even from this distance I spotted leaves in her hair, though I still could not tell whether that was because she'd had a run-in with a tree or because she'd placed them there decoratively. Her movements were so easy and the singing so like a lullaby, even though it didn't seem to have any words. One look at the other guys and I could see they were mesmerized too. Diabetes was on my right and he watched her openmouthed, his Adam's apple bobbing. He fell back onto his butt and a twig snapped underneath him. I turned back to Ashley but she stopped dancing suddenly, spinning to a stop in our direction.

"Is someone there?" she said.

More twigs snapped and leaves crunched and then Pika was there, staring down at us. A couple of the guys screamed, and some of them turned and ran. I tried to do both, but Ashley's bodyguard was closest to me. He grabbed the back of my shirt before I could get away.

Pika presented me to Ashley like I was a mouse he'd just caught, clamped triumphantly in his jaw.

"Gregor Maravilla. Hey." She was slightly out of breath and it was hard to see in the dark, but her face looked almost flushed. Maybe the dancing was some sort of exercise, like yoga—something that looked easy but took a lot of stamina. Her eyes were big with a sort of awed look to them, and I wondered if she really was stoned, though you could never tell with Ashley. This close to her I could see every outline and contour of her nightshirt/dress, and the mounds and swells that dwelled just underneath it. Was she not wearing a bra? I became laser focused on trying not to look directly at her, and Pika seemed laser focused on shooting arrows at me with his eyes. It was a good enough reason for me to keep my eyes firmly above Ashley's neck.

For a moment I forgot that she liked to eat dirt. I saw her just as she was: a blushing girl dancing in the moonlight. The beautiful star all the other guys saw.

"What are you doing here?"

I shrugged, and the motion reminded me that Ashley's bodyguard was still holding on to the back of my shirt. "Will you tell your bodyguard to let go of me, please?"

"Pika," Ashley said. Pika let me go and returned to the shadows from whence he came. "Were you boys spying on me?"

I pulled at the back of my shirt and tried straightening the rest of it out. "No. What were you doing?"

"Praying to Luna, the moon goddess."

Of course she was.

"We're mostly made of water, you know."

No, I did not know. I had absolutely no clue what she was talking about.

"And if the moon can control the tides, then it can control us too. I learned all about this stuff at a three-day intensive spiritual astronomy course in a mixed-used community space in Bushwick, Brooklyn. Pika and I really enjoyed it, didn't we, Pika?"

Pika nodded from the shadows.

"I was praying that Luna would be gentle with us," Ashley continued. "People tend to do strange things when the moon is out."

"You don't say."

"Like destroying poor ILP's mural," she went on. "Who would do such a thing?"

"I don't know," I said. I became aware of how awkwardly lanky I was, standing next to her in her loose shirt, her prancing-in-the-woods ways. I didn't know what to do with my arms. My feet. I wanted to go, mostly because I knew if I stayed here too long she would eventually ask me—

"Given any more thought to helping me with my Superman script?"

I sighed and smiled. There it was. "The answer is still no, Ashley."

She nodded, but she was smiling too. "I know what you need."

"What's that?"

"A spiritual journey to show you that helping me with this is good for the soul."

"Again, no."

"Well, I know what else you need. A little quid pro quo," Ashley said. "If I want your help with the script, I'm going to have to help you with something too."

"But I don't need help with anything."

"You need help with girls."

I froze, not because I was embarrassed but because what she said was incredibly accurate.

"I see the way you talk to Poe," Ashley went on. "You like her. It's obvious. But you clearly don't know how to talk to girls."

A minute ago Ashley was singing gibberish to a moon goddess, and now she understood me to the core. "You're perceptive."

"I'm an actress. It's my business to know how to read people. And you're very easy to read, Gregor Maravilla. You're a well-meaning boy, if a little directionless. You couldn't care less that I'm famous, and that's exactly the sort of person who would be perfectly honest with me. And you want Poe. So here's what I propose: You help me with my Superman script and I help you get Poe."

"Get? Get?" I said, suddenly disturbed by Ashley's totally on-point observations about me. "I cannot just *get* a girl. A girl is not something for a guy to possess. And who says I could 'get' her anyway? Poe is very probably gay, and if she is— which isn't even my place to say!—then your assumption that I could, what—turn her straight?—is totally wrong and very problematic. We shouldn't even be discussing Poe's sexuality right now, because it has nothing to do with anything and I am totally against thinking about a girl in terms of her sexual identity and you can't just turn a girl straight when she isn't, you can't just change someone's sexuality . . . I mean . . . right?"

Somehow, in this whole indignant rant, I'd ended things on a hopeful note. I now looked at Ashley like she was maybe some magic forest fairy who could indeed communicate with moon goddesses and help hopeless guys like me. For her part,

Ashley looked at me like she did not understand a thing I'd just said, which made sense since I barely understood it myself.

"Okay, you may not have a shot with Poe. But even so, I could teach you everything you want to know about girls. And that knowledge could be useful to you long after you leave this camp. I could help you with your general girl problem."

"General girl problem" sounded like the kind of affliction I had been hoping someone would diagnose me with just so that I could take the appropriate measures to remedy it. Suffice to say, I was listening.

"Lucky for you, I know all about girls," Ashley said. "I am a girl, after all. And my favorite comedy subgenre is the romantic comedy. I basically study romances. Everything you've ever experienced has already happened in a movie. And chances are I've watched that movie. We could use my encyclopedic knowledge of film to solve your general girl problem!"

"Me liking Poe has happened in a movie?"

"Sure!" Ashley said. "It's just like in *Chasing Amy*, the seminal Kevin Smith classic where Ben Affleck is in love with Joey Lauren Adams but Joey Lauren Adams only dates women. Ben's character is even into comic books, like you."

"And he gets the girl?"

Ashley shrugged/nodded, which didn't really answer my question, but I still considered her offer. "That's just a movie, Ashley. And I'm not Ben Affleck."

"Well, clearly. But have you got any other options?"

Obviously I didn't. But I shook my head. "I'm at this camp to win The Prize. I need to focus. People are getting pranked and thrown into the lake and—"

"And the flyers!" Ashley said. She zipped over to Pika, and he took a piece of paper out of his pocket without Ashley having to say anything. She brought it to me so I could read it. STOP INDENTURED SERVITUDE! the paper roared.

"Someone taped that to my door," Ashley said. "Are they accusing me of underpaying Pika? Because Pika is more than just an employee to me. I take this allegation very seriously."

"They're just the flyers that everyone is making, trying to get points."

At dinner earlier, PETA slid an EATING ANIMALS IS MURDER! flyer onto my table just as I took a bite out of my turkey sandwich. When I put my sandwich down and picked up my salad, Non-GMO slipped me a flyer telling me to EAT ORGANIC! Diabetes and Unity had started collecting the flyers and trading them like they were baseball cards. Unity's most prized flyer had been printed on scented neon-green stationery and had only appeared once. It was rumored to be part of a strictly limited set of ten. The flyer was coveted as much for its rareness as it was for its message. It read YOGURT IS ALIVE!

"Something to do with bacteria," Unity had told me. "Didn't you know single-celled organisms are people too?"

That was literally incorrect, but nobody seemed to care. Making flyers was activism du jour at Camp Save the World.

"The flyers are harmless," I told Ashley. "Ignore them."

The next morning, I found out that Diabetes Awareness was the latest lake-throwing victim. And also, you couldn't take one step outside your cabin door without landing on one of the rainbow-colored flyers that carpeted the grounds of the camp. I was pretty sure that loud, reverberating sob in the distance was Save the Trees stepping out of her cabin for the first time today.

I picked up the paper stuck to my sneaker and read.

My fellow campers,

I've noticed that a lot of us are acting out our frustrations with each other in ways that seem really counterproductive to what we came to this camp to do. I say we talk it out. Please join me tomorrow night for an evening of honesty and truth. (And possibly more!)

AN EVENING OF HONESTY AND TRUTH

When: Tonight after dinner

Where: The middle of the woods

Hosted by: Your friend, Ashley Woodstone

11

Ashley Woodstone lived in a yurt. Instead of sharing a cabin with other campers, Ashley Woodstone was spending her summer at Camp Save the World in a circular tent dwelling most preferred by nomads. It was big, though, to the point where I could imagine a bedroom, a kitchen, and even a small living room fitting inside of it. Though really, I had no idea what was inside. It could have been filled to the brim with sacks of mud for all I knew. Sustenance.

I was only seeing it from the outside, but the yurt looked like it was made out of a wooden frame with a bunch of different materials covering it. In some places the walls looked like they were made of green tarp; in others, animal hide. There were bits of woven mats and other large swaths of greenery that most resembled palm leaves, though that had to be wrong, since palm trees weren't native to New York. The yurt was kind of like a patchwork tent on acid, and I couldn't wrap my mind around how it had been constructed. It looked almost like it'd been there forever, like it had emerged from the earth whole, having collected its tapestries naturally over the centuries. It also looked like maybe a team of beavers had assembled it. Maybe they had. Who knew, with Ashley.

But the Evening of Honesty and Truth wouldn't be taking place inside Ashley's yurt.

About thirty of us campers had shown up. We sat in a circle around a campfire in front of the yurt, waiting for all the truth and honesty to begin. Ashley was nowhere in sight, but her bodyguard was here. He folded his arms over his wide chest and walked slowly and silently around us, like the bad cop in an interrogation room. He looked, as always, mildly bored and massively ticked off.

I was fully planning on not coming to Ashley's Evening of Honesty and Truth. Tonight was movie night at the rec room, and they were playing a movie called *The Stupids*. If its title was any indication, it would still be better than this. It was Win who'd convinced me to come to the Evening of Honesty and Truth. He said the camp could use some "honesty and truth" right about now. He also said that Poe would be there. Obviously, skipping movie night was an easy decision. Poe sat next to Win, who sat next to me, which basically meant that Poe and I were sitting together.

Ashley banged through the front door of her yurt and came to meet us. "Friends!" she said. "Welcome to an Evening of Honesty and Truth. I've been meaning to host an evening of honesty and truth ever since I got here, and this seemed like the perfect opportunity. I'm glad so many of you could make it." She circled the group of us, and her soft features were made harsher by the dancing firelight. "This is a safe space. I want everyone to be able to say whatever it is they want to say and not feel threatened. But in order for that to happen, you must all agree to *listen* and *feel*, openly and without prejudice. Why don't we talk about why we're here? At this camp. Let's remind ourselves of the beauty and significance of our true missions. I'll start. I'm here to spread the word about the economic and nutritional value of eating dirt. Who wants to go next?"

A girl raised her hand. I couldn't remember what her campaign was.

"I'm at this camp because there are so many screwed-up things happening in the world. And all any of my friends at home ever want to talk about are boys and clothes. I hate them."

Feminism raised her hand. "I hope you're not implying that girls who talk about boys and clothes are inherently stupid or vapid or something, because that is so not a good attitude to have."

"You of all people should agree with me," the first girl said. "Girls who only care about girly things aren't doing anything for the betterment of womankind."

"And just what do you mean by 'girly' things? It's people like you with your warped ideas of gender norms and what it means to be a 'real girl' that are—"

Stop Clubbing Baby Seals stood. "Can we get back on topic, please? S.P.E.W. is right." *S.P.E.W.* That was who the first girl was. I still had no idea what S.P.E.W. stood for, though. "The world *is* screwed up, and some of us are here trying to learn how to make the world a better place. Unlike some other people here with ridiculous campaigns that are basically just wasting the camp's resources."

"We all know you're talking about me!" Anti-Robotics said, shooting up with remarkable agility for such a large guy. Anti-Robotics had the physical shape of a linebacker and the high-pitched, shrill voice of an elderly woman stuck in a free-falling elevator. He directed all of his rage at Stop Clubbing Baby Seals. Something about the way they were looking at each other made it seem like this was not the first heated debate they'd had. "Everyone wants to ignore the inevitable, which is that by the year 2045 artificial intelligence will take over our lives, and if we don't do something to stop it *now*, we are looking at a world in which robots will dominate the earth!"

"Guys, I think we're getting a little off topic," Ashley said. "We're here to talk about the sabotage that's been happening around camp. And I don't think anyone knows more about that than I Like Paint, whose beautiful unity mural was destroyed in a callous act of hatred. Would you like to say something, ILP?"

ILP stood up slowly and looked around the campfire, his eyes seeming to settle on all of us briefly. I wasn't sure why Ashley was making him speak. All he was going to say was . . .

"I like paint."

We let I Like Paint's words settle over us. They were quiet but profound, and a reminder that people who don't speak your language have a voice too. Ashley squeezed ILP's shoulder. "I think those words are more poignant now than they've ever been," she said.

Rights stood next. "Ashley asked an important question: Why are we all here? Well, actually, let me explain it to you. I am here to win The Prize. And I intend to use my wealth of knowledge on the topic of my campaign to help those of you in need. Diabetes, you were thrown into the lake last night, were you not? If you accept my help, together we can combat those man-haters who put you in that lake. Heck, we can make you the stronger man that I know you can be. If being knowledge-able and helpful means I'm closer to winning The Prize, then so be it. And if that means partaking in a few pranks here and there, then I am perfectly comfortable with joining in the fun. And all of you should be too."

The way he spoke, it wasn't hard for me to imagine Rights

as a politician one day, one of those crooked ones who serves his constituents all smiles while dumping toxic waste into their water supply. He began to walk around us, the goose to our ducks. "I think you're all forgetting that we're here to win a trip to Florida. If you're just here to make friends . . . you're basically forfeiting."

I surprised myself by standing, but I couldn't just sit there and listen to the crap Rights was spewing. "There's a difference between promoting your cause and dumping on everyone else's, Rights. The latter is called sabotage. And that's what you're doing. You're basically inciting it right now." Speaking out against Rights spiked my blood with adrenaline. I felt like I'd just taken off running. It felt good. "We're working against each other when we should be working together. Well, technically separately, I guess. But separate and civil. The point is, all the sabotage is making this whole camp experience suck. And I'm not going to stand for it anymore."

The adrenaline was still there, even though I'd stopped talking. It felt suddenly like maybe coming to this camp was paying off. Like maybe I was learning how to become the leader I one day intended to be. I was pumped, but that feeling was quickly extinguished when Rights pulled the book from behind his back. My book.

"Are you people really going to sit there and listen to

someone who reads *How to Get a Girlfriend* every night before he goes to bed?" Rights said.

I could have set myself on fire. Literally: I jumped over the campfire trying to swipe the book out of his hands, but Rights was too quick.

"He underlined parts of it," Rights said. "Well, he underlined most of it."

My eyes darted to Poe. Her face contorted in a mixture of *squick* and pity. I lunged for the book again, and this time I managed to yank it out of Rights's hands, but something told me the only reason I got it back was because Rights let me have it. I tossed it into the fire without a second thought.

"I mean, is this really the kind of guy you're all going to listen to?" Rights went on, addressing the campers. "We all just watched him burn a book. He's a book burner."

"BOOK BURNER!" Books Save Lives yelled.

"So what if I sabotage your campaign?" Rights continued. "You are a *white boy* who thinks it's his mission in life to save the children of *Latin America*."

"I want to feed *all* children," I said. "Also obviously Latin American children, but——" My voice was drowned out by Rights, who spoke over me. Not that it mattered, since no one was listening to me.

"And did you hear what Children just said?" Rights asked.

"He said we need to be separate but civil. *Separate* but *civil*. Now, I don't know about you folks, but to me that sounds an awful lot like *separate but equal*. He's pretty much a low-key bigot."

It got very quiet very quickly. Even the embers in the flames seemed to stop crackling. "Are you kidding me? I'm not a bigot!"

"Sounds like something a bigot would say."

"This is ridiculous. I love everyone!" That sounded weird. I shook my head quickly and tried again. "I love children!" That sounded even worse.

"Next he's going to tell us that he's not a bigot because his best friend at camp is black," Rights said, pointing to Win.

There was so much tension in the air, and I thought it was because what Rights said was so inappropriate, but when I looked around, trying to find someone who I could share my shocked outrage with, everyone looked back at me with accusatory disappointment.

"Wait, I don't believe that," I said. "I didn't actually say that—Men's Rights did!"

I tried to catch Win's eye but he was whispering something to Poe. It was probably about how much of a bigot I was.

"I'm not a bigot!" I said. Though it didn't seem to matter. Once Rights said it out loud, everyone believed it was true.

Shit.

The camp thought I was a bigot.

"Thank you for a truly enlightening evening, Ashley," Rights said. Then he took a wad of bills out of his pocket and threw them at my face. "Go feed the children, dipshit." And with that, he left.

A quiet settled over us, but then people started to get up, as if Rights's exit signaled the end of the event.

"Where is everyone going?" Ashley said. "Pika made brownies! They're not dirt brownies!"

I was screwed.

12

Waking up in total darkness by a strip of duct tape savagely adhered to my mouth—that was the initial shock. But I couldn't say that I was surprised that they'd chosen to kidnap me in the middle of the night. It was three of them, all in black, and that was all I saw before they put a pillowcase over my head and hauled me out of the cabin. Two of them held me by my armpits, and the other one had my legs. It was a bumpy ride through the camp grounds with only the sound of my muted yells and their heavy breathing and occasional giggling.

The reason they'd chosen me was obvious. My three assailants said as much as they threw me sideways into the lake. "That's for being a bigot!"

I should also mention that they stripped me completely naked before throwing me in.

The water was icy, but only for a moment. There was too much else going on to really think about it anyway. Thankfully, the pillowcase had slipped off before I'd hit the water, but my duct tape was still on. I tore it off when I broke through the surface. It stung.

They were gone. The last of them disappeared through the woods carrying all of my clothes in their arms.

"Hey!" I shouted. Though that wasn't going to do any good. They weren't going to return my clothes just because I shouted at them.

I swallowed, treading water, and tried to focus my mind and figure out what to do. "I'm naked," I said to myself, stating the only relevant fact that I could think of. I couldn't worry about who'd done this to me or the fact that I was in the lake. All I knew was that I didn't have any clothing anywhere. I couldn't leave the lake naked. If I did—with my luck—someone would see me, and then I would forever be known as the camp's bigoted streaker.

"Hello?"

I stopped moving. A dangerous decision to make in a lake, considering that not moving would lead to certain drowning. But drowning didn't sound so bad right now.

"Gregor Maravilla?"

It couldn't be . . .

"Is that you?" Ashley Woodstone said. She was in the water, swimming right toward me from the other side of the dock, where I hadn't been able to see her.

"Are you kidding me?" I said. I only had my hands, but they would have to be enough to cover myself up, though I was sure she couldn't see down there. Just kicking underwater would have to keep me afloat. "It's the middle of the night. What are you doing here?"

"Swimming."

"*Swimming?*"

"Swimming."

This was just like getting kidnapped—seeing her was the initial shock, but once that passed, I wasn't surprised. Because *of course* Ashley Woodstone would be here right now. Where else would she be?

"Why is it always you?" I said. "You're constantly there with a front-row seat to all of my humiliations." Ashley was an exclamation point. I may have been the joke, but she was always the punch line. I could just imagine my brother, Anton, telling it: "*Gregor got thrown into the lake naked. But here's the kicker: Ashley Woodstone was there to see it!*"

"Humiliations?" Ashley said, swimming languidly before me. "Some people would kill to be where you are right now. Skinny-dipping with Ashley Woodstone."

"You're . . . naked?" In this darkness the water was black, and with Ashley's hair wet and heavy over her shoulders I couldn't tell that she wasn't wearing anything.

"Bathing suits are so constricting. I like to feel the water on my skin. Natural. Nothing in between."

I held on to myself tighter, reminding myself to keep kicking because I was starting to sink.

"But swimming without bathing suits isn't socially acceptable in this part of the world," she said in the sort of mocking tone of voice that sounded like she'd been reprimanded for this before. "So I have to do it when no one is around."

She was swimming so close to me, circling me. Her hair was plastered down her back whenever she surfaced, and swayed like coral behind her when she was submerged.

"I'm sorry about what happened earlier at my campfire. I can't believe Rights said those things about you."

"They aren't true."

"Of course they aren't. Who would ever try to find a girl-friend using a how-to book?" She smiled at me, and I could've sworn she winked just before dunking into the water. I waited for her to come back up before I continued.

"Do you think I'm a bigot now too?"

"You mean because you're a cis white kid trying to save the children of Latin America?"

"I'm half Latino," I muttered. "And I want to help *all* children." I lolled in place, letting the lower part of my face dip into the water. I opened my mouth and took some in, spitting it back out before I said what I was about to say. "I think I might be . . . offensive."

"What are you talking about?"

I shrugged. "I always thought I was pretty good at telling when something was offensive. Or at calling people out when they were being offensive. But I never stopped to consider the fact that . . . maybe I'm actually totally offensive."

"That's crazy."

"The word 'crazy' is offensive to those suffering from mental health issues." I always felt responsible to point something like that out. More often than not, people would roll their eyes in response. But I also felt that it was important to talk about this stuff and make people more aware of the things they were saying. Ashley didn't make me feel weird for saying it, though. She actually looked like she was considering never using the word "crazy" again.

"Maybe I do have a savior complex," I said. "And maybe Rights is right that it's offensive for me to try to be a hero for a whole group of people. But maybe me feeling sorry for myself right now is offensive too. It's like, who am I to feel bad if the people I'm offending feel even worse, you know?"

"Not really," Ashley said. "You might be totally right, but you also might not be making any sense. It's very hard to say." She disappeared under the water and then broke through the surface with such enthusiasm that I thought she'd come up with the perfect thing to say. Really, she just needed to breathe.

"I'm just tired of other people telling me who they think I am," I said. This was a heavy conversation. Probably too heavy to be having naked in a lake. But Ashley was a good listener, so it felt nice talking to her. She circled slowly around me still. "Sometimes I just feel like people look at me and make assumptions and snap judgments about who I am or who I'm not. People look at me but they don't really see me."

Ashley stopped swimming to paddle in front me. She looked at me with such wide-eyed intensity that for a moment what I'd just said felt like a lie. It didn't feel like she was looking at me, it felt like she was looking into me. "I know exactly what you mean," she said.

She was so close to me that if I were to let go of myself and reach out I could touch her. Skin on skin. Natural. Nothing in between. I was definitely starting to sink. And I let myself. I went under but when I opened my eyes everything was dark. When I came back up, Ashley had already started swimming away again, moving around me so that I had to keep turning in place to see her.

"There's a lot for you to think about here," she said. "But here's what I know: You are Gregor Maravilla. You love Superman. And you want to do good. You're not offensive."

"Yeah?"

"Yeah!" Ashley said. "And even if you are, we're all a little problematic sometimes. Trust me, I live under a microscope. Anytime I say the wrong thing—which happens a lot—I don't hear the end of it for weeks. All we can do is listen and learn and hope to be better. The Prize and the pranks and all the sabotage just have people on edge, making them say all sorts of weird things."

She continued to swim and I continued to kick, awkwardly holding myself. I thought about what Anton said, about experiencing firsts. Skinny-dipping with a girl was definitely a first for me, however arbitrarily it had happened. But this was definitely not what Anton had in mind. I didn't think I could stay afloat much longer without using my arms. "A lot of people would kill to be where I am right now, and yet, I gotta be honest, Ashley, all I want to do is get out."

Ashley laughed—actually *laughed*—and splashed me. "See! That right there is what I love about you, Gregor Maravilla! You don't care about me."

When she put it that way it sounded strange. "*That's* what you love about me?" It was preposterous and at the same time overwhelmingly sad. "Do you still want me to help you? With your Superman script?"

She stopped before me, treading in place. "Really?"

"No one else at this camp seems too fond of me at the

moment." I shrugged. "You might be the only person left willing to hang out with me."

It was true, but a bigger part of why I was agreeing to help her was because of what she'd said. That I didn't care who she was. That that was a good thing. It sounded so . . . lonely.

"Yes!" Ashley said. More laughing. More splashing.

"Okay, alright, I'll do it if you get me some clothes."

"Pika, get Gregor some clothes, please!"

13

There were a few hours left until daybreak, but I slammed into Cabin 8 loud enough to wake everyone in there up.

"What's going on?" Win said, sitting instantly and wiping the sleep from his eyes.

Rights was slower to wake but he eventually did. I think it was his own laughter that got him fully alert, like a dog who wakes himself up with his own farts. "What the hell are you wearing, Superman?"

Pika got me Camp Save the World sweatpants and an orange girls' Camp Save the World crop top. I stood over Rights's bed in a T-shirt that barely came down low enough to skim the bottom of my ribs. According to Ashley, those were the only clothes Pika could find. I wasn't sure I believed her.

"I know it was you, Rights."

"Man, it's four in the morning; what the hell are you going on about?"

"You threw me in the lake."

"You got thrown in the lake?" Win said. ILP's eyebrows shot up as though he understood too. Rights's laughter started up again. "Congrats, Superman! I know how exclusive a membership to the lake-throwings club is."

I didn't do violence. It was my firm belief that all conflict could be resolved with cooler heads. But something deep broke inside of me and came out as a roar. I jumped him, and Rights responded by rolling both of us off the bed and slamming me to the floor. Even before I jumped on Rights I knew this would be a losing fight. My biggest advantage had probably been the element of surprise, but now the tables had turned significantly, his knee bearing down on the back of my neck. Somewhere in my peripheral vision Win was trying to pull Rights off of me. But the guy was carved out of stone. I did everything I could to try to squirm away, but it was like a statue had fallen on top of me.

"You're an asshole!" I rasped between breaths. "The whole camp thinks I'm a bigot because of you!"

"Stop being such a bigot, then."

"I'm not a bigot!"

"Says the white boy who just jumped a Latino minding his own business."

"I'M HALF LATINO!"

"Shut the fuck up and feed some children, you stupid dick." Amazingly, Rights was able to pin me down and still sprinkle crumpled bills onto my head. How the hell had he gotten money in the middle of our fight?!

"You're going to kill him," Win said, his voice far too calm to convey those words. "You should probably get off of him."

"Not until he apologizes for ruining my beauty sleep."

"Never!" I shouted.

In the end it was ILP who ran to the counselors' house to wake Jimmy up. And now Men's Rights and I sat in the office as Jimmy slumped behind his desk, still half-asleep. "Fighting? Come on, guys. I thought you were better than that."

"Fighting?" Rights said. "I was giving Gregor a hug."

"I'm going to have to dock both of you two points."

"You can't dock me points," I said. "I don't have any points."

"And that's how I finally ended up on the scoreboard. With negative two points."

Ashley frowned. Though it wasn't really a frown—more like a frownie face. She was incapable of looking sad, apparently, but I appreciated the sentiment.

"I can't believe you got in a fight. There's a big welt on your cheekbone. Are you sure you're okay? How many fingers am I holding up? Who holds the record for most Golden Globe nominations?"

"I don't know, Ashley."

"Oh gosh, it's Meryl Streep!" Ashley said. "Should I get help?"

I stopped her before she got too worked up and ran for Nurse Patrosian. I looked back down to the open script in my lap, trying to focus again on the task at hand.

The two of us sat on the ground. We were in the clearing in the woods where I first found Ashley doing her moon dance. I'd told her I'd come meet her here after the day's activities to help her on the Superman sequel. But I only agreed to come under one condition: Pika could not be here. I'd had enough of constantly standing in the shade of his massive shadow while his eyes bore down on me, not so subtly telecasting the fact that he wanted to kill me. I wondered where Ashley's bodyguard went and what he did when he had an hour to himself. But no matter where I pictured him—fishing in the lake, buying snacks, running through a field of wildflowers—he was always scowling. And very possibly breaking a baby bird with his bare hands.

Unless he was hiding up in a tree somewhere, Pika wasn't here, and I could finally relax around Ashley. Unfortunately, the *Superman 2* script was—no surprise here—truly awful. It was so soul-crushingly wrong and terrible that I kept getting distracted, not that I knew exactly what I was doing here anyway. Ashley said she needed help learning her lines, so I played Superman and she did her part as Lois Lane. She said that my knowledge of the Superman canon could help inform her acting choices. But I couldn't exactly do much to help when there were lines like "*Save me, Superman! I don't think I can hold on much longer!*"

Ashley still threw herself into every scene, though, and her dedication was rubbing off on me. I figured if I was going to do this thing I better commit. I skimmed the page, trying to find my place again. *"Don't die on me, Lois. Don't let go."* I stopped, sighed. "Why did Lois fall out of the window?"

"She tripped."

I took my pen out of my pocket. "Can I change this?"

"Go for it."

Lois Lane does not trip, I wrote in the margin of the page. *She falls out of the window trying to save a baby from a vulture. She is a national hero.*

Ashley had been kind enough to let me rewrite the story in the margins of the pages. It was a good thing there was so much white space in scripts, because every page we'd rehearsed together was now a giant scribble of our handwriting. I knew this didn't change things, that when Ashley flew back to LA at the end of summer to begin shooting this thing, someone would probably take this script from her, burn it, and hand her a new one. But it felt good reimagining a Superman story.

We'd also renamed the movie *Superman 2: Lois Lane Is a National Hero*.

I continued to read the script. *"We are tight on Superman's CHEST. He flexes his PECS before FLYING out of the window to rescue Lois."* I tossed the script aside and lay back, staring up at the trees.

"You seem distracted," Ashley said. "Still thinking about the points?"

"Thinking about that, and getting thrown into the lake. I know it was Rights who did it."

"Why do you say that?"

"Because he hates me. And just physically, he's strong enough to carry me from my cabin to the lake. He probably masterminded the destruction of ILP's mural too."

"If only you could find out who really destroyed ILP's mural. Maybe Jimmy would reward you by getting you back up to zero points."

I sat up with a start. "And Rights would get in trouble."

"What?"

I was almost bouncing in place as the idea formed, coming quicker than I could put words to it. "I could kill a bunch of birds with one stone: help ILP by finding out who was behind his attack, get points for solving the biggest mystery at camp, and get Rights in trouble. It was obviously him who destroyed the mural. If I have evidence of that, maybe he'll even get kicked out."

"You really don't like Rights."

"You know he leaves me money under my pillow every night? He's like the douchebag tooth fairy."

"Okay, but how are you going to prove that he was responsible for what happened to I Like Paint?"

"The security cameras. I'll just do what none of the other counselors did: I'll watch the footage from that day."

"You're going to sneak into the counselors' office!" Ashley said, gleeful, giddy. "How exciting!"

I hadn't thought this plan all the way through, and the idea of sneaking into the office already had me worried. I'd never done anything like that before. It could all backfire. I could be the one to get kicked out instead of Rights.

"I've never snuck in anywhere before."

"I could help you!" Ashley said. "I know a lot about sneaking into places. I once broke into a pet store to rescue a baby chick on an episode of *Smarty Pants*. We could assemble a team, like Clark Kent does with Jimmy Olsen and Lois Lane. Oooh, we can live out the script and have a real adventure! Say yes, Gregor."

14

"Great morning workout, guys!" Jimmy said, catching his breath. It was another morning of calisthenics. Jimmy led us in extremely easy exercises that continued to challenge my lanky, flailing limbs. Win continued to execute all the motions in perfect form. Ashley's bodyguard continued to work out for her as she sat on the grass, making friends with a caterpillar. Men's Rights ignored the calisthenics altogether and was instead personally training Diabetes in some complicated-looking CrossFit workout or something. Rights wasn't doing anything particularly diabolical at the moment, but anytime I looked at him I was filled with an irrational hatred. No, not irrational, I had to remind myself. He'd thrown me in the lake and ruined ILP's mural. I just had to prove it.

"I have an announcement!" Jimmy said. "Tomorrow will be the second competition, so get ready! I won't tell you what it is just yet, but here's a hint: It's an endurance challenge! Exciting, right? So eat right and make sure to get your strength up! Anyway, you guys have been doing so well at this camp that I think you all deserve something special. What do you say, d'ya think you deserve a special surprise?"

A few campers answered him and cheered.

"Do you think Drill's here?" Win asked me.

"No way."

I couldn't trust Jimmy and his surprises anymore. But still, I hoped.

"We've got a very special visitor today!" Jimmy said.

"It could be Drill," Win said. "Today could be the day."

"No way."

Win, despite his better judgment, seemed to believe. And despite my own better judgment, I was letting his excitement get to me. I mean, was it really that hard to believe that Robert Drill could be here? A visit from him was way past due.

"Yes, boys, girls, and non-binaries," Jimmy said. "It's none other than . . . Mr. Robert Drill . . ." Jimmy pressed a button on a remote I hadn't noticed him holding. And suddenly, Robert Drill appeared before all of us, flickering, staticky, and completely transparent. ". . . the hologram!"

"No way," I said, but Win was laughing.

The hologram of Robert Drill shimmered before us, and the murmurs among the campers took on a tone of awe rather than disappointment, which explained why Jimmy looked pleased.

"Hello, everyone!" Robert Drill the Hologram said. "I'm so glad to be joining you on this glorious day." It was obviously a prerecorded hologram. He wasn't coming to us live from anywhere. "Here at DrillTech we're constantly improving the way people communicate, and that includes pioneering hologram technology."

Someone took off their shoe and threw it at the hologram. It went right through him.

"Amazing," Win said.

"Amazing" was one word for it. "Bullshit" was another. I raised my hand but didn't wait for Jimmy to call on me. "Uh, Jimmy, any word on when the real Robert Drill will be visiting the camp?"

"This is the real Robert Drill, Gregor," Jimmy said. "He personally sent this hologram over for us. He doesn't do that for just anybody, you know." More kids started throwing things, and Hologram Drill began flickering more than usual.

"I mean in the flesh," I said. "As in, a real live human person."

But Jimmy ignored my question. He was too busy pushing buttons on his remote, trying to fix the hologram, which had frozen, leaving us with an image of Robert Drill that looked like he was midsneeze.

"This blows," I said.

"It's kinda funny," Win said.

"Funny? That we've seen every possible version of Robert Drill here but the real one?"

"It's a little funny." He took a stick of gum out of his pocket and popped it into his mouth. Win wasn't totally wrong. Most of the campers seemed to at least enjoy this version of Robert Drill, as opposed to the other versions we'd seen. They'd started up a game, throwing any object they could find at the hologram. Getting something near Hologram Drill's mouth or crotch elicited the most laughter.

"Hey, Win? I'm thinking about sneaking into the counselors' office."

"Why?"

"I'm going to check the security footage to find out who destroyed I Like Paint's mural. He still seems pretty upset about it."

"Really? He seems pretty fine to me," Win said, smirking.

"Well, whatever, somebody's gotta look out for him."

"And you're that somebody," Win said, chewing.

"I guess."

"Noble of you, Gregor, but if you're looking for help breaking into the counselors' office, you can count me out."

I nodded slowly, slightly bummed but not totally surprised by Win's response. "Is this because of what happened at Ashley's campfire? Rights said a lot of stuff about me, but none of it's true. I mean, yeah, that book about how to get a girl-friend was technically mine. But it was a gift. Anyway, the rest of it wasn't true. You have to know that I'm not a bigot."

Win laughed. He actually doubled over laughing. "I don't think you're a bigot, Gregor. Even if I am your only black friend."

"You're not! I mean, at this camp you are, but that's only because I'm not really friends with a lot of people—"

"Calm down, Gregor, I was kidding. I'm not going to help you because if we get caught we'd probably get kicked out. And I'm in a really good position on the scoreboard right now. Can't risk it."

Win had a point. As ridiculous as this camp was proving to be—Hologram Drill was flickering in and out of existence at this point—I still didn't want to get kicked out.

Win shot his chewed-up gum straight from his mouth at Hologram Drill. It soared through the air in a perfect spiral and went right into the middle of the hologram's mouth. The campers erupted into cheers, and Jimmy was finally able to shut the hologram down.

"If you're really looking to assemble a team, it shouldn't be that hard," Win said. "There are people at this camp who hate it. They'd probably help you out."

*　　*　　*

As always, Win had been right—finding someone to help me break into the counselors' office turned out to be easier than I thought it would be. I knew just the person to ask.

I found Boycott Camp picketing his Outdoor Cookery activity. His picket sign read COOKING IS FOR FASCISTS, and I hadn't even gotten my full request out before he agreed to help.

"Will arson be involved?" he asked.

"What? No, of course not."

"We'll have to find another way."

So the team was assembled. It was me, Ashley, Boycott Camp, and ILP, who was not actually part of the team but endured us having our first meeting by his revamped mural as he painted.

"First order of business: sneaking into the counselors' office," I said to my team. "How do we do that?"

"I thought you had this whole thing planned out," Boycott Camp said.

"I thought we could brainstorm together to come up with the best idea."

"In that case I think we should embark on a spiritual journey," Ashley said. "The answer will come to us."

"No spiritual journeys, Ashley," I said. "We need to be in and out of there quickly, without being seen. Maybe you can tell us how you broke into the pet store on your show."

"I had the key."

I stared at her blankly. It took a few moments for a range of emotions to wash over me. Confusion. Frustration. Impatience. And worst of all, the realization that I'd hinged this entire endeavor on the experience of an *actress* playing a *character on a scripted television show*. I wanted to throw something. I wanted to quit. But Ashley smiled and continued.

"But!" she said. "I was in a movie with Sean Piss called *Cold Dark City*. Any of you saw it?"

We shook our heads.

"That's understandable; it came out ten years ago and was rated R. I was only six or seven when we filmed it, so I didn't even watch it myself until recently. I played Sean Piss's daughter. I remember him being quiet but nice—a very talented actor. Truly, I was lucky to be able to share some screen time with him. Though he did reek of alcohol, which was kind of unpleasant but also weirdly intoxicating in a way? It gave me some very confusing feel—"

"Get to the point," I said.

"Right. Anyway, there's a scene in that movie where Sean Piss has to sneak into a private detective's office to steal something. What he did was use a commotion outside as a distraction."

"A distraction," I said, nodding. "So what could we distract Jimmy with?"

155

"I could start a fire in the rec room," Boycott Camp said.

ILP must've understood the words "fire" and "rec room," because he suddenly looked at us warily, placing a hand protectively on his artwork. I was beginning to wonder if Boycott Camp wasn't actually *against camp* so much as *for arson*. "Let's just hold off on all fire-related ideas for now," I said. "But getting Jimmy to come all the way to this side of the camp is a good idea. How do we do it?"

"Leave it to me," Ashley said.

Half an hour later, as I crouched in the bushes next to the counselors' office, I wondered if leaving it to Ashley was really such a good idea. The plan was simple: Boycott Camp would stage a fake fight with ILP down by the rec room, and Ashley would make sure to get Jimmy there. Though the more I thought about it, the flimsier this plan seemed. I only now realized that ILP really had no clue what we were up to, and Boycott Camp staging a fight with him could prove traumatizing.

Well, there was no turning back now.

"You ready?" I asked her. Ashley was crouching beside me, and Pika was crouching beside her, though I don't think the bushes did much to camouflage him.

"As I'll ever be," Ashley said.

"Be convincing."

"Gregor, please," she said. "I'm an actress."

I watched as she took off, followed by Pika. The two of them stopped just in front of the counselors' office. She winked at me. Ashley looked way more cheery than I needed her to be, and the winking certainly didn't help. Jimmy would never believe there was an emergency that needed his immediate attention if Ashley Woodstone looked like she'd just baked him a birthday cake. But then she twisted her face up suddenly, her forehead crinkling, her eyes getting shiny. Her mouth drew open, and a giant sob wrenched itself out of it. "Jimmy!" she cried. It was a real, bloodcurdling cry, and I suddenly wondered if she'd ever played the victim in a horror movie before.

The scream was enough to get Jimmy to burst out of the office. "Ashley! What is it?!"

"Boycott Camp is setting fire to I Like Paint's mural! Only you can stop him!"

I thought "Only you can stop him" was a bit much, but it worked. Jimmy ran immediately in the direction of the rec room, Ashley and Pika close on his heels. Ashley needed to be there to convince Jimmy to stay when he saw that no real emergency was occurring. Unless Boycott Camp really was setting fire to an unsuspecting ILP's mural. Which, come to think of it, was a very real possibility. But I had no time to worry about that now. The door to the counselors' office was open and waiting for me.

"Come on, let's go!"

I spun around at the voice. Boycott Camp was right behind me, eyes laser focused on the door to the counselors' office.

"Dude, what are you doing here?!" I said.

"I thought you might need backup."

"If you're not at the rec room, then Jimmy has no reason to be there!"

"We better hurry up, then."

I bit down hard, but there was no time to be angry, because Boycott Camp—who wasn't even supposed to be here—was right. Jimmy would be back sooner than anticipated. We had to act fast. When we got to the door we were met by Blake, the sports counselor. "What are you doing?" she said.

"I . . . I . . ." I couldn't think. I was caught. It was for nothing. This whole plan was for nothing, and now I would get kicked out. "I'm sorry—"

"Just close the door on your way out," Blake said. She left the office.

I stood frozen for a minute, wondering what just happened. But Boycott Camp ran inside and I followed him.

The office was even messier than the last time I was here. There were documents everywhere: on filing cabinets rather than in them, posted to the walls, overflowing in the wastebasket.

"What the hell is this?" Boycott Camp said.

Jimmy's desk held a gigantic papier-mâché construction of what appeared to be a full-scale kingdom. There was a castle on a hill, barracks, a granary for food storage, stables, practice rings for swordplay and archery. A dog kennel. I knew what everything was because there were tiny signs next to every edifice, describing its role. A flag protruding from the highest tower of the castle told me that this kingdom was called JIMMYWORLD!™, with a subtitle explaining that JimmyWorld!™ was an "ideal utopian society of the future!"

We didn't have any time to waste, but also I seriously could not look away. The detail in it was *staggering*, and I didn't know whether to be saddened by Jimmy's pastime proclivities or deeply impressed. There was even a mini Jimmy standing in the middle of the castle grounds, with tiny yellow strips of paper curled like ribbon for his hair. Mini Jimmy's mini arm was frozen in a mini wave. He appeared to be looking right at me.

But the most surprising thing about JimmyWorld!™ was the writing on the wall. Literally. The castle walls were made of whole sheets of paper, so I could still read the writing beneath the glue.

The world is ugly right now. My biggest hope is to make it beautiful again. That's why I want world peace. Only after we achieve world peace will the world be the beautiful person I know she can be. Because beauty is important.

If I didn't know any better I'd say this was World Peace's admissions essay for camp. I looked at the stack of papers next to JimmyWorld!™ There was an essay on top of the stack. Either Jimmy was big on recycling or he really didn't care about our essays. I didn't mean to start reading, but the word "rights" stuck out at me. *Men are the only people on the planet who aren't allowed to ask for rights. And why is that? Well, let me explain it to you so that you understand.* Rights's admissions essay. I checked the name at the top of the page to confirm it. And then I started to laugh. Rights's name was *legendary.*

"What's so funny?" Boycott Camp asked.

"Nothing," I said, biting the inside of my cheek. I filed Rights's name away for later use and kept going through the essays.

I've struggled with diabetes nearly my whole life, so this cause is personal to me. The next essay started with *Where will you be when the robot apocalypse is upon us?* And the one after that read, *Why pot? I say, why not?* That was the only line in that essay. And it was written in crayon.

I'd spent three weeks working on my admissions essay, rewriting every word dozens of times, tweaking it over and over again with new statistics, all in the hope that my words would stand out. For the longest time I thought all that hard work had paid off, but now it appeared I could've just sealed it with a piece of chewed-up gum and that would've probably been attention-grabbing enough.

I picked up the Moleskine off the desk. I knew it was Jimmy's journal before I even laid my hands on it, because written across the cover was JIMMY DRILL'S JOURNAL. I had to take a peek.

I flipped through some early pages, scanning quickly until my eyes found the word "camp."

Gotta make Robert Drill proud. I mean, my new dad. He's my DAD!!! It feels so good to say that. I think this camp idea is really going to blow him away.

And then:

So many applicants. Really amazing response. But can't read it all. Considering choosing campers at random. Every cause is valid. Every potential camper deserves a chance. Pick applications out of an XL hat?? Procure a bingo cage?? Really must put effort into finding the perfect instrument with which to randomly draw names of campers for acceptance into CAMP SAVE THE WORLD.

Random.

All of it was random.

Maybe if Jimmy had put more effort into *reading* the applications instead of finding the *perfect bingo cage* to pull names out of it, I wouldn't have felt so let down right at this very moment. All of my hard work to get into this camp was for nothing.

Now I was starting to understand how people like Men's Rights or Save the World With Song had gotten in.

Speaking of people who didn't deserve to be here . . . "There's so much paper here," Boycott Camp said, a strangely awed look on his face. He shook me out of my thoughts. We were wasting too much time, and I had a mission. I headed for the TV and the tapes that were stacked by its side. There were only three tapes, and they'd been labeled even though nobody knew how to watch them. Using a VCR was a lot simpler than I'd thought. I popped a tape in and pressed play. It was the outside of the rec room. All of the footage just showed ILP painting his mural. I had to fast-forward for what felt like a really long time. There were hours left on the tape, and I didn't know if I'd have a chance to look through everything before we had to get out of there. But then I saw it. ILP slowly turned around to face someone out of the frame. And then he appeared. Just his back, so I couldn't see who he was. He held a bucket of paint in his arms and flung it at ILP, who threw himself against the mural, spreading his arms wide. The assailant turned to go, and I hit pause. I could finally see who had ruined ILP's mural.

"It was you," I whispered. I turned around to face Boycott Camp, but he wasn't even paying attention to anything on the

TV. He was too busy sparking his lighter, trying to set the papers on the floor on fire.

I lunged at him, taking the lighter from his hands, though one paper was already lit. I stomped the small fire out as quickly as I could.

"What are you doing?!" we both asked simultaneously.

"Why are you putting out my fire?"

"Why are you burning this place down?!"

"This camp is—"

"Fascist, I know," I said. "Is that why you ruined ILP's mural?"

"I didn't."

"You were caught on tape!"

"Okay, fine, I did," Boycott Camp said. "Is that what this is about?"

"Yes! That's why we snuck in here!"

"Well, you never told me that," he said. "I just thought you wanted to cause some trouble."

A noise startled both of us. A ringing coming from the open laptop on Jimmy's chair. The screen was on. I went to see if I could turn it off before any of the other counselors milling around outside or upstairs heard it and came in, but then I saw that it was a Skype call. And then I saw who it was from.

Robert Drill.

My heartbeat ticked up. Robert Drill was, for all intents

and purposes, just an arm's reach away. If I answered the call I could practically say I was in the same room with the guy. But obviously I couldn't do that. "We have to get out of here."

I looked up. Boycott Camp was already gone. I ran for the door, but then the knob started turning. Thinking quickly, I hid behind one of the filing cabinets, crouching down low.

Jimmy walked in. When he heard the ringing he rushed to the laptop and pressed a button on his keyboard. "Hey! What a nice surprise," he said.

"Please hold for Robert Drill," came a female voice from the computer.

"Of course, right."

"Jimmy?"

"Dad! I mean, Robert. I mean, hey, how are you?"

"Fine, great, look, I don't have that much time to talk, but I wanted to return your call. What is it?"

"Of course, thank you," Jimmy said. He was bent over the laptop in an awkward position, since it was still on his chair. "I just wanted to give you an update on what's been going on at the camp for the past week. It's been a little unusual."

"Unusual how?"

"Well, there have been a few . . . incidents, between the campers. Pranks that have been . . . escalating in scale."

"It's camp. Pranks are to be expected."

"Of course, Robert. Wise words. So true. I just wanted to ask you again about the unpaid internship—"

"How many times do I have to tell you, Jimmy?" Drill's voice said, stern, scary. "There is no unpaid internship. Now find a way to keep those campers in line. There's barely a month left."

"Of course, sir, I mean, Robert. Thank you so much for calling."

I watched Jimmy's reaction, trying to gauge what just happened. And then the crying began. It was coming from outside, and through the window I could see Ashley there, bawling her eyes out. She was acting up to start another distraction. She must've known I was still in here when I didn't meet the team at the assigned rendezvous.

Jimmy looked faint and ran out of the room.

Through the window I could see that Ashley was already leading him away. But I couldn't move.

Had I heard Robert Drill right?

There was no internship.

15

"Welcome to your second Camp Save the World competition!" Jimmy said.

It was after dinner, hardly any light left in the sky. Everyone in camp was gathered on the playing fields, sitting on the grass in random groups and clusters looking up at Jimmy, who had a golden retriever's enthusiasm for this announcement.

"Like I've already hinted at, this will be an endurance challenge. And now I can tell you that you will all partake in what we in the activist community call a sit-in. Sit-ins gained popularity in the sixties, when they were an effective method of protest for the civil rights and women's movements. Protesters would come together and occupy a space, sitting down and not budging for as long as it took to get their message heard. So tonight you'll all be sitting down for as long as you can. No getting up. No bathroom breaks. No sleeping. The camper who sits the longest will be awarded thirty-five points. So good luck, campers. The competition starts now!"

Boycott Camp was the first one up. He practically jumped at Jimmy's whistle and began marching around the playing fields. He hadn't had time to make a picket sign, but he already had a chant. "Competitions. Are. For. Fascists! Sitting. Is. For. Fascists!"

I followed him with my eyes as he circled around us, providing the soundtrack to this competition. I looked at him in a new light. Boycott Camp was no longer just a nonconformist arsonist. He was also a mural vandalizer. When I'd told Jimmy what I discovered on the tapes in his office, he'd awarded Boycott Camp ten points for what he called "an inspired act of outside-the-box activism." He then docked me another two points for breaking into his office. I tried to appeal, bringing up the fact that Feminism had broken into the counselors' office just last week. "And you practically threw her a party for it," I'd told Jimmy. "She broke in through the skylight, Children," Jimmy had said. "She broke *the glass ceiling.*"

So I was still in the negative-points range. Not that it mattered at this point. Thanks to that video call, I now knew that these competitions were bullshit.

Ever since I'd overheard that call I kept thinking back on the time I met Drill at that book signing when I was thirteen. He'd told me I had the potential for greatness. He'd told me I could feed the hungry children of the world one day. I never forgot those words. But for the first time they sounded wrong. This time I knew they were coming from a liar.

"Are you sure you heard him say that?" Ashley asked. She sat beside me. She'd come dressed for an endurance challenge, wearing a dugout T-shirt with yellow sleeves, knee-high socks, a sweatband like a crown tamping down her wild hair, and bright red short shorts. Pika sat beside her, wearing an identical getup, though he faced away from us. Ashley used his back as a leaning post.

"I know what I heard, Ashley. Robert Drill admitted that there was no unpaid internship."

I tried to go over all the possibilities of why he'd lie. Was it to build character? To make us work harder than we otherwise would have and then make us realize that it wasn't for a prize after all, but for our own good?

But if that was the case, then Drill had turned what should've been a nurturing and inclusive place for like-minded young people to come together into a total cutthroat environment where everyone was out to get each other.

Even now, there were a couple of campers who'd quit the competition but had come back to throw water balloons on people to get them to stand up. The only reason I hadn't been hit by a water balloon yet was by virtue of sitting next to Ashley, whom nobody dared bother because she was a celebrity. In fact, I think there was a balloon meant for me, but since I was so close to Ashley, Pika caught it in his hand as delicately as if he were catching a raw egg. He hurled the balloon right back at the assailant and it exploded in his face with enough force to knock him down to the ground.

Not to sound too petulant about it, but Drill not giving us an internship just wasn't fair. We were promised something. And it wasn't right to promise something and then just take it away to teach us a lesson.

"I can't believe Drill would do that," Ashley said. "But I believe you."

"You do?"

"Yeah," she said. "Of course I do."

My small smile mirrored hers. "Thanks." With all the shittiness I'd discovered about this camp in the office, it was nice that somebody was there to listen, and to believe me. "That means a lot."

A group of people were getting up, distracting me from Ashley. It was the camp's resident cool kids—Poe, Win, Balthazar-Adriano. Even Rights had joined them. At least ten of them had gotten up together and slinked away, arms draped over each other's shoulders and waists and laughing like they were in a Levi's commercial. "Why are they leaving?" I asked.

"Pika," Ashley said, "can you find out why they're going?"

Pika dutifully left, and Ashley and I watched as he followed the group and then came back to us moments later. He whispered in Ashley's ear so low that I couldn't hear his voice.

"They're throwing a party!" Ashley said. A few people sitting close by turned to look at her, suddenly interested in our conversation. "Since all of the counselors are tied up here, they're free to throw a shindig. Come on, Gregor, let's go!"

With one spritely jump to her feet Ashley effectively shook off the last half hour of this competition. "What about the sit-in?" I said.

"Who cares about the sit-in? It's not like they're giving out points for every hour you remain seated. Only one person is going to win."

"And that person will be me!" Anti-Robotics shrieked, eavesdropping on us. "I will piss myself if I have to."

"A real, underage, and unsupervised party, Gregor," Ashley said. "Like in the movies."

The way Ashley said "movies" was the way other people said "magic," though I guess for her those two things might be synonymous. I watched her go. It didn't take long for others to follow her. The rumor of the party was spreading through the field like a brushfire. Slowly and looking slightly uncertain, campers began to rise and follow the path that the cool kids had paved. By throwing this party, Poe and Win and all the other first-namers were engaging in their own kind of

170

sabotage. It may have been unintentional—or not—but this party was luring everyone off the field, because why stay in a competition when you could party with the cool people?

Wait a minute, why was I still here? I sat in the grass like an idiot when I knew there *was* no internship. Who cared about points anymore?

I stood, patted my jeans down, and walked away.

"It's alright, Children," Jimmy called after me, sitting so erect and cross-legged it looked like he was meditating. "Not everyone can sit still for long periods of time."

No, not everyone could. Sometimes you had no choice but to get up and move.

The party was being held in the rec room. There wasn't music blasting from a stereo, but I could hear Save the World With Song strumming on his guitar before I even walked in. I didn't do parties. I'd never been invited to any house parties in school, but this was my summer of firsts, so here I was.

Unity came at me so fast he didn't have time to properly stop, and full-on bumped into me.

"Children, you made it!" He handed me a plastic cup. I really hated that nickname, but I let it slide and sniffed the contents of the cup he'd just given me.

"Does this have alcohol?"

"No!" Unity cheered. "This party was last-minute. No time to sneak in contraband."

"Then why is everyone acting drunk?"

The room was getting pretty packed, and people were bumping into each other more than seemed strictly necessary. A few people were bopping up and down, and others were full-on dancing even though Save the World With Song's music output was more of the indie-acoustic variety. I Like Paint was one of the people dancing, and it instantly lifted my mood, seeing him out, socializing, being happy.

"Everyone's just having fun," Unity said.

I nodded, embarrassed that that needed to be explained to me. "Have you seen Ashley?"

He shook his head. "I think she was signing Free the Nipple's nipple."

"That's a little on the nose, isn't it?"

"No, it was on his ni—"

"Never mind," I said quickly. I scanned the crowd for Ashley. Farmers of America was in the corner making out with Underwater Noise Pollution. Recycle collected empty bottles, trying to make it look fun. Diabetes Awareness and Men's Rights were talking intensely on one of the couches. Finally, I spotted Poe next to Win. She was lounging back on the armrest, her legs dangling over Win's knees. She played with his hair. Both of them were laughing.

"Tonight's the night to make a move."

"Huh?" I turned to Unity. He was talking to me but he wasn't even looking at me. All of his focus was trained on the beautiful girl across the room.

"Me and World Peace," Unity said. "Tonight I'm going to talk to her."

I took a gulp from my cup. It was Mountain Dew. "Oh yeah?"

"Yeah, Children. I hear it in your voice—your doubt."

"I didn't say anything."

"You think a girl like that can't like a guy like me?"

"Dude, I didn't say anything. I think you've had too much Mountain Dew."

Unity shook his head and bounced on the balls of his feet like a boxer getting ready to spar. "Naw, man. Tonight's the night. I think World Peace could be the one."

I nodded, though I wasn't sure what he was getting at. "Like . . . your first?"

"No," Unity said. "Well, yes, eventually, but like the girl I'm supposed to spend the rest of my life with."

Funny there could be such a difference between "the first" and "the one."

"I'm going to talk to her tonight, and then we'll get together, and after camp's over, we're going to FaceTime every day and I'm going to send her flowers on the weekends. We're going to try to go to the same college, and if that's not possible, then we're going to go to college as close to each other as we can. We're going to have a rough patch after we graduate—I'll get a job on the West Coast, but she'll want to stay close to her family in the South, and I'm going to let her go because I care about her so much. But then we'll come back to each other, like in that movie *The Notebook*? We'll compromise and it'll be beautiful. It'll be the best it's ever been between us—better than it was in the beginning. After a year we'll get engaged. We'll get married in Central Park, like in all the best movies. I'll invite you to the wedding. And Ashley too. She could be your date."

"Why would me and Ashl—"

"Ashley will sing at the wedding."

"Ashley's not a singer."

"She'll sing anyway. It's going to be perfect, Children. And it all starts tonight with me talking to World Peace."

"Do you know what her real name is?"

Unity looked at me openmouthed, his bottom lip glistening with the very nonalcoholic sheen of Mountain Dew. "That's the perfect opening. Thanks, man. Real quick, do I have any dirt in my teeth?"

He flashed his teeth at me. "What? Why would you have . . . dude, have you been eating dirt?"

"It's just dirt, man."

"Exactly, Unity. It's dirt."

"It's actually not that bad. Plus, it's supposed to be great for your hair and nails."

I was too stunned to even respond to that. What the hell was happening at this camp? Was everyone eating dirt but me?

"You need to loosen up, Children. Live a little." Unity patted me on the shoulder. "I'm about to go live a little myself."

He went to talk to World Peace. As ridiculous and drunk on love (and dirt) as Unity was, I was jealous of his nerve. He was going to go talk to the girl that he liked—even if he didn't know her real name. I knew Poe's name and I couldn't even do that. But this was my summer of firsts. Like Unity had said, tonight was the night, and I needed to loosen up. I took one last swig from my Solo cup and turned toward the couches, but Rights stepped in front of me, blocking my way.

"Who invited Superman to the party?"

At that moment, Save the World With Song started playing a new tune. "I Kissed a Girl." ILP stood on top of the Ping-Pong table and started singing it. He knew every single word. Count on Katy Perry to crush the language barrier. The crowd went wild. They were so loud that I couldn't hear the rest of what Rights was saying to me, but the expression on his face made whatever it was seem threatening.

"Get out of my way, Rights."

"Don't think I won't get you back for getting my points docked."

"It was two points. I think you'll survive."

"I know that two points means nothing to you because you're so out of the running at this point, Superman. But for me two points could be the difference between spending the next summer at home or spending it in Tampa."

"Aren't you from LA? I'd think LA trumps Tampa."

"Whatever, Superman. I'm onto you. When you least expect it I'm going to get you back. In the meantime, you know what to do with this, dumbass." Rights shoved me out of the way while pressing several bills into my chest. He walked away and I caught the money before it fell to the floor. With him out of the way I could finally make my way to Poe. I had a clear view of the couch she was still sitting on. Win was nowhere in sight. Someone new had taken his place, and this time Poe wasn't just sitting next to them playing with their hair. Poe and Ashley Woodstone sat together, kissing. All I could do was stand there and stare, holding Rights's money to my chest as ILP provided the perfect soundtrack to my heartache.

Hello, Mother, hello, Father, here I am at Camp Save the World.

I know that you guys never really believed in this camp. You didn't understand it. You didn't get the whole activism angle. And you definitely didn't understand how/if it would help me become a better person.

I just wanted to let you know that I see your side of things now.

P.S. Ashley Woodstone is an amazing actress. I never should have trusted her.

16

Anti-Robotics won the sit-in, and he didn't even need to piss himself to do it. It shot him up to sixth place on the scoreboard, behind Win, Poe, Ashley, and Men's Rights. That same night, Anti-Robotics was thrown into the lake. He held the distinction of being the first camper to be thrown in twice. The next few days saw Save the Trees and Anti-Globalization join the lake-throwings club. Jimmy's response to the lake-throwings was to introduce pacifist activities to quell our violent tendencies. Arrowless archery was about as exciting as it sounds, though two people were still sent to Nurse Patrosian with bow-related injuries.

Throughout this time I avoided Ashley. Or tried to. But it was a small camp, and I knew our next meeting was inevitable. It happened when I went to see ILP's mural. Before it'd been destroyed I'd liked to watch him paint. It had helped clear my head. Now that he was working on it again, it seemed like the perfect thing to do. I just didn't know Ashley would be there helping him.

"Gregor Maravilla!" she said when she saw me. "What a nice surprise!"

She and Pika were helping ILP with the artwork. Ashley wore overalls that were splattered with an obscene amount of paint even though the paintbrush she held in her hand was smaller than a pencil. She was happy to see me, smiling big.

"What are you doing here?" I asked.

"Helping I Like Paint. I don't know the first thing about painting, but I did win an art competition once in an episode of *Smarty Pants*, so I think I've got this. Plus, I find that painting works wonders to relieve stress. Isn't that right, Pika?"

Pika nodded but did not look away from the intricate design of the flower he was painting. The tip of his tongue stuck out of the corner of his mouth as he concentrated. The world took over most of the wall, looking similar to how it had before, but now there were arrows that almost circled the globe. There was an arrow that started at a point in what looked like the Mediterranean and stretched all the way to New York. And there was another arrow that went from New York to California.

"What's with the arrows?"

Ashley stepped back to contemplate them, biting down on

the end of her brush. "I'm not sure," she said. "It must have something to do with bringing the world together. Perhaps arrows have a special symbolic meaning where ILP's from. I'm just going to embellish them a little."

She began painting over one of the arrows, decorating it with her own flower designs. "How's that look?" she asked ILP.

ILP looked at her flowers and frowned. He shook his head and got down off his stepladder to paint over them. Ashley sighed. "He's a little difficult to work with, but the collaborative process is often choppy. One must navigate it carefully."

"Maybe he's trying to tell us something with the arrows," I said. "Maybe we should listen."

"Maybe," Ashley said. "And maybe people like flowers more than they like random arrows. It's one of life's mysteries." She tossed her paintbrush into one of the cans on the ground and wiped her hands on her overalls. "Why have you been avoiding me?"

The directness of her question startled me, even though I was expecting it. Ashley's eyes bore down on me, waiting, and my response was to step back. I found an overturned bucket close by and sat on it. "You know why."

"I really don't."

She was going to make me say it. Fine. "I saw you kissing Poe."

Her lips formed a little O, but then they went back to their usual state, with corners upturned, and she sat on the ground beside me. "You're not really angry about that, are you?"

"Not really angry?" I repeated, indignant. "Ashley, you kissed Poe. You knew I . . . liked her."

"I was doing recon for you," Ashley said, "finding out if Poe likes girls. Turns out she does. But good news for you, she could still like boys. She does hang out with Win a lot."

That hadn't gone unnoticed by me, but I shook my head, getting back to the point. "You kissed her for *recon*?"

"Well, no. ILP was singing that song, and Poe really did want to kiss me, so I went with it. You'll never be closer to someone than when you kiss them for the first time." Ashley's eyes twinkled and her voice took on that mystified tone it sometimes did, like she was amazed simply by the memory of it. I could feel it myself too, hearing the music Save the World With Song was playing and ILP's voice as he sang. I could see Ashley's and Poe's faces, tilted and pressed against each other, parted lips connecting perfectly. I could see their cheeks, rosy and tinged with that summer glow that girls seemed to get. I could see the underside of Poe's bottom lip, shiny with smeared clear gloss. Ashley had a quintessential camp experience. The one I was so desperate for. I'd never considered that my summer of firsts could also be Ashley's summer of firsts.

"So you kissed Poe because you felt like kissing a girl?" I said, carefully considering this. It wasn't like they liked each other, which made me feel less bad about it. But still. "That seems so . . . dishonest."

"Why?" Ashley said. "Poe kissed me because I'm her celebrity crush. She told me so."

"Oh," I said. "Really?"

"Yeah," Ashley said. "My *New York Times* Eat Dirt ad is hanging in her cabin."

"It sounds like you were using each other."

"We were enjoying each other's company," Ashley said. "It's camp, Gregor. If movies are to be believed—and it's my philosophy that they always should be—everyone kisses everyone at camp."

And I had still managed to kiss exactly zero people.

"So you're not mad, right?" Ashley said. "I'd really hate it if you were angry with me. You're too good a friend for us to fight."

I shrugged. Now that we'd talked about it, I actually did feel better. Ashley didn't want to stab me in the back or anything. She just wanted to kiss a girl. And really, who among us didn't? Who was I to make her feel bad about that? "It's fine," I said.

"Great!" Ashley said breathlessly, slapping both of her knees. "Now, you haven't come to the clearing in a while.

What do you say I hold up my end of the bargain and help you with that talking to girls problem?"

How could I say no?

Since the last time I was in the clearing, Ashley had outfitted it with weatherproof throw pillows and coolers full of snacks and drinks. There were even string lights that hung in zigzags through the branches all around us. I was pretty sure I could thank Pika and some hidden portable generators for that. Per Ashley's instructions, it was the only time Pika was allowed into our little circle in the woods: when we weren't in it. Right now, the light around the trees was caught in Ashley's eyes. She scooted so that we were now directly facing each other.

"When you kissed Poe," I said, "you had your hand in her hair."

"Yes," Ashley said. "It was a proper make-out."

"Right. Of course," I said. "Is that what makes a proper make-out? Hands-through-hair moments?"

"Duh, silly."

I nodded. Of course I absolutely already knew that. "I absolutely already knew that."

It felt strange, talking about this, the technical side of how to properly kiss a girl. We'd met in the clearing so that Ashley could teach me the finer points of talking to girls, and somehow we'd landed on the physical side of things. It felt strange but I wanted to continue. Ashley scooted even closer, which automatically seized me with fear, but I did not scoot away. "You *have* had proper make-out sessions, haven't you, Gregor? You've run your fingers through a girl's hair?"

I had definitely made out before. Vanya Reechles in eighth grade. We would meet every day for a month in the playground behind school. She very adamantly wanted to make out with me, and I very adamantly wanted to make out with a girl, so the arrangement worked out. But our kisses, on reflection, were of the chaste variety, with my hands, useless and inexperienced, jammed into my pockets every time. Vanya Reechles had beautiful, long black hair. In our monthlong courtship I had never once touched it.

"No," I admitted. "Not really."

"Well, maybe we should start with how to be with girls, before I school you in the art of attracting them," Ashley said.

"How to be with girls" sounded incredibly vague and incredibly like exactly what I needed to learn. It sounded like an impossibility and yet like it might solve every single problem I've ever had and would ever encounter. I wasn't sure how Ashley planned to teach me that, but she moved even closer to me and I wasn't about to stop her.

"Lesson the first: how to be close to a girl." Ashley was so close that she was practically on top of me. "When people get this close, one of two things happen. One person totally jumps all over the other, *or* one person totally clams up, closes off, and gets really awkward."

I guess I knew which category I fell into. "I'm not totally awkward."

"You're sweating." Her fingertips were suddenly on my temple. I flinched involuntarily.

"It's hot out."

"Your heart is beating really fast."

"How do you know?"

"I can hear it from here."

She couldn't possibly, but she took the hand that was at my temple and brought it down to my hand, her fingers slipping over my knuckles. "Feel for yourself," she said. She brought up my hand with her own and pressed it against my chest. My T-shirt was on the verge of damp, and my heart was indeed clattering against my chest cavity. Of course she could hear it. I wouldn't be surprised if all of the creatures in the woods were skittering away from us, thinking there was an imminent earthquake where I sat.

"Relax," Ashley said.

"I am," I lied.

"You can't even look me in the eye."

So I looked her in the eye. She was so close. Just a few inches from me. It was a weird thought, but it dawned on me that she had "close-up" eyes. The eyes of an actress. She looked the way girls in movies looked when the camera zoomed in on their faces at crucial moments in the story and we were just viewers, separate but invested, locked on their gazes. I looked in her eyes, feeling invested but not so separate. I was lost in them.

"You're fine, Gregor. You're a great guy, and you happen to be really cute too."

"You think I'm cute?" I'd always had doubts about this. My mother always told me I was handsome, but she also told that to Anton, who definitely wasn't. Objectively, I had a pretty symmetrical face. Everything was in proportion, though I wasn't sure if that really amounted to anything.

"You're very cute, Gregor." Ashley probably thought everyone was cute, but I chose to believe her, and my heart slowed down.

"Try putting your hand in my hair."

Her word was law. I reached up behind her head to touch her hair, but she smirked and shook her head slightly.

"Not on my hair, *in* my hair," she whispered. She moved my hand from its resting place over her shoulder and placed it on the side of her neck, so that my palm touched skin but my fingers were deep in the strands of her hair. As tangled as her hair always looked from the outside, inside it was smooth, thick. Lanes of locks between my knuckles. I never knew long hair could feel like this.

I didn't even realize her hand was over my heart again. "A nice, steady rhythm," she said. "Only a little quick."

I didn't stop looking in her eyes, and only briefly lingered on the quickly fading moment of Ashley Woodstone saying the word "rhythm," which should have been a totally innocuous word but only made me want to move even closer to her.

Looking at her, with my fingers in her hair and the side of my hand touching her warm skin, I realized this was just the cusp. This was just a peek at something I'd never been privy to before. I was standing at a door and behind it, there was truth, and I'd only just turned the key. There was so much about girls that I didn't know.

"Are you comfortable?" Ashley asked, voice low, not much more than a breath.

"Yes," I said. And the thought hit me like a bolt of lightning. I could kiss her if I wanted. I was close enough. Even the sky wanted me to. It clapped for me. And then it broke open and beat us with rain.

Ashley yelped, but not without delight. "It's a rainstorm!" She leapt to her feet, but I stayed frozen to the ground, rusting. Ashley grabbed my hand and pulled. "Let's go!"

I chased her through the forest, winding through pitch-black trees and bullets of water. The woods really were her home, and I had the distinct feeling that even blindfolded she'd be able to lead the way. We burst through the door of her yurt and didn't stop until we fell onto the bed. We caught our breath in the thick silence of the room. Ashley sat up. "You're soaked."

I sat up too. "So are you."

She laughed and swept her hand over her arm, past her elbow. "I love the rain. It makes the world smell like earth."

Of course she would love the rain. Truth is, I was kind of loving it too at the moment. The first time we met up in the clearing, I asked Ashley why she lived in a yurt instead of in one of the cabins with the other girls. She'd said that it was because she was a late addition to the camp and there wasn't any more room in the cabins. She'd wanted to join the other girls, but Jimmy had this yurt made especially for her. She couldn't turn it down. It was good that she had a place to herself. "So are we going to continue the lesson?"

Lightning exploded outside. The yurt lit up in a flash, revealing Pika, standing in a shadowy corner of the kitchen. I nearly jumped out of my skin at the sight of him: arms crossed and scary pale in the sudden blaze of light. "A place to herself" wasn't exactly correct. The room went dark again.

"I think we pretty much covered it," Ashley said. "You don't want to be the guy that jumps on top of a girl too quick." The lightning hit again and Pika appeared again, inches closer now, looking way too hungry. "But you don't want to be closed off either," Ashley went on. "Just be comfortable. When you're comfortable, the girl you're with will be too. And then you can both figure things out together."

The lightning again. Pika again. He was right behind Ashley, leaning over her and staring directly down at me. His teeth were bared. This time, a loud clap of thunder accompanied his countenance.

"Comfortable," I said. "Got it."

17

At calisthenics in the morning, Jimmy told us all to expect "something special." And then he said a "certain someone" might be paying a "surprise visit."

You haven't seen someone stretch until you see them doing it while using air quotes.

Jimmy's announcement was pretty big. So obviously, I knew not to expect anything. But the rest of the camp was abuzz about Robert Drill coming. Whispers bounced around between activities. I, of course, didn't believe any of them. But they got louder as the day wore on, and by the time I was finished with Mindful Basketball the rumors had materialized into fact: Robert Drill was here, on the premises, taking a tour of the grounds.

No one knew where exactly. He could've been spending the morning taking care of business matters, holed up in the counselors' office, or taking a tour of the cafeteria. But a little after lunch a whole group of campers swarmed together near the main entrance. They moved slowly and in unison as if they were in a hive, all reverently surrounding someone in their center. It had to be Drill.

I set out toward them, quickening my step the closer I got. I tried to wedge my way past some people, though my height was definitely an advantage. But I couldn't see anyone. And then someone stepped aside and there he was: Robert Drill.

Well, his face.

On a screen.

Mounted on a telepresence robot. Nothing more than a tablet on a stick, which in turn was on a couple of wheels, reaching the height of a middle schooler and rolling itself over the bumpy terrain of the main dirt road.

"And over there are the girls' cabins," Rights said. He was jockeying for space in front of the screen, effectively cutting off any view as he played tour guide.

"Wonderful," Drill said.

I stepped back, leaving my place in the hive, and watched as the rest of the campers followed a telepresence robot as if it were the real thing. Jimmy stood beside me, watching the hive of campers too, but with a much more satisfied expression on his face. "He made it, Children. He finally came."

"I'm pretty sure he's still in his office."

"He's taking time out of his lunch to do this," Jimmy said. "Do you know how many times I've asked to see him for lunch and he's said he's too busy? This is huge for me. I mean, for this camp."

I'd known this for a while, but now it was finally starting to hit me.

This camp was fucking weird.

And I'm not just saying that because Robert Drill deigned to visit in the form of a telepresence robot. Or because out of the corner of my eye I spied a trio of girls sharing what appeared to be a snack bag of dirt. Everything about here was weird. The people. The camp itself. The way it made me look at things. After lunch we had a brand-new activity, and it proved my point. It was run by Jimmy, and he called it The Art of the Handshake.

"I bet you guys never thought about having to fund-raise or network or meet important people," Jimmy said, addressing us from the head of the clubhouse. More than a few murmurs around the room suggested that that was exactly what people had already been doing for their campaigns. "But guess what!" Jimmy continued. "That's an important part of activism! And the way you shake someone's hand will say a lot about you."

He paired us all off and now weaved through us as he spoke. "You're going to want to be firm, but not *too* firm," Jimmy said.

I was paired with Legalize Marijuana, who was currently using the entirety of his palm to wipe snot from his nose.

"You want to look them in the eye with a fair amount of confidence, but don't be intimidating," Jimmy said. "So go on and try it with your partner. All different styles and speeds are recommended until you find what feels right to you."

"That's what she said!" someone called out from the group, his comment followed by titters and snorts from everyone.

"Come on, guys, I thought you were the most mature teenagers in America," Jimmy said.

I could see Rights shaking Diabetes's hand so fiercely that his whole body shook. Next to them, Poe and Win had bypassed shaking hands altogether to play an impromptu game of what looked like Miss Mary Mack. In front of me, Legalize Marijuana looked annoyed at having to stop wiping his nose so that he could present me with his hand.

I spotted Ashley. She was shaking hands with Pika. Why was she always paired off with her bodyguard? I wondered if it was because she wanted to or because her presence at any camp activity caused the campers' numbers to be uneven.

I left Legalize Marijuana standing with his hand sticking out and made my way to Ashley.

"Can I cut in?" I said to Pika. As was her custom, Ashley's eyes lit up. And as was Pika's custom, his eyes tried to kill me with the force of their stare. He stepped aside, though, and I took his place.

"Hello, Gregor." She held out her hand and I took it.

Firm but not too firm. Confident but not intimidating. Her hand was soft, but then of course it was—huge stars and their perfect skin care and all that. Though I wouldn't be surprised if it was just a result of the exfoliating properties of dirt.

The internship was a ruse, Drill was never coming to visit, camp activities were a joke; at this point I was going through the motions at this camp, but this was a motion—this simple act of shaking Ashley's hand—I could live with. Ashley was probably the weirdest thing about this weird camp. And yet, she didn't weird me out anymore.

I smoothed my thumb over her skin as we shook, my eyes locked on hers. Somehow, impossibly, my time with Ashley had become my escape from this weird camp. Somehow, I now understood, Ashley was my closest friend here.

"So I'll see you at the clearing later?" I said.

Ashley continued to shake my hand, her face set in a mode I could only describe as *serious business*. "Definitely."

I couldn't wait.

Really.

Like I said: fucking weird.

18

The third competition was moved up because this would be a busy week at camp, Jimmy explained. In a few days' time our families would descend upon the Catskills for Visit Day, so we needed to get the third competition under way before then. And while I no longer cared about the competitions (knowing there was no prize to speak of), I especially did not want to participate in this one.

"You're probably asking yourselves why I loaded the entire camp into buses and brought you all here, to the center of town," Jimmy said to us. He stood in front of his hybrid, which he'd driven here separately. All of the campers were lined up in front of the buses, parked along Main Street in the sleepy town of Swan Lake. "You will be given a clipboard with a few sheets of paper. You'll write your cause's mission statement at the top of those papers. And then you will be unleashed upon the lovely people of Swan Lake to collect as many signatures as you can for a competition I like to call PETITION RELAY!"

See? Totally did not want to do this.

"Real activists often have the difficult task of getting in front of people's faces and convincing them that it is in their best interest to sign a petition," Jimmy continued over the excited murmurs of the campers. "You all have one hour to get as many signatures as possible. Two points per signature. Now let the games begin!"

Everyone swarmed Jimmy, diving into the backseat of his hybrid to get their hands on the clipboards. I just leaned against one of the buses and watched.

"Aren't you coming?" Ashley asked, appearing suddenly at my side, as she so often did.

"You and I both know these competitions don't mean anything."

"Well, that's one way to look at it. Another is that you're being given permission to run around town without supervision. You have an hour to break free and do whatever you want." Her eyebrows wiggled like dancing caterpillars, and beneath them her eyes twinkled with what could only be described as mischief. Sometimes you have a choice, and sometimes a girl will smile at you like that, and you know that you never actually did.

*   *   *

"So where are we going?"

"I have no idea," Ashley said. "But we'll know instantly when we see it."

I didn't know what we were supposed to be seeing. For now, Ashley and I walked down Main Street, farther and farther away from the mayhem of the competition. It'd barely started and already campers were ambushing passersby, cornering the unassuming people of Swan Lake at the grocery store when all they wanted to do was buy their milk in peace.

Ashley had explained to her bodyguard that we intended to have a fully unsupervised hour to ourselves, so Pika stayed back. We'd left Main Street behind for the less populated terrain of Swan Lake, where the cracked roads were hugged on both sides by overgrown weeds and the occasional bait shop.

"So why are you in a funk?" Ashley asked out of nowhere.

"I'm not in a funk."

"I can tell when you're in a funk, Gregor."

I listlessly kicked a stray pebble down the road, which I guess seemed like the type of thing someone in a funk might do. "Doesn't this all just seem like a joke to you?"

"Define 'all.'"

"I mean literally everything. This competition. The fact that Robert Drill is a liar and there is no internship. It's Visit Day in a few days and my family's going to come here and I'm not going to have anything to show them. My biggest accomplishment this summer was sneaking into the counselors' office to try to get Rights kicked out of camp, and I couldn't even do that. It's all a joke . . . I'm a joke."

"I don't think you're a joke."

I appreciated that but did not look up from the pebble I was now apparently playing a one-man game of soccer with. "This isn't activism. This isn't what I came to this camp for."

"So why did you to come to this camp, Gregor Maravilla?"

"I'm here for the same reason as everyone else. To win The Prize."

"The internship was announced after camp started. So that can't be it."

She was right. I'd almost forgotten there was more to this camp than just The Prize. "I came here to make a difference," I said. "Or to learn how to."

"Why?"

"What do you mean 'why'?"

"Lots of people want to make a difference. What made you want to come to this camp so badly? What drove you to start a Feed the Children fund?"

I shrugged, not sure of what to say. She was right, though—people were inclined to do good. But only a certain brand of us were so driven that we'd go to a summer camp to do it. "I think it really started my freshman year," I said. "There was this kid in my school, his family lived really far out in Brooklyn, close to the water. And this superstorm hit and his whole house was basically destroyed. I didn't even know the guy, because he was a junior, but his friend—this girl named Cherry—she started this campaign to help his family out. She rallied the entire high school for months, constantly asking people to donate just a dollar every day to try to help her friend rebuild his house so he'd have a place to live again. And she got people to do it. Even I donated a dollar every day. It became this big thing that everybody came together for. And at the end of that semester, the school held a huge assembly where Cherry announced that they'd raised almost ten thousand dollars for this guy's family. And it was amazing. I'd never seen anything like it. Cherry had managed to bring people together to do something really good for someone. I guess that was when I realized I could try to do the same thing for a cause that was important to me."

"That's very noble of you," Ashley said. "Do you know why I came here?"

I shook my head. I'd wondered that. A lot.

"To make friends," she said simply.

Ashley Woodstone may have been a lot of things. Advocate of the all-dirt diet, megastar, nighttime nude swimmer. But there was no way she was lacking in friends. There was only one reasonable explanation for this. "Are you one of those people who loves to collect friends? Because there's a kid in my school like that. He bends over backward trying to get people

199

to join his 'squad.' Especially the people who don't like him. He's even got three pen pals."

"No," Ashley said. "I don't collect friends. Making friends in Hollywood isn't as easy as you might think." She got to the pebble before I did and kicked it herself, watching as it skidded down the empty road. "People in LA love to inject fat into their lips and surgically implant muscles in their bodies, but the idea of eating dirt is really weird for them. Go figure. Plus, it's kind of hard to meet kids my own age sometimes. My costars are almost always older than me."

"But you were on those kid shows."

"You never watched them."

"No."

She nodded knowingly and smiled. "Anyway, I realized I've got less than a year left before I officially turn into an adult, and I've let so many milestones of childhood pass me by. I've never been to anyone's birthday party—which is a real bummer, because I've always wanted to bust open a piñata. I've never played tag with anyone. I've never even skinned my knee. So I thought, *Hey! I'll go to camp!* It seemed like the perfect solution to all my problems: Do a bunch of fun activities that normal kids do and meet people my age who share similar interests with me. That's why I came here. And I think that's why you came here too."

"I've skinned my knees before."

"Yes, but do you have many friends, Gregor?"

I thought of school. Of lunch sitting at my foldout table to collect money for my Feed the Children fund. I knew I was trying to do some good, but it also preempted sitting alone at one of the regular lunch tables. "No. I guess I don't."

Ashley jumped, surprising me with her abruptness. "Rejoice, Gregor Maravilla! For we are at an amazing place, enjoying each other's company and living magnificent, blessed lives. We should not feel sorry for ourselves. Plus, we just found exactly what we were looking for."

I stopped, taking in our surroundings for the first time. In front of us was an abandoned store. You could tell it was abandoned because some of the windows were boarded up, while shrubbery obscured the rest of them. Also, you could tell it was abandoned because it was a Tower Records.

"The town's eyesore is what we've been searching for?"

"Trust me, Gregor. It's perfect."

Nobody bought CDs anymore—nobody even wanted them—and we knew that, because as soon as we snuck in through the unlocked front door, we saw that the abandoned music store still had CDs on display. Not many. Most of the popular stuff was gone, but there was still a pretty good selection of '80s-era jazz-rock collecting dust on the shelves.

"Isn't this amazing?" Ashley said. She stood with her arms spread out in the center of the store, where the light coming through the cracks in the shuttered windows haloed her in sunshine.

"Define 'amazing.'"

I picked up a CD and wiped the dust off the plastic. A spiky-haired blond guy holding a saxophone was on the cover. He was wearing a braided headband across his forehead. And he was winking at me. Ashley plucked the CD out of my hands. "I think I see a CD player back there."

"I don't actually want to li—" But she was already gone, collecting more CDs on her way to the back of the store. I turned my attention to the shelves, searching for more bad music, when a shadow darkened the music display.

"What's the matter, Superman? Not a fan of jazz-rock?"

Rights stood in the doorframe, and I couldn't help but wince upon seeing him. It was only when he showed up that I realized how nice it was to get away from the rest of the camp for a while. "What do you want, Rights?"

"I just wanted to show you my list of signatures." He held up his clipboard, covered in scribbled names. "It's amazing how many people will support the Men's Rights cause once you explain to them that it's all about equality. I'm so winning this comp."

"I'm elated."

"Thank you. I'm also here to lock you in." He stepped back outside and closed the door before I had time to react.

"You can't lock me in here!" I said, pounding the side of my fist against the door. It was made of glass, so I could see Rights laughing as he stuck a pipe though the handles of the door. Where the hell had he gotten a pipe?

"Well, actually, I can."

I tried the door again, but it wouldn't budge. "What the hell is your problem?"

"I told you I'd get you back for docking my points."

"It was two points, Rights!"

"We're even now, Superman."

I threw my shoulder into the door a few times, but the pipe wasn't moving. The uselessness of my attempts were punctuated by Rights calmly retrieving his wallet from his pocket and smashing a five-dollar bill against the glass. "How do you like dem apples?"

"That really doesn't mean anything!" I yelled back at him.

Ashley must've found the CD player, because just then the sound system broke into "The Final Countdown."

"I could just break the glass, you know!" I shouted at Rights.

He laughed. "We both know you won't."

I turned and knocked the back of my head against the door. When I opened my eyes, Ashley was standing in front of me. "What just happened?"

Ashley and I spent the next half hour debating whether or not to break down the door. Although it wasn't much of a debate. I was adamant that we not break anything. If we broke something, someone would hear it and call the police, and yes, we'd get rescued, but then we'd also go to jail for breaking things after breaking in here, and if we went to jail my chances of getting into a good school would plummet. But then again, I didn't want to spend all night in here either. Basically it was a debate I was having with myself. Ashley just wanted to smash something. But if she couldn't do that, she was perfectly content surrounded by the world's worst music castoffs.

At the moment, a tune that sounded like it should've been a family sitcom theme song played throughout the store. I sat slumped against the wall. I wondered if the buses would leave without us. Nobody would notice me missing, but Ashley's disappearance could warrant a full-on search. "Bet you regret telling Pika to stay behind. He probably could've helped in this situation."

"Nope, no regrets," Ashley said. "I think we were meant to get stuck in this place. It was fated."

"What's the deal with him? Why do you need a bodyguard?"

"Oh, lots of reasons." Ashley sat on the floor, against the wall next to me. "He's been working for me for three years. At first he was assigned to me on *Smarty Pants*. We shot on location a lot, so I needed someone to accompany me from my trailer to the set. You'd be surprised how many people will come at you out of nowhere if you're walking alone on the street."

"That doesn't sound too pleasant."

She took a little baggy out of her pocket. Not dirt. Chia seeds. "That's why I have Pika." She held up the bag in offering, but I shook my head.

"Can I tell you something?"

Ashley's eyes lit up, just as I knew they would. "Yes."

"Pika kind of terrifies me."

She laughed. "Pika's a teddy bear."

"I don't know what kind of teddies you had as a kid, but . . ."

"He's just trying to keep me safe," Ashley said. "He was the only one who saw that this guy on the show a couple of years ago was bad news."

"Bad news?"

"Yeah," she said, munching on a pinch of seeds. "A costar. Anyway, Pika was there when no one else was. He's my protector. My own private Superman."

I knew she'd brought up Superman for my benefit, a

buzzword to distract me. But I was stuck on her. Stuck on "bad news." A couple of years ago Ashley was fifteen. What kind of bad news could she have seen at fifteen? At sixteen I still hadn't yet lived enough life to garner a single headline. Not even a byline. Not even a paid classified. "What was the bad news?"

"Just a guy," she said through her smile. "Now you tell me something."

"Me?"

"Tell me something true."

Tell me something true. It sounded like a movie quote or something, but then Ashley had that quality that made little things feel bigger than they were. I racked my brain for something to say. Something that would make me sound interesting and deep. But you were hardly ever interesting and deep when you were honest. Honesty meant being stripped bare, exposed, showing your real self. My real self was the opposite of interesting and deep. Not that it mattered what I said. The way Ashley looked at me I was already stripped bare.

"Remember when I told you earlier that I wanted to come to camp to make a difference? That was only partially true. I also came because of my brother." My honesty made me petty. But it was real. "Anton is kind of famous on the internet."

"Have I heard of him?"

"Not unless you play Minecraft."

Ashley, thankfully, shook her head.

"He's got this YouTube channel where all he does is broadcast himself playing this video game. It sounds ridiculous, but people actually tune in. A *lot* of people. People care. My *parents* care. They're so proud of him for figuring out a way to make ad money out of his dumb gaming hobby. To them, if people care enough about something, then that makes it worthwhile. So I thought, *People care about this camp. I'm going to show my parents what I could do with my passion.* And then they'd see that I was good at something too." I looked at Ashley. "I came here for superficial reasons."

"Nah," Ashley said. "You shouldn't be jealous of your brother. Being famous isn't all it's cracked up to be. And you definitely shouldn't do something just to make your parents happy. It's the opposite, Gregor. Whatever *you* choose to do should make *them* happy. My general philosophy on parents is, if they're not supportive of you, screw them."

"Screw them?"

"Screw them."

"Is that how it is with your parents?" I asked.

Ashley opened her mouth for a second, not saying anything. I could tell that she didn't want to, and that when she did say something, it wouldn't be in answer to my question. But then she was saved when a new song started playing. Her eyes went wide and she jumped up. "I love this song!"

I sat on the floor, leaning against the wall, watching Ashley dance. Her moves were much the same as when she'd done her moon dance in the woods. She languidly swayed and dipped in and out of the window's light beams. It looked like the sun was dancing with her. Even the dust played along, swirling around her, sparkling like suspended glitter in the rays of light. This new song was something foreign, which felt appropriate. Watching a girl dance was a foreign experience for me. I was frozen, watching her. Utterly ineffective. But I couldn't say I wasn't enjoying it.

Ashley floated closer to me and caught my gaze. As a French woman sang a slow jam, Ashley's eyebrows did their thing again, asking me a silent question.

But I shook my head. *I don't dance.*

She came to me and pulled me up. *You will dance.*

She twisted on the balls of her feet and I looked down at her, trying to emulate her. No one would consider my shifty steps dancing, and yet somehow we moved in sync.

Ashley laid her temple against my chest, leaving me with little more to look at than the top of her head. It was a good view. I held her hand the way you're supposed to when you dance slow with somebody. Ashley used my palm as a sketch pad for her thumb. She drew her finger lazily over my hand,

and my mind was laser focused on deciphering the invisible pictures she scratched. A star? A flower? An *A*? I hadn't even noticed that the CD had stopped. The only music came from Ashley's humming, though soon that stopped too. She looked up at me. Her smile was close-lipped, serene.

This had to be what Ashley had talked to me about that night in the clearing before the rain came down. How to be close to a girl, how to be comfortable. Because this was the most comfortable I'd ever been with a girl, or anybody. My heart beat at a steady rhythm, even as Ashley continued to look at me. Even as her thumb grazed the soft part of my hand.

And then she let go of me and made her way over to the door.

"Where are you going?"

She knocked on the glass. "Pika's never too far."

A moment later he was there, Ashley's enormous body-guard, pulling the pipe out to open the door. I shouldn't have been happy to see him, not at this very moment when I could still feel a tickle in my palm where Ashley had touched it. But I was happy to see him, not because he'd saved us but because Ashley, knowing that he'd been right outside this whole time, had waited so long before getting him.

19

Amazingly, Men's Rights did win the petition relay. It put him in second place on the scoreboard, behind Win. And since she didn't collect any signatures, Ashley fell to fourth place. But more surprisingly, Boycott Camp rocketed into the top ten after getting the residents of Swan Lake to sign a petition in support of closing down Camp Save the World so they could get their peaceful town back. I was still in last place with negative four points. Not that it mattered to me. There were more pressing things on the horizon.

"Tomorrow is Visit Day," Jimmy said. Calisthenics were over, but instead of letting us get to our activities, Jimmy wanted to have a short chat with us. He invited Diabetes Awareness to come stand next to him. The two stood before us, matching dour expressions on their faces. "I thought that yesterday we had finally come together as a camp, but I know that there have been some—let's call them *shenanigans*—

happening here. Diabetes, why don't you tell the campers what happened to you last night."

"I almost died," Diabetes said.

"And why did you almost die?"

Diabetes didn't look up from the floor, but his voice was loud enough for all of us to hear. "Because War on Drugs took away my insulin."

War on Drugs was standing right next to me. His plump face reddened and his eyes narrowed to slits. "I saw contraband in a camper's pack and acted accordingly," he said in his slow, Southern drawl. "I was only trying to save him from a lifetime of drug dependency."

I had assumed taking Diabetes's insulin was an honest mix-up, but now I wondered if War on Drugs wasn't the type of antidrug protestor that detested Tylenol as much as cocaine.

"I appreciate your determination to rid the world of drugs," Jimmy said, "but the fact remains that Diabetes here is near death *daily* from the shenanigans some campers are pulling under the guise of protest. Now, parents and family are coming tomorrow, and it's important that we cool it a little bit, okay, guys?" Jimmy's short chat was turning into a full-fledged speech, and he went on and on about the importance of "respect" and "common sense" and "not killing your fellow campers." I tuned out at the obvious stuff.

"So let's be kind to each other," Jimmy concluded. "Let's be cool. And when your families come tomorrow, let's show them that Camp Save the World is the most normal camp in America! And I wasn't supposed to say anything, but there might be an extra-special visitor here tomorrow. I'll give you one hint: His name rhymes with Crawbert Shrill."

You know how you can sometimes wake up and not know where you are or what day it is? That wasn't the case today. I woke up with the instant realization that today would be the day that my family would come to camp and see my total failure at it. And it filled me with dread.

I tried to convince myself that today was just a normal day, that everything would go fine. And that was when I heard the unmistakable sound of an elephant blowing his trunk.

I hopped off the top bunk, suddenly very awake. Everyone was still asleep: Rights snoring lightly, Win peacefully snuggled in his sheet, ILP fitfully kicking at his. It must've been early, because it was still gray and chilly when I ran outside.

In front of me, on the path that stretched before the row of boys' cabins, was a veritable parade of wagons being led across the camp. Through the open windows of every car, I could see the animals being kept inside. One car had ostriches, another camels, and another had the aforementioned elephant I'd heard through my window.

There were rumors about this yesterday. That Jimmy was planning on bringing a petting zoo to the camp so that the campers and their families could enjoy a special treat only five-year-olds would appreciate. But now, as the parade passed me by, I couldn't help but think that Jimmy hadn't commissioned a petting zoo for the day but instead had bribed a traveling circus to come to the camp for a pit stop.

I half expected a troupe of clowns to spill clumsily out of one of the cars. But all I saw was Jimmy hanging off the back of the last car, waving wildly at me.

"Good morning, Children! We've got an exciting day ahead of us!"

"This is a very bad idea," I said. I tried to say it loud enough for Jimmy to hear, but my voice was drowned out by the yawp of a goose.

"I know!" Jimmy said, bright, happy, obviously mishearing me. "Isn't it great?!"

"So great it's ridiculous."

"Remember, Children: This is the most normal camp in America!"

He stretched the word "America" out so that it sounded like "AMERICAAAAAA!" and I wasn't sure if it was because he really was that enthusiastic about this or because the screech of the llamas was overpowering his voice.

Win, Rights, and ILP finally joined me outside. "Did I just hear an elephant?" Win said groggily.

"It was the petting zoo. I think."

"Fantastic," Rights said. "I want to ride a horse."

"I didn't see any horses. You'll have to settle for a camel."

"Horse, camel, whatever. No one is going to stop me from being a cowboy today." He turned to me, angry, accusatory. "*No one.*"

It was too early in the morning for this fuckery.

Before I came to this camp, I went on about it for a long time. I couldn't stop talking about it when I'd first heard of its inception. I couldn't stop talking about it when I was trying to convince my parents to let me go to it. I couldn't stop talking about it when I found out that I'd been accepted. I talked a big game about how instrumental this camp would be for setting me on the course to acquiring the necessary skills to be a better leader—heck, a better human being. I said this camp would set me on my way to achieving all of my dreams to save the world.

And what had been my biggest achievement so far?

"It's a lanyard," I said. I held up my most recent arts and

crafts project to my parents, who looked at it with the right
amount of skepticism.

"Three weeks at this camp and all you have to show us is a
friendship bracelet?"

My family had been here for half an hour. I'd taken them
on a tour of my cabin, the clubhouse, the mess hall. It was all
pretty uneventful except when we stopped by the rec room.
ILP was there with a family that wasn't his own, showing off
his mural to them. He was speaking very passionately about it
too, gesticulating wildly at the arrows that spanned the painted
globe and rambling in his native tongue. I wondered if the
family he was talking to even understood him or if he was just
caught up in the moment. I pointed him out to my family as
one of the more passionate examples of a camper at Camp Save
the World.

Now I stood with my family in the playing fields, where
picnic tables had been set up for the impending Family Fun
Lunch. So far, shockingly, things at the camp were running
smoothly. None of the campers had pulled any pranks or tried
to kill each other. Actually, the only moment thus far to really
give my family pause was the tiny spate of protesting at the
petting zoo. The petting zoo had been kind of a success;
nobody seemed to be wondering why they were petting a seal
instead of a goat. Jimmy put the animals in the all-purpose
sports rink so they'd have a natural enclosure, or as natural as

traveling-circus-animals-at-a-sleepaway-camp could get. My family didn't find this circus attraction strange—it was the campers marching in front of the enclosure, brandishing picket signs, that caught their attention. "Why are those kids protesting the petting zoo?" my father asked.

I shrugged. I wasn't too surprised by the kids protesting (circus animals kept in captivity were always controversial), but what was normal for Camp Save the World was new to my family. "We protest things here. A lot."

Despite the day going well (or maybe because it was going *too* well), I was constantly on the lookout for sudden calamity at every corner. Anytime someone ran someplace, I thought for sure the zebras must have escaped or that Boycott Camp had set something on fire. But so far so good.

"I think I'm getting better at becoming a leader," I lied to my parents.

"Leaders make friendship bracelets?" my mother said.

"Yes, Mom."

"I think your friendship bracelet is beautiful," my father said.

I wouldn't have called it a friendship bracelet. Most of the friendships around here were actually more like alliances. But "alliance bracelet" didn't exactly have the right ring to it.

"That bracelet would make a great gift for a girlfriend," Anton said. He put his arm around Darcy, who did not look up

216

from the thick notebook she was scribbling in. "Oh, wait, you still don't have one." Talking to my brother was a lot like talking to a garbage disposal. I had no idea why he was here.

"How do you know I don't have a girlfriend? Maybe I met a girl here."

"Who are you kidding, Gregor?" Katrina said. "You don't have a girlfriend. You don't even have a single friend here, do you?"

"Leave your brother alone," my mom said. "I'm sure he has friends at this camp. He's a leader with a friendship bracelet—of course he has friends! You have friends here, don't you, sweetie?"

"Of course I do."

"Any friends you want to introduce us to, son?" my dad said.

I looked around, trying to spot someone who I could feasibly call a friend. Win wasn't around, probably being carted around on his family's shoulders, in celebration of his perfectness. I saw Poe, standing with a pair of smartly dressed adults who must have been her parents, but there was no way I could introduce her to my family. I wouldn't even know what to say. Unity was busy talking to World Peace's parents, though I had no idea if that was by invitation or not. Out of the corner of my eye I spotted Rights walking toward us as if he could read my thoughts and was about to answer them with a cruel joke.

217

"You can't ride a camel!" PETA was saying, chasing after him. "It's unethical! And potentially harmful!"

But Rights just shrugged and kept walking, passing me and my family by. He was wearing a cowboy hat and had a piece of straw dangling between his lips like a lit cigarette. "I'm ridin' that camel and there ain't nothin' you can do about it."

I saw Diabetes close by out of the corner of my eye and grabbed him. "This is my friend Diabetes."

"Is that your name?" my mom asked, slightly horrified.

"It is here, ma'am." He swayed. Diabetes was a small guy, but there was no way the force of my mom's handshake was strong enough to sway him like that. I pulled him back out of earshot.

"You okay, man?"

"I'm great," he said. "I'm on a cleanse."

"You're on a what?"

"I haven't eaten anything in the last twelve hours."

"Why?"

"I wanted to get rid of my diabetes before my parents show up. Surprise them. Rights thinks I can do it."

I pulled Diabetes even farther away from my family. "Rights doesn't know what he's talking about," I hissed. "As much as he likes to say he does, he doesn't have the answer for everything. He doesn't care about you—he only cares about The Prize. This isn't safe, man."

"I have guns now, Children," he said, showing me his pathetically small flexed biceps. "Rights and I have been working out. I've been getting stronger. So yeah, he does know what he's talking about."

"You're talking like the disciple of a cult leader, dude."

"Men's Rights is a leader I can believe in!" Diabetes said. He squirmed out of my grasp. "You're just sticking the word 'cult' in there to be controversial. But buzzwords don't work at this camp, Children."

"Our *names* are literally buzzwords," I said. "Men's Rights is brainwashing you."

"There you go with your buzzwords again. Rights is *helping* me. You aren't." He stormed off, leaving me alone and friendless in front of my family again.

"Nice friends," Katrina said when I went to rejoin them.

I had no choice but to pull out the big guns. "I'm friends with Ashley Woodstone."

My entire family stared at me. Even Darcy looked up from her notebook.

"¡Mentiroso!" Abuelo Maravilla said. He sat in his wheelchair. I didn't think he'd been listening to anything that we were saying, but apparently he had and he had something to say about it.

Great. Even my grandfather didn't believe that I could feasibly be friends with a megastar like Ashley Woodstone.

"It's just that you've been giving us conflicting reports about Ashley in your letters home," my father said. "How can we be sure what to believe?"

"There's no way you're friends with Ashley Woodstone," Katrina said. "Ashley Woodstone is rainbows and Dipsy Doodles, and you're lame. Dad, can we go to the petting zoo already? I want to see the flamingos."

"Why would I lie about that?" I said.

"Because she's not here to deny it," Anton said. "Classic move. Before Darcy, I called a lot of girls my girlfriend when they weren't there to deny it."

"Well, you are an awful human being," I said to Anton. "Ashley Woodstone is my friend. I'm as surprised as the rest of you, believe me. And I don't have to prove it."

"Prove it," Anton said.

"Yeah, prove it!" Katrina said.

My father squeezed my shoulder and looked at me pitifully. "Perhaps you should prove it, son."

I often wondered if I was a hard person to be friends with, and if it was because of the family I came from. Because no matter how much I loved them, I really wanted to dig a hole in the ground right now and stick my head in it, much like the ostrich at the petting zoo. "She's probably in her yurt," I said, sighing. "Why don't you guys get us seats for lunch while I go find her."

*　　*　　*

There was no answer at her yurt, but when I turned around I found Pika, back against a tree, arms crossed over his chest, watching me. He startled me, like always.

"Pika. Hi. Is Ashley around?" I waited but he didn't say anything. It was a long moment of him staring me down and me trying not to wither under his glare. Then he looked up into the trees, and I followed his gaze. It definitely wasn't a bird or a plane. Ashley sat on a thick branch, one foot flat on it, the other dangling off.

"Hey!" I said. Her head swiveled around, and she looked down at me from over her shoulder.

"Gregor Maravilla! What a wonderful surprise!"

"What are you doing up there?" I said, my head craned back to look at her. "You could fall."

"But what if I fly?"

The last thing I needed right now was Ashley Woodstone's dime-store pearls of wisdom: the Tumblr edition. I looked at the tree. It was long and high and did not have a lot of protruding parts that would make it easy to climb. But I couldn't just stay down here either. Damn Ashley Woodstone.

I couldn't ask Pika for a boost because he would very likely catapult me into the sky. I climbed on my own. My shirt kept getting caught on the rough bark and my knees got scratched every time I took a step. I also realized I had no upper body strength at all, but I made it. Scratched and out of breath. I sat on a branch next to Ashley's, not wanting to add my weight to her already slim-looking tree limb.

"Gregor. You made it!" Relief and happiness flooded her face. Yes, I made it. But I didn't dare let go of the tree. I wrapped both my arms and legs around the trunk. Ashley looked so at ease, like she belonged in trees. Like, unlike the rest of us humans, she didn't have to worry about falling out of them. Though I guess having a bodyguard down below to catch you if you fell let you live life a little more recklessly.

"I don't think your bodyguard likes me." I looked down and caught the glare off Pika's shiny bald head. He was too far below to hear us.

"Pika? He's a teddy bear."

"You know, you keep saying that, but all I see is grizzly. Like, if I make any sudden movements he'll pounce on me."

"He doesn't trust boys. Not after my last boyfriend."

I nodded. The boyfriend. The more he came up, the more it nagged on me. "Are you ever going to tell me what happened with him?"

Ashley shrugged and fixed a smile on her face. "Wouldn't you rather talk about happier things? Tell me about your family."

From this high up I could see into the playing fields,

between the leaves. I had a clear view of all the families and campers spread out among the tables. Lunch was being served, and while most families shared tables with each other, my family took up one entire table. "That's my family at the second table from the left."

"The Family Maravilla," Ashley said through a grin. "What a delight."

"There's my parents; and then the old man in the wheel-chair is my grandpa; the lady in the blue scrubs next to him is his nurse; the big guy is my brother, Anton; the girl next to him with the stack of books is his girlfriend, Darcy; and the twelve-year-old girl is my sister, Katrina. She's a big fan of yours."

"You have a wonderful family."

"You say that because you haven't met them."

"And still, I know it to be true."

She was so sure, I almost believed her. I scooted closer. "So why are you here, in the trees, and not out there?"

"I love seeing all of this," Ashley said. "So often, because of who I am, I can't observe these things, you know? I can't sit in a crowd and watch normal people interact with each other. So when I find a way to do it, even if it means sitting in a tree—well, *especially* if it means sitting in a tree—I jump on it."

We were high up and I was still terrified, but I was getting more used to being up in a tree. It was nice and quiet up here, the only sound coming from the chirping birds around us.

Ashley turned to me. "Do you think I'm weird, Gregor?" she asked suddenly. "I mean, I know I'm a little weird and I'm fine with that, but do you think I'm *too* weird?"

I didn't know what she was getting at or what this had to do with anything. And I especially didn't know how to answer her question. She was sitting in a tree, wearing a navy-blue mechanic's jumpsuit rolled up to just over her ankles. Her hair was sprinkled with gold confetti stars. Of course I thought she was weird. But in the time I'd gotten to know her, that word had taken on a new meaning. "Why are you asking me that?"

She shrugged and I held on to the tree more strongly. "I see all those people out there and . . . sometimes I wonder if I'm really different than them. My job creates this big divide. I wonder if I'm so different that . . . I alienate some people."

"You don't alienate me," I said. "I'm in a tree with you."

She laughed.

"Aren't your parents coming?" I asked.

She was still smiling, but it was different this time. "Don't be silly."

I hadn't realized I was. Even though I felt like I was dangerously close to stepping on a land mine, I pressed on. "Do you not want to talk about them either? Because you can tell me anything. We can gripe about our weird parents together."

"That's okay, Gregor." She was still smiling, and yet the smile filled me with the overwhelming need to hug her. I would let go of this tree and risk falling to the ground, right at Pika's uncaring feet, just to put my arms around her, comfort her somehow. I didn't know anything about her family or home life, but Ashley could so easily telegraph everything she was thinking just by the expression on her face. And that smile was sadness. I never knew a smile could break my heart. I wanted to hug her, but I couldn't even move my hand on top of hers. And not all of it was because I was afraid I might fall.

"Do you want to meet my family?"

Her smiled flickered into something brighter. "Really?"

Ashley and I walked out of the woods together, but I slowed down. I had to tell her something before we reached the rest of the Maravillas. "I told them we were friends. They don't believe me."

"Then we'll make them believe," Ashley said. She looped her arm through mine, which instantly and irrationally made the back of my throat dry up. When we marched up to my family they froze at the sight of us.

"Hi, Gregor's family!" Ashley said. She gave everyone their own individual hug. Even Grandpa Maravilla, whom she had to bend down to hug in his wheelchair. She talked to them like they were old friends. She even signed Katrina's forehead. We all sat down together to eat. During a rare quiet moment, when my family wasn't barraging Ashley with questions, I leaned over, close to her neck.

"Thank you," I whispered.

"For what?"

"For showing up. Showing them that we're, you know, friends."

"But we are," she said, her grin as big as ever. Mine was much smaller, but it was there.

Jimmy finally came out. He stood before a curtain that was set up earlier in the day, just for Visit Day.

"Welcome, family, friends, and campers, to the first-ever Visit Day at Camp Save the World!" he said into his microphone. Parents and campers clapped. "I think we can all agree that today was a rousing success! And that Camp Save the World is the most normal camp in America!"

He tried to get the clapping going again, but people were mostly too busy eating their hot dogs.

"Now, I promised the kids that Mr. Robert Drill himself would be here to show his appreciation. Unfortunately he can't stay too long, but he did want to wave! So here is Mr. Robert Drill, waving hello!"

Jimmy pulled the curtain back from its frame and there he was: my (former) hero. Robert Drill. He waved and smiled, and despite everything, I was excited for a second. Until I realized that something seemed off. His waving seemed mechanical somehow. Like his elbow wasn't just an elbow but a point of articulation, like my Superman action figure. I could see Anti-Robotics stand up slowly. I could hear his shrill old-lady-like scream before he even opened his mouth.

"That is not Robert Drill!" Anti-Robotics yelled. Everyone turned to look at him. "That is Robot Drill!"

Robot? I turned to look at Robert Drill again. It couldn't be . . . but he hadn't even stopped waving.

Anti-Robotics ran straight to the stage and charged. With a big warrior yell, he pulled his arm back, formed a fist, and came with all his weight at Robert Drill, socking him in the chin.

Robot Drill's mechanical head snapped off.

There was a moment of awed silence. Some people stood up in shock. Diabetes passed out. And then the screaming began.

"I knew I never should've let you come to this camp," my mother said.

20

Robert Drill sat at his desk in his Palo Alto office, the sun bright and shining through his floor-to-ceiling windows, when his secretary knocked on his door and popped her head in.

"Mr. Drill, there's been an incident that needs your attention."

Robert Drill looked up from his computer screen and lifted his glasses to the top of his forehead. "Yes?"

"A camel broke its back at your sleepaway camp, sir."

"Excuse me?"

"One of the campers decided to ride a camel at the camp. He apparently rode it too long, sir. Also, there is a slight international kidnapping situation. Apparently the camp has been holding a young man from Croatia captive. He goes by the name of 'I Like Paint'—also known as ILP—and was meant to go to an art camp in California but was somehow diverted to your camp earlier in the summer, sir. We only found out

228

after a parent at Visit Day who spoke Croatian was able to communicate with him. Plus, your top secret robot design prototype had his head torn off by one of the campers in front of every parent and child at the camp."

Robert Drill slowly put his glasses down on his desk. *"What?"*

Hello, Mother, hello, Father, here I am at Camp Save the World.

I know that Visit Day may have seemed very strange to you guys and the rest of the family, but trust me— that's just how this camp works. There is no need for alarm. You probably want to pull me out of camp, and while I wouldn't argue with you if you did, I think you should reconsider. You saw that I made a friend. Also, after everything that happened at Visit Day, Robert Drill is finally going to come to the camp. And I actually kind of want to see him.

P.S. Ashley Woodstone says hello. She didn't find you guys strange at all.

21

Robert Drill was going to come to camp tomorrow. For real this time. And to think all it took to get him here was an injured camel, a kidnapped Croatian minor, and the decapitated head of the cyborg that bore his likeness.

Robert Drill wasn't just coming alone—he'd invited numerous media outlets and scheduled a press conference in order to spin the bad press the camp had gotten these last few days. I wasn't sure how he was going to pull that off, though. If things continued to go the way they were going, chances were good the camp would explode as soon as Robert Drill set foot in it.

I couldn't stop thinking about the fact that he was going to be here. And that I was finally going to see him. After the disaster that was Visit Day, my parents actually contemplated making me leave the camp. A lot of parents must've felt like that as they witnessed Anti-Robotics tackle a beheaded Robert Drill robot to the ground. But then Ashley stood before the crowd and gleefully said, "What an amazing performance!"

I have no idea if she thought it was really a performance or if she was just quick on her feet, saving the camp's ass, but everyone started following her lead. She clapped enthusiastically, and then campers started to clap. Then parents. After a moment of recovering his wits, even Anti-Robotics began to clap, confused but also happy that he'd destroyed one of his mortal enemies.

Whether or not the parents bought it, Robert Drill certainly knew it wasn't planned. And now he was on his way. The man I'd once idolized for so long. In the flesh.

"Other people idolize athletes or musicians or actors, you know?"

"I know," Ashley said.

"But I idolized him. He's just a regular guy, but he's using everything he has to make the world a better place. He's making an impact."

We were in the clearing again. Ashley had managed to weave two wreaths from twigs and leaves. She called them our enchanted forest crowns as she put one on my head. I'd promptly taken it off and looped it over a tree branch. Ashley didn't mind, though. She said it made our clearing look more welcoming. An evening of working on the Superman script and recounting *Chasing Amy* (which was starting to sound like a really problematic movie) had been sidelined in favor of doing absolutely nothing.

The two of us lay on blankets and pillows on the ground, eating from the same tub of Twizzlers and staring up into the trees.

"Do you know what my biggest fear is?"

Ashley shook her head.

"It's not making an impact," I said. "Time is just passing by, and if I don't figure out how to make a difference *right now*, then before I know it I'll be old. I'll have done nothing of any worth."

"Dreams take time."

"Not for you. You're already leaving a legacy. And not for Robert Drill either. He was my age when he started his company. He knew exactly what he wanted to do." I fished around absently for a Twizzler, but I was too distracted to actually pick one up. My mind was swimming with too many thoughts. "I just want to live a life that's of use to others. And I don't know how to do that."

Ashley found a Twizzler on my behalf and threaded it between my thumb and forefinger. "Gregor, you are going to make a big impact. You're already making one. Every day."

Maybe she was like this with everybody, but Ashley always made me feel like a hero when I was with her. And I didn't even need to be saving anyone's life to feel that way. We could just be lying here in the grass—lazy, doing nothing, talking about big or stupid things—and she could so easily make me feel that way. It was in how she listened, I think. It felt like I could tell her anything. I hoped I could make her feel like that too.

"You're obviously conflicted about Robert Drill coming to camp," Ashley said.

A Twizzler drooped from the corner of my mouth like the suction at the dentist. "On the one hand, Robert Drill was my hero and I modeled my life after him. On the other hand, he's a liar who's deceiving everyone at this camp."

I thought of the injustice of false promises. It was wrong to manipulate young people. Just because we were young and adults thought we had "lessons" to learn didn't mean it was right to toy with our emotions. That was bullshit.

Ashley turned onto her stomach, lying perpendicular to me so that our bodies formed the letter *T*. There were a few leaves embedded in the strands of her hair. I gingerly plucked one out, but she looked all wrong suddenly. I stuck it back in its place. Better.

"You'll do something to make this right," Ashley said.

I bit off the end of my Twizzler, my forehead scrunching as I fixed her with a questioning look. "How do you know?"

"Because I know you. I know you want to make a difference in this world. This is your time, Gregor! You can be the hero this camp needs."

That sounded a lot like what people told the hero in superhero movies. It was so trite and so Ashley. She had a way of talking in inspirational posterspeak, but she infused it with so much sincerity that you believed her. You had to believe, because you could tell she believed it wholeheartedly herself.

I took the Twizzler out of my mouth and pointed it limply

at her. "Or maybe I should just stop trying to be a superhero because I'm not eight years old and probably should've grown out of my obsession with Superman a long time ago."

"But . . ." Her fingertips dipped into the strands of hair that had fallen over my forehead. She brushed them back. "That's what I like about you."

No one had ever played with my hair before. It felt nice. Soothing. I could feel what her fingers were doing; she was giving me the Superman *S*. I watched her lips stretch slowly into that familiar smile. I wondered what her smile tasted like. Would her mouth taste like mud? Where once that thought would've totally grossed me out, now it just sparked curiosity in me. I leaned in.

And then I froze, suddenly realizing that I was alone with Ashley with blankets and pillows and her hand casually in my hair as if it'd been there many times before. I didn't know what was weirder: the fact that I was fantasizing about kissing Ashley or the fact that I was fantasizing about tasting mud. "I have to go," I said, standing.

Ashley sat up. "Are you going to stand up to Drill tomorrow?"

"I don't know." I seriously didn't know anything anymore.

"I think you should, Gregor. If anyone's going to save this camp, it's you."

22

The press conference would be taking place on the basketball court, the clubhouse apparently too small to accommodate all the journalists and campers who'd be attending. Rows of folding chairs had been set up in the morning, facing a podium where Robert Drill would presumably address the crowd.

The camp was still pressing on with its normal routine of activities for the morning, but only just barely. Everyone's mind was on the impending press conference and Robert Drill. I skipped the activities altogether. Instead, I went to the basketball court early and made sure I got myself a good seat.

I thought about what Ashley said, about being the hero this camp needed. What if she was right? The camp needed to know that the internship wasn't real. If I told them about it, they'd just laugh at me, but if I confronted Robert Drill in front of everyone, then he'd have no choice but to respond.

The truth would be out. People could stop being horrible to each other.

In that sense, this press conference could turn out to be the most important event in my life thus far. If I made a change—if I took down my idol and showed the world who was really behind the mask—this could very well be the moment I'd been waiting for my whole life. My moment of real impact.

"Earth to Gregor." Win was in the chair to my right. I hadn't even noticed him sit down. Actually, I hadn't noticed that other campers had trickled in and the seats were filling up. I didn't see Ashley anywhere, but that didn't matter. Her words still rang in my ears. *Be the hero.*

"Your hero's about to show up and you look totally lost in space," Win said.

"He's not my hero anymore."

"You think he's not gonna show? Another robot? Because it'd be pretty hard to fool the press." Win gestured toward the men and women in the front row, busy with recorders and phones. "But also pretty funny."

"I think maybe I was wrong about him," I said. "I'm going to do something about it."

Win stared at me for a long moment. I was looking straight ahead, so I couldn't actually see him staring, but I could feel the force of his stare hit the side of my face. "What are you going to do?" he asked.

"I'm going to get up there and tell the whole camp that he's up to something."

"Gregor, I wouldn't ever tell you not to do something you have your heart set on, but I think on this occasion it might be necessary. I want you to listen to me carefully, buddy. *Don't sabotage the press conference.*"

Sabotage. It was funny he used that word. This whole summer I'd been trying to take a stand against all the acts of sabotage happening around camp, but now I was about to commit the biggest act of sabotage of all.

"Look, I'm upset with the stuff that's been happening too. The whole situation with ILP? That was bogus. And the way he left?" Win took a moment to take a deep breath. "I didn't even get to say a proper goodbye. He was—"

"I'm sad about our bunkmate too. But this is bigger than what happened with ILP."

"Am I getting through to you at all?" Win said. "Look, Poe's sitting over there. Do you really want to do something potentially humiliating in front of her?"

I watched Poe, sitting a few rows farther up, her hair split down the middle, straight and shiny, as always. I'd been humiliated in front of her before, but this time would be different. This time I was standing up for something that would make a difference and impact all of us, and that couldn't be wrong. But Poe wasn't who I really wanted to see anyway. I looked around for Ashley. She wasn't in any of the seats. Or in any of the trees, from what I could tell. I turned back to Win. "I have to make things right."

Jimmy appeared behind the podium and greeted the members of the press. I guess it was time to start.

"First of all, I just want to say, the rumors about this camp have been greatly exaggerated," he began. "You've probably heard that there has been one hospitalization at this camp and two fatalities. Well, those figures are simply flat-out *wrong*. There was only one fatality, and we gave the goldfish a beautiful burial. And I can confirm that the camel that was injured a few days ago did not in fact break its back. It was only dehydrated and needed to rest. Who knew camels could get dehydrated, amiright?" Jimmy's uncanny skill for trying to make an audience laugh and failing was as strong as ever. In a low and rushed voice he concluded, "Camper Michael Kremsler, however, was in fact taken to the hospital for diabetic ketoacidosis. The point is . . . Robert Drill is here, everyone!"

I almost couldn't see him for the sudden standing ovation, but there he was, pulling back the curtain and walking to the podium. His movements were not translucent or robotic. He was the real Robert Drill. My one-time hero.

"Hello, campers and press. I just want to say right off the bat how happy I am to be here at Camp Save the World, the most normal camp in America!"

A media person's hand shot up. He didn't wait to be called on before he started talking. "Is it true that conditions in the mess hall have gotten so bad that star camper Ashley Woodstone has been reduced to eating dirt?"

Drill laughed. "Ashley Woodstone does not eat dirt."

Jimmy stepped forward and whispered something quickly into Drill's ear that wiped the smile off his face. Drill took to the microphone again and quickly said, "I have no comment on Ms. Woodstone's eating habits."

Another member of the press raised her hand and asked a question. "Mr. Drill, can you address the issue of the international kidnapping that occurred at this camp? Is it true that the camper in question, who did not speak English, tried to draw his way to freedom, effectively painting a map showing where he was from and where he was supposed to be heading this summer—a camp in California—but was largely ignored by campers and staffers alike?"

"What happened to that camper was a simple mistake with his travel itinerary," Drill said. "The good news is that he was sent to his art camp in Palm Springs as soon we were alerted to the incident. We hear that I Like Paint is very happy there." Robert Drill's eyebrows crinkled as he read over his

paper, and then he turned to Jimmy once again before return-
ing to the audience. "Excuse me, the camper's actual name is
Alec Pent."

I couldn't believe it; I Like Paint had been telling us his
name the whole time. We were all just too stupid to hear it.

Another press person raised his hand, but Drill stopped
him before he could go on. "Okay, I know you all have a lot of
questions, but I feel I need to make clear that this is still a normal camp. Camp Save the World has an emphasis on civic duty
and leadership. All of our campers are accomplished activists
with their own personal campaigns, trying to make the world
a better place. The camp has provided them with opportuni-
ties they wouldn't have had anywhere else, with counselors
who are activists themselves that have taught them what it
means to be out in the field. With activities that are uniquely
focused on activism."

Lies. Lies. Lies.

"Aside from this wonderful camp experience, one lucky
camper will have the opportunity to work with the Robert
Drill Foundation in Florida for an internship opportunity
unlike any other."

I couldn't take it anymore. I found myself walking, my feet
moving of their own accord, down the aisle, right through the
center of it, ignoring all the looks I was getting. I caught a
glimpse of Poe, staring right at me, and although she wasn't

saying anything, I found courage in the way she watched me. By the time I got to the podium it was too late for anyone to stop me.

"ROBERT DRILL IS A LIAR!"

I had definitely shouted that too loud, but I had to take advantage of the shocked silence around me. "The internship is a lie! Tell everyone, Mr. Drill! I heard you tell our head counselor that there was no unpaid internship! It was all a lie, wasn't it? And for what? To make everyone at this camp turn against each other?"

Mr. Drill smiled, but it was an uneasy smile, like he was just plastering it on for the cameras. "Son, I think you're mistaken."

"No, I'm not," I said. "I met you when I was thirteen years old. And you told me I could feed the children of the world someday. But that was a lie too, wasn't it, Mr. Drill?" I walked to the microphone, which made Mr. Drill take a step back. "It's time you tell us the truth," I said. "We deserve that, at least." With the microphone in front of me and everybody's undivided attention, I decided to throw in one last thing before I let Robert Drill have the stage back. "Also, I just want to state for the record that I am not a bigot."

I stepped away, and Mr. Drill took my place behind the podium. "Okay. I'm not sure how you heard that conversation between Jimmy and I, but you're right. I did tell him that there was no unpaid internship."

Gasps everywhere and murmurs from the press. It was the chorus of my validation.

"But," Mr. Drill continued, "it was only because The Prize is actually a *paid* internship. In the amount of a full four-year college tuition."

Well, shit.

23

"You ever going to get out of bed?"

No. The answer to that question, for now and always, was no.

Win pulled back my sheet anyway, exposing my head to the harsh light of nothing. "You missed calisthenics."

Didn't care. "Are people talking about me?"

"Nobody is talking about you."

"Are you kidding? The whole *camp* is talking about you!" Rights said. Activities had already started, so I didn't know why he was even here. Probably wanted to gloat. Probably wanted to see what humiliation looked like in low-quality human form.

Well, here it was: lying in bed with a sheet over its head, stewing in its own self-loathing.

"Pathetic," Rights said.

"Don't listen to him," Win said. "It doesn't matter if some people are still talking about you. Just remember—"

I pulled my sheet back over my head again and shut myself off from the world.

I didn't know how much time had passed before I heard a knock on the door. I ignored it, but the knocking was persistent. I rolled over onto my stomach and reached for the window curtain next to the bed, pushing it aside to see who was out there. Pika stood outside the window, staring straight at me. I almost fell off the bunk bed when I saw him. If he was at the window, that meant that the person at the door had to be . . .

"Ashley," I said. Pika was making his way up the steps behind her, but I closed the door on him before he could make it in.

"Gregor Maravilla!" Ashley said. "I heard."

She was dressed in a ballerina-type skirt that was too long to be a tutu but strawberry-ice-cream-colored enough to remind me of the ballet anyway. Her hair was tied in a messy knot at the top of her head. She wore a chunky sweater even though it was a hot day. "What did you hear?"

"I heard you stood up to Robert Drill. I'm so proud of you."

"What?"

"I didn't go to the press conference because, well, I hate those things. I go to enough of them for work. Had I shown up they would've made it all about me, and it wasn't about me. It was about you and Robert Drill and your big moment. Pika was there, though. He told me all about it. He said you went up to the podium and really told Drill off."

Pika. That bastard.

"You didn't come to the clearing, or dinner, and today you missed calisthenics, so I came to see you. Tell me everything!"

"What your bodyguard didn't tell you is that I'm the idiot who accused Robert Drill of making false promises, but it turns out it was an even better promise, and now I have no chance of getting that paid internship—of my *dreams*, I might add—which would've not only fulfilled me on a deeply personal level but would also have, as it turns out, paid for my entire college education."

Ashley's ever-present smile dimmed. "What?"

"'Be the hero,' you said. But you know what, Ashley? I'm never going to save the day. I'm never going to feed the children, because heroes aren't real. *Superman* isn't real. Superman never had to live in the real world. Superman never had to go to this camp!"

I only realized I was out of breath when I found myself trying to catch it. I had come to this camp with a mission to do good. I thought I could change the world. I thought I would find my *pathetic* origin story. But this camp changed all that. It broke me. I was done being an idealist. Living with my head in the clouds never got me anywhere. In fact, it had made everything worse.

"What are you talking about?"

"I humiliated myself!" I said. "Not only in front of the man I idolize, but in front of the *press*. Do you know what my brother sent me today?" I went to my bunk bed and dug under my pillow for the fax that Anton had sent first thing in the morning. "*The five most embarrassing moments from the Robert Drill press conference at Camp Save the World*," I read. "Let me just skip to number one: *A camper totally lost his shit and stormed the podium, accusing Robert Drill of 'injustices' that all turned out to be completely made up. It'll probably be a while before that kid ever lives that tantrum down.*"

I crumpled up the paper and threw it on the floor. "And it's all your fault."

Ashley took a step, her face a picture of confusion. "Do you really think that, Gregor?"

"You know what? Yeah, I do." I was getting even angrier, the last four weeks of this clusterfuck of a summer finally coming to punch me in the gut, making me vomit up all the vitriol that had been cooped up. "I actually came to this camp with a good cause. Not like Save the World With Song or Zombie Attack or that girl who wants S.P.E.W.—which I still don't understand, by the way. And I certainly have a better cause than you. All you do is eat dirt, Ashley. I mean, what the fuck even is that? Nobody is going to start eating dirt just because a Manic Pixie Dream Celebrity going through a fad diet is telling them to. And I'm

247

sorry to break it to you, but I'm not altogether sure that your eating dirt isn't just a case of undiagnosed pica or at the very least a serious eating disorder. Either way, you obviously have an iron deficiency and you need to get that checked out."

Ashley didn't say anything. She just looked upset, and that, weirdly, made me even angrier. "Everything about this camp is so screwed up that you're probably going to be the one to win the internship. And you don't even need it! You said yourself you're only at this camp to make friends. But guess what—you can't make friends if you don't open up about yourself. You might be famous, but I don't know anything about you. Or your family. Or your 'bad news' exes. You just shut me down anytime I ask you about them. And you can't make friends when you've got a bodyguard following you everywhere you go. You asked me if I thought you were weird, and you know what? Yeah. I do. You're freaking weird, Ashley."

I breathed. It only took a second—just that one breath—but in that moment I found out that hating yourself could happen instantly. I hated myself with a force so strong that it knocked me back a step. I was winded with how big of a jerk I was.

I wanted to eat my words, find them all, gather them up and swallow, pretend they hadn't ever been out in the world.

But they had.

I could see it on Ashley's face. No smile, not even the hint of one.

"Sorry you were humiliated, Gregor."

"Ashley . . ."

"I brought you this." She held up a bag I hadn't even noticed she'd been holding the whole time. "Which was . . . stupid of me. But here it is." She set it on the floor.

"Ashley, wait."

She left, despite my stilted moves to try to reach out, explain, take it back.

I felt like running headfirst into the wall. Instead, I pulled my shirt over my face, plopped down onto the floor, and breathed hard to try to dissipate my new anger. This time it was all directed at myself. I wasn't even thinking about Drill anymore.

I pulled my shirt down. There was the bag she'd left. Inside was red fabric. I stretched it out, trying to make out what it was. The letter G was sewn onto the top center of it. And then it hit me. A cape.

There was a note too.

For Gregor. Now that you're a real hero you'll need this.

24

I sat in Nurse Patrosian's office. Just like the first time I'd been there, I had to wait to be seen. The kid before me had taken up a lot of the camp nurse's time with a bleeding thumb. It didn't look that bad when he walked out with his hand bandaged up, but Nurse Patrosian's white uniform was splattered all over with blood.

"Is he going to be okay?" I asked her. "Are *you* going to be okay?"

"No," Nurse Patrosian said. "Now, how can I help you?"

I sat up and combed the hair falling over my forehead off to the side. "I think I'm having a heart attack."

"I see," she said, sighing. "Why do you say that?"

I felt for the space in my chest where my heart was. "It feels like an elephant is sitting on me. I can't breathe right." I took a deep breath to show her just how hard it was for me to take a deep breath. It came out all shaky. "Just . . . My chest hurts. Can you help?"

Nurse Patrosian sent me on my way with a lollipop, a bottle of Tums, and instructions never to bother her with a nonsense illness again.

I had felt awful since the moment I woke up, the memories of the day before smashing into me the second I hit consciousness. There was the piercing, twisting agony of the things I'd said to Ashley in the cabin. I pressed my fingertips into the center of my chest and rubbed.

I was a colossal idiot. The certainty of that fact heavy like a weight, pinning me to my bed. But I knew I had to get up. If there was any hope for me to make things right with Ashley, I'd have to find her and do my best to apologize.

My first stop was the mess hall. It always seemed that anytime I sat down to eat, Ashley would appear and come straight for me. Before, in the first days of camp when I'd been stupidly predisposed not to like her, it felt like a nuisance. Now I'd give anything to see her make a beeline for my table. She wasn't anywhere, though.

I took my tray, ready to make my way through the crowds, when the whispering all around me reminded me of the press conference. I was so deep in thought about Ashley that I'd almost forgotten I'd made an ass of myself in front of everyone. I tried not to listen to the whispering going on behind my back, but I couldn't help but pick up on a few things, and everything I could make out had one common denominator.

Ashley.

After a moment I realized no one was talking about me. The buzzing all around me mirrored the thoughts in my brain exactly. All anybody was interested in was her.

I took my regular seat, grateful that Unity was already there so I could ask him. "What's everyone talking about?"

"You haven't heard?" he said. "Ashley Woodstone left camp."

"What?" He was wrong. She wouldn't just leave. Not without saying goodbye. But worse, I thought: *Not because of what I said to her.*

"Rumor has it she went to see her boyfriend in jail," Unity said. "Upstate New York: nothin' but jails and summer camps, man."

Her boyfriend in jail? The rumors I'd forgotten from the start of camp came crashing back to me. A cluster of three girls walked by my table and I stood abruptly, blocking their way. "Is it true that Ashley went to see her boyfriend— ex-boyfriend—in prison?" I didn't know why I thought they'd know better than anyone else, but I needed to hear from other people. I needed confirmation and second opinions before I put any stock in this.

"Oh yeah, she def went to see Rupert L.," Clean Air said.

252

"I think it's so sweet that she wants to get back with him after everything," Censorship said.

"If my boyfriend was as ripped as Rupert L., I wouldn't care if he was in jail for murder," Fracking said.

Clean Air slapped Fracking's elbow. "He's not in jail for *murder*," she said. "Only an accessory to it. Or something."

The girls walked on and I took my seat again, feeling dazed, my knees weirdly weak.

"I heard she went up there to marry that Rupert dude," Unity said. He was stuffing his mouth with a breakfast burrito, so I couldn't understand him too well, but having gotten the gist of it, I didn't want him to repeat himself.

"She can't—she can't get married. She isn't even old enough," I said. "Right?"

"She can do whatever she wants. She's an adult."

"She's seventeen," I corrected.

"Emancipated minor," Unity said. "Once she marries him they can have conjugal visits."

"Conjugal visits?"

"Yeah, they let you have sex—"

"I know what it means."

"They do it in like a trailer or something, for privacy. That Rupert dude is getting so lucky right now."

I pushed away from the table, letting my untouched bowl of cereal go soggy. "I gotta go."

I almost didn't recognize our clearing anymore. The blankets and pillows were gone, no ice bucket or snack chests. The branches looked naked without their string lights.

Pika stepped out from behind a tree.

"Pika!" His name was a gasp when I said it. I was relieved to see him. If he was here, then Ashley couldn't be too far. "You almost gave me a heart attack."

He walked up to me slowly, and any relief I felt was brief, being quickly replaced by fear at the expression on his face. He looked angrier at me than usual. Ashley must've spoken to him. "You deserve more than that."

His words were meticulous and slightly accented. I didn't think Ashley's bodyguard could get any more intimidating, but hearing Pika speak for the first time was a new experience. My feet moved backward. I was literally cowering before him.

"I never liked you, Gregor. And now I know why. Ashley was so happy, thinking she had a friend, but I knew you for who you really were. Just another little shit."

"Look, I'm sorry, okay, Pika? I know I messed up."

"It is not me who you need to apologize to."

"I know that. All I want to do is apologize to Ashley. Can you tell me where she is?"

"I don't know where she is. She left, and I can't call her

because she doesn't own a cell phone. But she told me what you said."

Was he going to kill me? Would this be the moment my life ended? If a Gregor got killed in the woods and no one was around to hear him, did he really scream?

"You do not know anything about Ashley," Pika said. "But I know her. I am her father."

Plot twist. *What?*

"I am her mother," Pika continued, confusing me further. "I am her brother and sister. I'm even her grandmother. I am her shoulder and her rock. I am there when she is happy and *I* am there when people like *you* make her sad. I am all she has." He was close enough to chew my head off if he wanted to. "I have seen what boys do to that girl. I have been there when they break her heart. My job was to protect her from everything, but especially from boys like you."

He scoffed and then stepped back, and I felt like I could breathe again. "I don't want to see you," Pika said, swishing a dismissive hand my way. "Get out of my face."

Now that I'd done it once before, breaking into the counselors' office was easy. Made easier by the fact that this time I didn't care about being caught. No one was there, and the office door was practically swinging wide open for me, waiting for me to get online on the only computer at camp and check out Ashley Woodstone's Wikipedia page.

Pika was right. Well, he was right about me being a little shit, but mostly he was right about the fact that I didn't know Ashley at all.

Ashley became an actress at nine months old, after her mother saw an ad that said they needed a baby for some formula campaign. Then, from ages three to eight she was the adorable child of the two gay dads on the sitcom *I Love My Two Gay Dads*. From ages nine to fifteen Ashley was on *Smarty Pants*, where she played Vivian Pants, a little girl so smart that she skips ahead to high school. All of her costars were teenagers when the show started and adults by the time it was over. Of her experience on the show, a precocious Ashley was quoted as saying, "Everyone is so great, but we don't really hang out off set because I'm still too young to get in anywhere." *Smarty Pants* abruptly ended when one of its stars, Carla Owens, got busted for growing large amounts of cannabis in her basement.

It wasn't until she was fifteen that Ashley's life really hit the tabloids. Having discovered that her parents were squandering all of her money, Ashley petitioned to get emancipated from them and won her case. She left television altogether and decided to try her hand at feature films, where she went after the meatier roles that her parent-managers never bothered to send her. She found great success playing roles as the daughter of some of the more important actors of our day, quickly working her way up to lead roles. Last year she'd been the "it girl" of Hollywood, with five movies in the can.

Her most prominent and public relationship had been with Rupert Lemon of the musical group The Ruperts. The relationship was short-lived and ended when Rupert L. was arrested.

I stopped reading, and the pit in my stomach that I'd felt all day got larger and deeper. All she wanted was a friend. It was obvious that her lifestyle of growing up as the only kid on soundstages had never afforded her one. She came to this camp looking for real experiences, and all anybody cared about was her celebrity.

All she'd wanted was a friend, and I'd failed her.

Like I said. I was a colossal idiot.

Hello, Mother, hello, Father, here I am at Camp Save the World.

There's not much to report.

Ashley was the best person at this camp. A much better person than I am. This whole time I thought everyone at this camp was ridiculous. But I think Ashley was the least ridiculous of all of us. She was the best of all of us. And I drove her away.

I really screwed up.

25

I Like Paint—Alec Pent—had been sent to his art camp in California where he truly belonged. But even though he was gone now, I still liked visiting his mural.

I went to see the mural for the first time after Visit Day. ILP was already gone by then. It was weird, seeing it so quiet, without the flurry of ILP's delicate paintbrush constantly touching it up. A world with arrows pointing from Croatia to New York, to California, with a bunch of exclamation points all over LA and question marks over New York. (In the last week that he was here ILP had added even more detail, painting three self-portraits at different points on the globe: himself in Croatia with his bags packed; himself in New York with tears springing out of his eyes like fountains; and himself in California, happy.) His message seemed totally obvious now. ILP—Alec—had been lost, and he'd painted himself a map to get himself found. I felt lost too, and even though his map wasn't tailored to me, I still went to see it, hoping it'd bring me the peace of mind it normally did. But tonight it seemed like I wasn't the only one feeling lost.

Men's Rights sat on the ground, his meaty legs splayed out before him, probably too packed with muscles to be comfortable cross-legged. He faced the mural, staring up at it like it held the answers to all his unasked questions. It seemed impossible, but Rights looked almost . . . sad. I knew what sad looked like. It took one to know one.

"What are you doing here?"

Rights looked up at the sound of my voice. "Superman. I'm glad you're here. I could use a friend."

"We are the opposite of friends."

"That's fair. But I could really use some advice right now. I know you're bummed that Ashley left. And that you humiliated yourself in front of Robert Drill and the press and you have absolutely zero chances of winning the paid internship, not that you ever had any to begin with. I need to know: What's it like being such a failure?"

I guess I wasn't going to get my peace of mind here.

"Wait!" Rights said as I was turning to go. "I'm sad."

I stopped. As much as I disliked him, I had to admire Rights for his candor. He wasn't ashamed to admit when he liked somebody, and now he wasn't ashamed to admit something that most people would probably not say out loud. I sat down on the ground, keeping some distance from him. "What have you got to be sad about?"

"Diabetes is in the hospital because of me."

Diabetes Awareness had been taken to the hospital after he collapsed on Visit Day. None of us had seen him since. "Diabetes is in the hospital because he made some bad decisions."

"That *I* led him to make," Rights said. "I worked him too hard. He starved himself because I told him he could get rid of his sugar illness."

"He had type 1 diabetes. You can't just 'get rid of it.' You knew that, right?"

"Well, I know that *now*." Rights dropped his head, letting it loll between his collarbones. "Diabetes almost died. And it was my fault. It's got me shaken up, Superman. Shaken to my perfect core. I need to make some changes."

I'd never seen this side of Men's Rights before. Serious, reflective, accountable. And then, with no small amount of shock, I realized what I was witnessing. This was a major moment in his life that was serving as a catalyst for change. Almost killing Diabetes was the defining thing that would launch Rights into his destiny. Just like in the movies when Superman and Spider-Man and Batman all realized their destiny, this was Rights's origin story.

"I gotta clean up my act," Rights said. "I need to do better. I have to rise above."

"Does this by any chance mean you're going to stop throwing money at me?"

"Oh, *poor* Superman. *People are just throwing money at me!*" He pulled some bills out of the pocket of his hoodie and threw them at my feet. "Get out of here with your white people problems, you dumb shit."

"I'm half Mexi—"

"I know, I know," Rights said. "Sorry. Reflex. It's going to take some time for me to get used to this. This . . . *nice* thing."

"So you're going to stop pranking and sabotaging everyone?"

"Absolutely. Just after Color War's over."

I wasn't there when it happened, since I'd been unceremoniously escorted out before it was over, but at the press conference, Robert Drill had tried to maintain the illusion that Camp Save the World was the most normal camp in America by declaring a most normal summer camp activity: Color War. Color War wasn't part of the official competitions to win The Prize, but it would still incorporate them into the game. A particularly overzealous reporter had apparently used his one opportunity to ask Drill a question to inquire what the teams were going to be.

Drill, knowing nothing about the bunks or the dynamics between the campers, shrugged and said, "Boys versus girls?"

So those were the teams. Boys versus girls. A number of campers were protesting Color War because it divided people into antiquated gender groups without considering the plethora of humans that fell between the assigned gender normative roles of male and female. But just because they were protesting didn't mean they weren't still participating. The members of the losing team would be ineligible to win the paid internship, making the stakes for this very normal camp activity impossibly high. By declaring Color War, Robert Drill had effectively made the situation at camp worse. Before, it was sabotage. Now, it was cutthroat.

Obviously, all I wanted to do was stay in bed. I want to be clear that the only reason I was doing any of this was to forget about Ashley. I was standing in the bushes behind the row of girls' cabins strictly to forget about her.

I still wasn't sure what the plan consisted of, or if there even was a plan, but all the guys who were present—Win, Rights, Unity, Anti-Robotics, War on Drugs, Seat Belt Safety, Boycott Camp, Gun Control, and Legalize Marijuana—seemed very determined to do whatever it was we were about to do. It didn't put me at ease at all when Rights dunked two fingers into a flat tin can and smeared eye black under my eyes. I squirmed out of his reach when I realized what he was doing, so I was pretty sure the inky stuff was now an abstract design down the side of my left cheek.

"There," Rights said. "Now you're one of us, Superman."

"Can someone please tell me what the hell we're doing?"

"There's ten of us," Win said. "One for each cabin. Gregor, you get Cabin Three."

"Our intel tells us that the girls are off having a secret meeting in the playing fields all the way on the other side of camp," Rights said. "So we're in and out in one minute flat."

"We have intel now?"

Rights ignored me and swung his backpack off his shoulder. It made clinking sounds, like glasses coming together for a toast. "Quiet as church mice, spry as cats on their ninth lives, you got that? Make sure you hide these well. We can't have the girls finding them before we alert Jimmy."

He was placing a bottle in each guy's hands, all of them a different shape and color. And all of them small enough to fit in our fists. It wasn't until Rights handed me mine that I realized just what kind of bottles these were. "Minibar liquor bottles? We can't have liquor."

It came to me in that moment that perhaps what I'd just

said was exactly the reason I was never invited to any parties. Rights stared at me like the loser that I was. But now I understood the plan. Possession of alcohol was one of the three offenses that would get you kicked out of camp. We were going to plant bottles in the girls' cabins and then tip Jimmy off. He probably wouldn't kick out the entire female population of campers, but it would surely get them eliminated from Color War. "Planting booze? Are you serious?"

"Serious as a heart attack, Superman."

"This isn't right," I said. "The girls don't deserve this. And also, how did we get booze?"

"There's no time for perfectly rational questions right now!" Unity said. He was bouncing on the balls of his feet, his large, deep-set eyes looking particularly crazed above the eye black. It might've had to do with the fact that he'd smeared the stuff not only on the tops of his cheeks but also over the entirety of his forehead. "The girls aren't in their cabins right now, which means there's nothing between us and their dressers. And do you know what's in their dressers? Panties."

I grimaced as soon as he said it. I knew he was going to go there, but still, the optimist in me had hoped for the best. "A panty raid? Come on, Unity, what is this, a bad eighties college comedy?"

Unity shrugged. "You have your reasons for being here, and I have mine."

"What happened with you and World Peace? I thought you two were going to be an epic couple."

"We had a fight. Never play Settlers with a girl you love, Children. It can get ugly."

"I told him not to put the robber on her six, but did he listen?" Rights said. "Just because I wasn't playing with you guys doesn't mean I still wasn't offering expert advice."

"Alright," I said. I no longer had a reason to be here. I put my bottle of Scotch down on the ground but didn't get too far before Win stepped in front of me.

"Come on, Gregor, we need you. One guy per cabin."

"Win, how are you of all people on board with this?"

"It's Color War," he said. "All bets are off."

"Look, everybody knows that when girls aren't wearing underwear they go a little insane," Unity said.

"What?" I said.

"It's totally factually true, man," he continued. "Rights told me. Plus, this could be my only shot at getting close to girls' panties."

"You're definitely right about that."

Win pulled me aside and spoke in a low voice that the rest of the guys couldn't hear. "I think this could be good for you," he said.

"Yeah, and why's that?"

"Because this whole time we've been out here I bet you haven't spent a single minute thinking about Ashley."

I stood in the middle of Cabin 3 with the bottle of Scotch in my hand, not thinking about Ashley Woodstone.

I probably should've put the Scotch down and gotten the hell out of there immediately, but I had to stop and marvel at the neatest cabin in camp. I didn't know who it belonged to, but nary a shoe was out of place. Were all girls this tidy? Should I stop generalizing about girls so much?

I had no clue where to hide the bottle. Any place I tried to position it seemed out of place. Obviously. A bottle of Scotch would always seem out of place in a summer camp cabin. I decided to put it under one of the beds.

Except there was already a bottle of Scotch under there. A larger, full-sized one. I tried putting my mini bottle in a drawer, but there was booze in there already too. Actually, there was a bottle of alcohol in every drawer I opened. I began to wonder if the girls of Cabin 3 weren't actually all alcoholics.

"What are you doing in here?"

I spun around. Down With Styrofoam stood at the door and locked eyes with me. Then she shrieked.

I ran out of the cabin as fast as I could, shrieks ringing out outside. Whoever had timed this scheme was an idiot or we'd had some faulty intel, because practically every girl in camp was chasing after us. "GIRLS!" Marijuana yelled, his voice taking on a desperately paranoid edge. Boys dressed in blue and eye black ran like they'd just lit a fuse, but not all of them got far enough. Feminism tackled Unity to the ground, and a flurry of brightly colored underwear flew out of his arms like a spray of blood from a gunshot wound.

I was finally grateful for my long legs. No one was going to be taking me down.

I was taken down. She came at me so quick it blindsided me, and the two of us collapsed in a tangle, tumbling on the grass. I was getting ready to get up and run again when the black hair tipped me off. "Poe?"

She was on top of me, pinning me to the ground, the tips of her loose hair brushing against my cheek. All thoughts of running left my mind immediately. This wasn't the worst way to get caught, all things considered.

"They were trying to plant liquor in our cabins!" Feminism said, holding up one of the bottles. She stood with one foot on the ground, the other on Unity's chest.

"Gee, Gregor, I didn't know you had it in you," Poe said.

"What can I say? I'm a badass."

She actually laughed, and it didn't matter that we'd

failed at our mission because Poe was on top of me and happy to be there.

"Girls, girls!" I could hear Win's voice call out. "Maybe we can work something out."

I wondered what Win had in mind. Poe apparently did too. She waggled her eyebrows at me, questioning but not disinterested.

Sometimes it felt almost like all the counselors up and left for the night. Tonight was one of those times.

Because there was no doubt that we probably could've used some adult supervision right now. Even though it was way past lights-out, it was relatively easy sneaking over to the playing fields. Much easier than it should've been for practically every camper to go unnoticed with a bottle of booze in hand. Poe got the party started by standing before everyone and declaring, "The world is fucked! Let's get drunk!"

We'd only just begun partying and people were already going wild: dancing too erratically to the mellow musical stylings of Save the World With Song, flopping onto the ground and rolling around with each other, hooking up, of course. Rights had stripped off his shirt and was now swinging it over his head, to the questionable delight of a group of girls around him, like they were all playing out a scene from *Magic Mike*.

And I sat and watched them, wondering if Jimmy would wake up tomorrow to find that instead of calisthenics, everyone's morning workout would consist of trying to get up off the ground.

I'd taken a few sips of beer, my first one ever. I did it partly to fit in and partly because this was another "first." A first drink seemed appropriate right now. The beer tasted gross—it being room temperature probably didn't help—but I could already feel it getting me buzzed. My brain was beginning to swim. I wasn't yet sure if I liked the feeling, but I was leaning toward yes.

"Hey," Poe said. "Wanna go somewhere?"

I stared blankly. "Okay."

She presented her hand. Her small, lovely, soft-looking hand. I put mine in it. Definitely soft. She helped me up and then pulled me along.

We walked through the woods. I did not like walking through the woods at night, but apparently my superpower was gravitating toward girls who did.

"I just wanted to get away from all that noise," she said.

"Uh-huh." I almost tripped on an overgrown root but found my bearings again. Luckily, Poe hadn't seen.

"That's a lie. I really just wanted to get you alone."

I swallowed. "Me?"

We stopped walking and she took a swig from her beer can. Her lips twisted in a smirk, that beauty mark on her lip practically twinkling. She looked at me quizzically, like if she studied me long enough she could read my mind. Maybe she already could.

"You and me, we have a lot in common," she said.

"Yeah?"

"Yeah," Poe said. "We both think this camp is a joke. And we both really like me."

"What?" I had to stop with the monosyllabic comments, but it was like my mind couldn't form long words in her presence. Also, I was mostly confused whenever I was around her. Like now. Especially now.

"There's this rumor going around that you like me."

"Oh." There I went again. "I couldn't possibly like you," I said. "I mean, even if I did like you, it wouldn't matter because . . . you know . . ."

"I don't," she responded, walking closer to me. Her hair could've been a single piece of cut velvet. It was so uniform, not a strand out of place.

"It wouldn't matter if I like you because you're . . . you know." If she wasn't going to say she was gay, then I definitely couldn't say she was gay. That'd be like outing her. Or something. Except she was walking even closer to me. So close that

I could smell vanilla in her hair and beer on her breath. An intoxicating combination.

This was dangerous territory. I couldn't look directly at her. If I looked directly at her I might do something stupid. I looked anywhere else. And then my eyes caught something on a tree. A circle of entwined twigs and leaves.

My crown of leaves. The one that Ashley had made me, the one I'd promptly taken off and hung on that tree like a welcome wreath.

I looked around and realized where we were. We were in the clearing. *Our* clearing—mine and Ashley's. She'd wiped it clean, but she'd forgotten that wreath.

I took a step back from Poe. At the beginning of the summer I would've done anything to be in this very situation with her. Anything to be as close to her as I was now, anything to make her as interested in me as she seemed to be at this very moment. But now I realized I didn't want any of that at all.

"I have to go," I said.

I left Poe and the clearing.

26

I needed to take my mind off things. Which was the only way I could explain my attendance at Talent Night.

For our fourth competition to win The Prize, Jimmy explained that we could get up on stage and perform a talent. Something about how being a good activist meant being creative and how being creative meant having talent. I wasn't too clear on the details, but I did know that Talent Night would now be connected to Color War. The counselors would award five points to every camper whose talent was—what they would liberally deem—remarkable. But for the first time, all points gained for this competition would also go toward rewarding the Color War teams. Also for the first time, this competition was optional. I decided to partake as an audience member only.

So I sat in the clubhouse, watching as Stop Fracking twirled her baton with gusto. She wasn't as good as Trigger Warning had been before her, who had passionately sung a sad Adele song. Now Unity, dressed in a tux, was at the mic.

He'd talked to me about his talent. He said he didn't have one but that it was okay because he'd gotten World Peace to help him out with that. He said she'd competed in tons of talent portions in plenty of pageants and that he had this in the bag. I looked at the program in my hands to see how long this was going to take.

Unity will be wearing his finest evening wear and answering the age-old question: "Why America really does need unity through multiculturalism."

"I am American," Unity said into the microphone. "And I personally believe that unity through multiculturalism is important and also the fabric of this nation. Because unity is part of the American Dream. But sometimes we have nightmares." The spotlight on Unity must've been intense, because sweat was starting to sprout on his forehead and he was squinting. "And nightmares happen, such as thinking about clowns and others. It's up to our leaders like the dreamers who dream to help educate our American students—especially the youngsters as such kindergartners and more littles—to never stop dreaming of unity in places like Texas and Alabama and New Hampshire as well as Old Hampshire. Not to mention my birth state of Illinois, where the pizza was invented. Because America."

I had no idea what he was saying, and part of me wondered if World Peace had actually tried to help him or sabotage him. It really was a special talent to not be able to answer a question you asked yourself. I clapped, if only to aid Unity off the stage quicker.

I looked down at the program again. There was only one participant left.

Down With Styrofoam puts on a one-woman show of her original play, Death of a Styrofoam Salesman.

Time to go. No offense to Down With Styrofoam, but I was really not in the mood to sit through an entire play right now. Plus, her stance on Styrofoam was made even more unclear when the curtains went up and all of the scenery and props for her play were made entirely out of Styrofoam. Did "down" mean "with" or "against"? I got up and squeezed through the seated audience members to get to the aisle.

Down With Styrofoam took the stage. "Thank you all for joining me tonight in bringing the story of a doomed Styrofoam salesman to life. I wrote and directed this one-woman show, and I am happy to announce the return of Ashley Woodstone in all of the roles!"

I stopped in my tracks and turned. There she was. Ashley. Styrofoam salesman. I sat down at one of the empty seats in the back row.

The seven-minute play was an abomination, but Ashley was

amazing. She acted the crap out of all six roles, playing a variety of people, from a little old man yelling at his cup to the title salesman, a fortysomething man in the midst of a debilitating depression. I sat on the edge of my seat for all of it, eyes wide, jaw unhinged. I couldn't tell if we, the audience, were meant to root for the Styrofoam salesman or applaud his demise. And the death-by-elevator-shaft ending seemed entirely beside the point. But as soon as Ashley "fell" off the stage and the lights went down, I jumped out of my seat and clapped.

It was a standing ovation of one, and when the lights went back on, Ashley stood there onstage, her eyes locked on mine. I clapped, I cheered, I was the loudest person in the clubhouse. But she did not return my smile, or my excitement at seeing her. She broke our eye contact and walked off the stage.

I was seized with a sudden fear—that I'd really blown it, that she would leave camp again, that I would never get to properly apologize to her. I acted on instinct and ran down the aisle, throwing myself onto the stage just as Jimmy was walking to the center of it.

"Wait!" I said, standing up. "There's one more act."

Jimmy was confused but excited. "It looks like we have a last-minute entry. Children, the stage is yours."

Jimmy left the stage, and a spotlight shone directly on my face. I had to shield my eyes for a moment until they adjusted to the light. I searched the room for Ashley. "My talent," I said into the microphone that Jimmy handed me, "is being a terrible friend."

It was dumb, I know it was dumb, but I had no idea what else to say and I was desperate to say something—anything—that would get her to listen. I found Ashley in the crowd. She'd taken a seat all the way in the back. To me, she could've been the only person in the room. "It's something I discovered about myself at this camp. I didn't know if I'd make any friends this summer, but I did. And I didn't realize that making friends means that sometimes you can hurt them almost as much as you care about them. I discovered at this camp just how painful missing someone can be. And that it can consume you. And that every little thing can remind you of them. Like a salamander in the woods. Or the smell of the earth after it rains. My talent is saying things I don't mean and being an idiot and ruining a really good thing. The *best* thing." I watched Ashley, trying in vain to read her unreadable expression. "I'm so sorry," I told her. "I know I don't deserve your forgiveness. But I hope you'll at least consider it."

I didn't move. No one in the room seemed to. I just watched Ashley, waiting for her to give me a sign, waiting for that patented Ashley Woodstone smile. She stood up and walked out of the clubhouse.

A lone voice in the audience shouted, "YOUR TALENT SUCKS!"

* * *

I crashed through the double doors, into the night. I'd jumped off the stage and run down the aisle after her. She was heading in the direction of the woods. "Ashley, wait!"

Her back was turned to me, but I could see her sigh in the way her shoulders moved. "I'm not here for you," she said. She turned to face me. "I didn't come back for you, and I wasn't at this camp for you. I know it may have seemed that way, but my time at this camp wasn't just to be your sidekick or some girl you found really strange but drawn to for whatever reason. My camp experience wasn't just to validate yours, Gregor. I was here to make friends. And I thought that was what I was doing with you. I guess I was wrong."

Her voice got small at the end there, and it made my heart feel even smaller. Tiny enough to topple over and break.

"You might think that eating dirt is weird, but I don't think that a sixteen-year-old boy who likes Superman is weird. Sorry if my so-called weirdness ruined your camp experience. But you kind of ruined mine."

She walked off again, and I could do nothing to stop her.

27

"So she walks up to it, slowly. She doesn't know what to do, she doesn't know where to go. And then she opens the door and sees . . . that the pantry is full of grains and pasta and does not contain a single gluten-free option!"

This was Gluten Freedom's idea of a scary story.

We were sitting around a small campfire, some other campers and I. It was Campout Night. Two days after Talent Night, two days after Ashley, in so many words, had told me she didn't want to talk to me anymore.

Tonight, campers were spread out through the vast playing fields, some of them building tents, others learning the finer points of outdoor cookery. Tonight, we left the comforts of our cabins to sleep under the stars. A real camp experience.

Ashley and I had managed to stay away from each other these last couple of days. But now we sat at the same campfire, listening to the same ghost/gluten stories. Sitting across from each other and avoiding eye contact at all costs. Pika wasn't anywhere in sight, though, so at least I didn't have to worry about also avoiding his piercing gaze.

"Spooky!" Jimmy said. He was our group's counselor for the night, heading up the ghost stories and sitting with us. "Let's try talking about something else. It's the last week of camp, and I want to get to know you kids better before it's all over. I want to know the origin of your causes. Children, why don't you start off by telling us why you want to feed the . . . children?"

I started, caught off guard. "Why I want to feed the children?" Ten pairs of eyes were trained on me, waiting for me to answer. "Well, I mean, I want to do good."

Jimmy nodded thoughtfully. "But why that specifically?"

I picked a blade of grass from the ground, rubbing it between my fingers. "Well, a few years ago I actually met Robert Drill." I guess I was expecting some gasps or awed looks on people's faces or something, but then I remembered that everyone here had met Robert Drill when he'd come to camp for the press conference. "Anyway, he told me that I could feed the children of the world one day if I put my mind to it. So I decided to put my mind to it. I read up on children who are going hungry all over the world and decided that if I

280

could do something about that, then my life would really be of some worth. That I wasn't just taking up space." It felt good, talking about this, about something real, something that mattered. But nobody seemed very impressed by anything I'd just said. Actually, I was pretty sure I caught Feminism rolling her eyes.

"That's nice, Children," Jimmy said. He scanned the rest of the campers until his eyes settled on Gluten Freedom. "Why don't you go next," he told her.

"Okay," she said. "I started getting sick a lot a couple of years ago. I never felt good. Ever. It wasn't just stomachaches, it was all-consuming. I would miss school a lot because of how sick I was. And the worst thing was, I had no idea what was wrong with me. No one did. Some doctors even told me it was all just in my head, like I was actually *trying* to make myself sick on purpose. Before I got diagnosed with celiac disease I thought I was dying; that's how bad I felt. People think going gluten-free is a stupid fad diet or a joke, but it isn't a joke to me. I can't eat the same things as everybody else. I have to be extra careful anytime I go out that there isn't any cross-contamination in my food. And if I get just one person to be a little bit more sensitive to the needs of others, then I'll feel like everything I'm putting into this cause will be worth it."

The sounds of the other campers at the other activities still filled the fields, but it was quiet enough here, with us, that the crackling of the flames drowned them out. We all stayed listening even though Gluten Freedom was done talking.

Jimmy nodded and smiled. "Win, tell us about your campaign."

Win cleared his throat, his eyes locked on the fire. "It's just me and my mom in California. She has a job now and everything is good, but for a while there, when I was in first grade or so, she was unemployed. I was hungry a lot. That's the most prevalent memory I have from that time in my life. Other kids were learning how to ride bikes or how to read or whatever, but all I remember is being *so hungry*. What that felt like. I'm grateful that my school had a free breakfast and lunch program. My mom would drop me off extra early so that I could eat before school. It made a big difference."

He rubbed the pad of his thumb over his bottom lip, and I caught a glimpse of his fingernail, chewed almost to the stub.

"Ending hunger is the most important thing in the world to me because I know what it's like to be hungry," Win went on. "And nobody should ever have to feel that way."

Jimmy nodded. "Thank you for sharing that with us, Win. Unity, why don't you go next?"

Unity's big eyes shifted, looking around at all of us but not settling on anyone for too long. "I'm originally from Chicago, but my dad moved us to Missouri three years ago for his job. In Chicago we had family and friends and a community of people. In Missouri, though . . . I'm the only brown kid at my school. It's a small private school, and me and my sister are the only Indian kids in the whole place.

"I know there's not going to be a big, diversified population everywhere I go—that's not realistic in some places—I've accepted that, but it's important that people like me—people with different customs or from a different culture than you're used to—it's important that we're visible and that we're included in the conversation. I know it probably sounds cheesy but I really believe that if we can all unite and accept each other we'll be stronger together. Because sometimes I feel so apart from the people around me, you know? And I just don't want to feel like an alien in my own town anymore." Unity picked at the edges of his cast, where it was fraying close to his thumb. "It's lonely being the only one."

World Peace, who was sitting next to him, placed her hand on top of his cast. She linked her fingers with his.

There were plenty of times this summer that I thought I had a pretty noble campaign, that what I was fighting for was more important than what a lot of other people here were fighting for. But looking around the campfire, I was starting to realize just how wrong I was. I'd been a snob about this. Maybe my campaign was not the most important one here.

And the campaigns that I thought were just jokes could actually be meaningful to a lot of people.

I needed to put things in perspective. Because no matter what I was going through, there were bigger problems out there in the world. I found Ashley staring back at me. I wondered if she was thinking about perspective too.

28

Things were different after that campfire. No more wallowing in bed, no more being sad about the state of my life and Ashley. I was going to do something.

My bunkmates were happy to see this new initiative.

"Glad to see you're finally taking Color War seriously, Superman," Men's Rights said as he put down his barbells. "I wouldn't normally count on you, but we're going to need as much manpower as we can get if we want to win Capture the Flag. Who am I kidding? We're going to need very little manpower, because we are playing against girls. Amiright?" He raised his hand in a high five toward Win, but Win let him keep his hand in the air.

Capture the Flag. I'd forgotten all about that. The final act of Color War.

"Sorry, guys, I've got other things to do." I grabbed whatever was in my drawer and put it on quick.

"Good luck, buddy," Win said. "I hope she gives you a break."

I wasn't sure how Win knew I was going to talk to Ashley, but then, of course he did. He was Win.

"Whatever," Rights said. "Like I said, we need manpower, and you clearly don't have any, Superman."

"I'd reconsider calling me Superman if I were you."

"And why would I do that?"

I hadn't made too big a deal about him calling me Superman before, but I was a different person today, a more confident one. I was a man on a mission. And anyway, he needed to hear this.

"Because we've all got real names, *Top Gun*."

My smile was directly proportional to Rights's sudden scowl. Win couldn't know what I'd just unleashed but he understood it was something big by the way everything suddenly stilled. He pulled his fresh shirt over his head and watched us silently. Rights took a step toward me, his head bowed forward, his voice extra low. "Why did you call me that?"

"What's the matter, *Risky Business*? Can't handle a nickname?"

"I can handle a nickname!" His voice projected the opposite.

"Nah, that's a *Mission: Impossible*. I don't think you can."

"Wait, why are you calling him a bunch of Tom Cruise movies?" Win said.

"Because that's his name. Rights here is actually Tom Cruz."

Admittedly, it wasn't that funny. But Win still laughed, and I joined him. It helped that Rights still looked so pissed off. Lesson one of doling out obnoxious nicknames: Don't have a funny name yourself. Guess Rights never got that memo.

"How'd you find out my name?"

"So Ashley Woodstone isn't the only celebrity at this camp?" Win said.

"How'd you find out my name?!" Rights demanded again.

"Gentlemen, I have places to be."

"It's a family name, Gregor!" Rights called after me. "I go by Tomás!"

I left the cabin feeling more confident than ever. It helped that the soundtrack to my parting was Rights's haunted screams.

She could've been anywhere. Since today was all about Capture the Flag, regular camp activities were suspended. Campers were finishing breakfast and heading to the playing fields to start the official game. And even though Ashley had said that all she wanted was a normal camp experience, something told me to check our clearing first.

She was there. Her back was to me as she sat on the fallen log. I wasn't dumb enough to think she was waiting for me, though. Seeing her was instant relief, and I held on to that feeling as proof that I needed to make things right with her, no matter the cost. I loved the way I felt when I saw her. Even when she was mad at me. Selfishly, I wanted to keep feeling that way.

I rounded the log so I was standing in front of her. I expected a look of disappointment on her face, but when she looked up at me she wasn't even surprised. And there was a tiny smile hidden behind her lips.

"You're wearing it," she said.

My hands, at my sides, felt for the cape. Red and long enough to reach the backs of my thighs. Easy to grab and spread out behind me. "It is a pretty excellent cape."

"You don't have to wear it."

"I want to," I said. "No one has ever made me a cape. You're the only one who's ever looked at me as . . . a hero. I don't deserve it." I waited for her to say something. This would've been the perfect opportunity for her to call me out, tell me she still didn't want to talk to me, but Ashley only looked at me, waiting. "I was a gigantic asshole to you. I'm sorry. If I could fly around the earth backward to turn back time and erase all the awful things I said, I would. If there's something I don't deserve, it's your friendship. Because you were my best friend at this camp and I treated you like shit."

"Let's not say the *S* word."

"Okay, I treated you like dirt."

"But dirt is marvelous."

I sighed. She was going to make this difficult. But I deserved that. "I treated you like garbage."

"Compostable garbage . . . ?"

"Unrecycled, smelly-garbage-juice garbage."

"Better."

I sat next to her on the log, not knowing what else to say, but wanting to be nearer to her.

"When you left, there was a rumor that you'd gone to visit your boyfriend in jail." This was probably not the right thing to bring up, and even if she chose to roll her eyes or stop talking to me, I had to know. "Is it true?"

"Rupert is no longer my boyfriend. He hasn't been for a long time. And no, I didn't go see him."

I let go of the breath I'd been holding.

"I left because I needed to figure some things out. You were right when you told me that in order to make friends I needed to be more open. It made me think about things I wasn't even telling myself. I needed to figure out why everyone I care about ends up leaving in one way or another. Like my parents. At first I didn't believe that they just wanted my money. And to prove that they didn't, I gave away most of it. I gave away all of the money that I didn't need. I thought, *This'll prove that they love me anyway, despite the money. If they stay with me when I have nothing, this will prove it.* But they didn't. They fought it in court. So I got myself emancipated. You can imagine how much they liked that."

"I'm sorry, Ashley."

"It's okay. It just means no parents at Visit Day for me," she said, shrugging. "And then Rupert left, but obviously he didn't have much control over that, being arrested. We weren't together that long, but he was my first . . . public boyfriend. I know that probably sounds weird, but when everything happened—and how public it was—it was pretty hard to handle."

As much as I'd wanted Ashley to open up, it was still hard to hear her this upset and not know what to do to make her feel better. But I knew that being a good friend wasn't always about trying to make the other person feel good. A wise person once told me that sometimes it is best just to listen and learn.

"And then I made a friend here, and I was so happy about that," Ashley said. "But you put a stop to that too."

"I came back," I said quickly. "I'm here. I'm sorry."

"I know. And I forgive you, Gregor."

Relief. I was flooded with it.

"You were right about things," she said.

"Pretty sure I've never been right about anything in my life."

Ashley laughed and shoved my shoulder with hers. "You were right that if I want to make true, meaningful friendships,

I need to open up more. I'm going to work on that. And that if I wanted to be a normal camper like everyone else here, I shouldn't have brought a bodyguard along. I gave Pika the rest of the summer off."

No bodyguard to potentially bash my head in? The relief was too much. "This is going to sound totally corny, but . . . can we be friends again?"

Ashley stuck out her hand, ready for a handshake. I shook it. "Friends."

She sighed, and I could tell she was relieved too. Her smile came back in full force. It was blinding. Captivating. Hypnotizing. I hadn't realized how much I missed that smile. I would've followed her anywhere so long as she smiled at me like that. I would say and do anything she wanted.

"Now that that's out of the way, I think it's finally time for you to go on a spiritual journey, Gregor Maravilla."

I laughed. "You're not still on that, are you?"

29

She was still on that. Since the start of camp, Ashley had been talking a big game when it came to spiritual journeys. And every time she brought it up, I had no clue what she meant. I always turned her down, partly because I had absolutely no desire to go on a spiritual journey, partly because I was pretty sure it was somehow offensive, but mostly because I didn't think she was serious about it.

But she was serious about it. I was now discovering just how serious she was as I stood inside her reassembled yurt, watching her stir a brewing pot of murky brown liquid.

"What the hell is that?"

She produced a halved coconut husk and poured the liquid into it. "A vine, a leaf, and a root of plants with names that I can't pronounce, but don't worry, they're totally natural and safe."

"Usually when someone has to add that something is totally natural and safe, there's reason to believe that maybe it's not," I said. "Where'd you get the plants? Where'd you get a *coconut* husk?"

"All very good questions," Ashley said. "Perhaps you'll find the answers on your spiritual journey."

She held out the husk, clutched in both of her hands.

"You don't actually expect me to drink that."

Her arms fell a little bit but she did not let any of the liquid spill. "You said you'd do it."

This was true. For reasons I could not explain but that probably had something to do with wanting to make Ashley happy and cementing our new and improved friendship, I had agreed to do the one thing I'd been telling her all summer that I would not do. But I wasn't just going to go on this journey totally blind. I never did anything without fully knowing what I was getting myself into. Camp Save the World being the only exception. And look how well that turned out.

"Is this, like, even legal?"

"Yes!" Ashley said, laughing. "This tea is legal in some countries."

I took a step back. "I'm not drinking that."

Ashley walked over to her bed, a few feet away. She sat and tapped the space next to her. I joined her. The way she sighed, I knew she was about to impart one of her many weird and wise stories.

"Did I ever tell you that I lived in the Peruvian Amazon for a time?"

"Somehow that never came up."

"I was there to film *Today Is Yesterday's Tomorrow*, playing the kidnapped daughter of William Gleeson. It's a very good action film if you've never seen it, by the way, and even though I spend most of the movie tied up in the villain's lair, I get rescued at the end. Anyway, I was living in the Amazon, with the Amazonian people, eating the local food and playing with the local children, when one day a shaman invited me to a spiritual awakening ritual and told me to drink this very special tea. And what do you do when a shaman invites you on a journey and tells you to drink a very special tea?"

"You absolutely do not drink it."

"I drank it," she said, scooting closer to me, her eyes going wide as if she herself were hearing this story for the first time. "And when I drank this tea I basically understood the entire meaning of life."

"Only that, huh?"

She pushed the tea forward, holding it out enticingly. "I would never make you do anything that you weren't comfortable with, Gregor. And I wouldn't have even made this for you if I didn't think it could help you. But I know you're looking for something. I know you're searching for meaning and purpose. You were hoping this camp would provide that, but it didn't. Don't you want answers to your questions?"

I stared at the tea. I did want answers. I wanted to know if this whole camp experience was for nothing. I wanted to know if I was ever going to live up to my potential and make anything of myself. I wanted to know if I could save the world—if it was even possible to. I wanted to know if I would go my whole life—or even just this whole summer—without doing anything interesting or daring, or legal only in some countries.

I looked at Ashley. "Doesn't William Gleeson blow up the Amazon in *Today Is Yesterday's Tomorrow?*"

"Yes."

I drank the tea.

Ashley had some too. We sat on the bed and waited. "So when does this stuff usually kick in?"

"Usually immediately."

"And how long does it last?"

"Just a few hours or so," Ashley said. "Your whole life if you're lucky."

I nodded. "Wait, what?"

But Ashley pressed her index finger against my lips and shushed me with a whispered, soothing "Just let the tea take you."

I already regretted swallowing. I tried preparing myself

for whatever it was I was about to experience. I'd never done anything so illicit before, and my insides were suddenly swirling in a cocktail of fear and excitement . . . Or it could've just been the tea. It was a pleasant feeling. A buzz that made me instantly giddy. Definitely not the uncontrollable high I had feared. "This is it?" I said. "This is nothing. I don't feel anyth—"

I pressed my hand against the yurt's wall and the wall moved back. "WHOA!" I yelled. "THE WALLS ARE MOVING!"

I turned to Ashley, having never been so amazed in my life, but she simply nodded and smiled, her head lolling from side to side as though she were listening to a song that I could not hear. "They do that sometimes," she said.

Right. Ashley's walls were made out of bedsheets or endangered animal hides or leaves or something. Of course they would move if I pressed against them, so that wasn't so impressive. The fact that the walls were talking to me, however, was.

"What?" I said. They were just whispers at first, and I had to make myself concentrate really hard to understand what they were saying. "You want me to what?"

"Leave," the walls said.

Now, I was still lucid enough to think that maybe Pika had stuck around and was hiding outside the yurt and pretending to be the walls just to spook me. Because the walls and Pika seemed to agree that they didn't want me around. But I was already high enough to be thoroughly spooked anyway.

"Ashley, your walls hate me." I turned to her but she was gone, the space she occupied on the bed suddenly empty.

Ashley wasn't outside either, or maybe she was and I just couldn't see her. Didn't matter, because the trees were calling my name and sparkling in bright neon colors and there was nothing I could do to stop myself from basking in their glory. They wanted me to dance. I'd never had the requisite moves, but now I knew that I not only possessed the moves—I had the *right* moves. My body was made for dance, and I swayed to the rhythm of the wind, letting it fill my ears in the delicious way that air filled my lungs. Every tree in the forest was my dance partner on our very own dance competition show, and we were all about to win the grand prize.

The idea of time felt suddenly fluid. It was like it lay at my feet one minute, expansive and clear, and then was tugged from under me so I lost whole swaths of it. Life felt like a movie with some of the frames cut out of the reel. Like how I'd just been dancing with the trees but now I stared into space, standing still and feeling the strange and sudden compulsion to create something beautiful. I knew what my subject would be, and I looked around to find the right materials to make it. I only had to look down.

My Ashley Woodstone statue was now complete. My medium?
Dirt. (Plus a couple of sticks and stones that I'd used for her
arms and eyes, respectively.) I'd molded her with my own two
hands, shaping the mud like clay. It was only in the edges of my
mind that I wondered if this was objectifying Ashley. But no,
this was art. There was Venus de Milo, and now I'd created
Ashley de Woodstone. She was so beautiful. I mean, like,
really beautiful. I don't want to toot my own horn or anything,
but I was pretty sure there had never been a more beautiful
and lifelike statue of a girl ever created in the history of art.
Looking at my artwork I was certain of two things: I was an
incredible artist, and my Ashley Woodstone statue was *hot*.

I caressed her dirt hair. So lifelike.

"Children?"

I spun around. Jimmy was standing in the woods, staring
at me.

"Oh. Jimmy. Hey. I'm not doing anything weird."

"What are you doing, Children?"

"Just minding my own business, Jimmy. Hey, check out
my amazing Ashley Woodstone statue," I said, gesturing
behind me.

298

"That's a pile of dirt."

I looked at my Ashley statue. Curiously, Jimmy was right. I was looking at a pile of dirt.

"You're covered in dirt," he said.

I looked at myself. My palms were filthy. Crusted clumps of mud clung to my knees. And there were dirt stains all over my shorts, mostly in my crotch area. "This isn't what it looks like."

"Why are you wearing a cape? And why are you shirtless, Children?"

"WHY AM I SHIRTLESS?" I said. "WHY ARE YOU CRYING?"

Because Jimmy *was* crying. There were tears on his cheeks, and once I asked him about it the streaming started up again.

"The camp is in utter chaos," Jimmy said. "I came into the woods to hide. I'm hiding from my own campers! Have you seen what it's like out there?"

I shook my head.

"It's horrific. And it's all my fault. When I had the idea for this camp, all I wanted to do was make my new dad proud, you know?" he blubbered. "I wanted to make a difference in young humanitarians' lives the way Robert Drill had made a difference in mine. I thought that maybe I could be a sort of Robert Drill for you kids."

"THAT'S VALID," I said. "TOTALLY NORMAL."

"But I've failed you. It's madness out there. Capture the Flag has totally gotten out of hand. And so has this camp."

It took every ounce of strength I had to concentrate on the words coming out of Jimmy's mouth. I squinted, zeroing in on his eyes. I bit my lips together and breathed deeply through my nose. I could tell by the expression on his face that he was distressed about something, so I tried to match his face and show some empathy, like any normal human being would. Because I was a normal human being. My hands were on the side of my face, stretching the skin back as far as it would go.

"Is everything alright with you, Children?"

"Jimmy, I can help you. I've got all the answers now and I have one thing to tell you and it's going to blow your mind, so listen carefully." I grabbed his shoulders and leaned in. "Don't worry. Be happy." I laughed and laughed and lau—

Were my nostrils getting smaller?

I could swear my nostrils were getting smaller. Jimmy was gone, so I couldn't ask him to confirm, and I spun around, searching for someone else to help me. There must be someone else in the woods.

"You almost stepped on me!"

I froze and looked down, searching for the tiny yet deep voice that had just spoken to me. "Ashley?"

"Do I sound like an *Ashley* to you?"

A rock. I dropped to my knees, slack-jawed, staring at this egg-sized gray stone. Had it just spoken to me? Was I that high? "Was that . . . you? Did a rock just talk to me?"

"No, you idiot. It was me." A salamander scurried by, and I nearly fell back at the shock of his bright orange color. And the shock of him talking to me. He looked exactly like the salamander that had been on Ashley's shoulder the night I had first talked to her.

"Yep, that was me that night."

"You can hear my thoughts?"

"Obviously."

"I'm tripping balls," I said.

"You and me both, kid," said my new salamander friend.

This was incredible. I'd never spoken to a salamander before. And one had never spoken back. I wondered if Ashley spoke to salamanders. She probably had long conversations with them all the time. I wondered if they all sounded like Allan Sherman.

"Hey, what's your name?" I said.

"Gaspard."

"GASPARD!" I said. "WHAT A WONDERFUL NAME."

I sat back, realizing what I'd just said. It was exactly what Ashley said anytime anyone ever told her their name, even if it was a shitty name.

Whoa.

Was Ashley always on this stuff?

Is this what she felt like all the time?

Because what I felt was serene peace. And also wisdom. I knew everything there was to know in the universe, and I knew no shame. Also, I felt acutely aware that me and Gaspard were about to become best friends forever and I was excited about that. Maybe Ashley *was* on this stuff all the time.

"Kid, I don't got all day," Gaspard said.

"WHAT ARE YOU EVEN DOING HERE?" I said. "IN MY DRUG-INDUCED SPIRITUAL JOURNEY, I MEAN?"

"I'm here to answer your deepest questions," Gaspard the salamander said. "You only get five and you already wasted 'em all."

"WHAT?" I said. "THAT'S TOTALLY NOT FAIR. I DIDN'T KNOW."

Gaspard crawled around in a circle, thinking of what to do with me while I sat, distraught over this arbitrary five-question rule. The weird thing about this tea was that it could make me feel so good one minute, but when I felt bad, I felt really bad. My stomach was starting to hurt with the idea that I'd just squandered all my questions. I thought I was going to cry.

Also, all of my words were coming out in capital letters. I had to tone it down.

"Alright already, calm down," Gaspard said. He stopped moving and faced me, slamming his little salamander hand into the dirt, which didn't even make a sound at all, though I could tell by his exasperated tone that that was his intention. "I'll give you one more question."

"THANK YOU!"

"I got all the answers to the universe, kid, so you better think hard about what you wanna ask."

There was so much I wanted to know. Would I ever make anything of myself? Would I have an impact on the world? Would I be great one day, like my heroes? Did my life have meaning? But maybe most important, the question that I asked myself all the time and that weighed most heavily on my mind was this one: Was I ever going to get laid? But when I thought all those things through, I realized they were selfish questions. I couldn't just ask about *me*.

I couldn't be selfish. I had to ask about others—about my friends, about this camp, the world, the universe. I locked eyes with Gaspard, and we were practically nose to nose. I got ready to ask the most important question of my life.

"Are we going to be okay?" I whispered.

Gaspard stared back at me hard, and I held my breath in anticipation of what he would say.

"Yes," Gaspard said. "You and Ashley will be okay."

I froze in place and so did the rest of the world. The trees stopped dancing and the wind stopped singing just as all of my breath left me, because now I knew. Thanks to what Gaspard had just said, I knew.

I was in love with Ashley Woodstone.

It was so clear to me. Maybe it was the tea, or maybe it was just a truth that I'd been too blind to see, but I loved Ashley Woodstone. The realization hit me like a stick crashing against my skull.

And then I stood up and a stick literally crashed against my skull.

I blacked out.

30

I blinked my eyes open, trying to get my bearings. I had no idea how long I'd been out. I was in a tent, that much was clear. I was sitting on the ground with my hands tied behind my back. Actually, they were tied to a pole behind my back. I didn't know where the pole came from or what it was attached to. Was it the tetherball pole? Probably.

Before me stood my captors, Feminism, Down With Styrofoam, and Clean Air, their stony faces hidden behind a generous slathering of red face paint. Or, I hoped it was face paint. Were they part of my hallucinations? Was I still high? I wanted Gaspard back.

"I found him trying to infiltrate the girls' headquarters," one of the girls said. I wasn't sure who it was. I had a headache from the blunt trauma to the head, and I was growing increasingly hungry.

"Girls' headquarters?" I said. "What the hell are you talking about?"

"Are you really trying to act all innocent?" Feminism said. She was close enough to me that I felt her spittle landing on my cheek. She yanked on my cape. "How do you explain this?!"

"It's a cape," I stammered. "Lots of people wear them, okay?"

"It's kind of weird when you're shirtless."

Right. Forgot about that. "That I can't actually explain."

Feminism let my cape go and went back to stand next to her friends. "A *red* cape, which just happens to be our team color. Obviously he was trying to cross into our territory unnoticed. Lucky we got him."

Down With Styrofoam came to stand over me, her short blonde hair jutting out from underneath the red bandana tied around her head. "What was your objective here?"

"I have no idea what's going on," I said.

"What's the boys' plan?"

"Boys' plan? I do——" Oh. It was coming to me. In all the hoopla with Ashley's magic tea and meeting Gaspard, I'd forgotten what was going on today. "You tied me up for *Capture the Flag?*"

"Don't answer my question with another question!" Down With Styrofoam yelled. Feminism held her back with an outstretched arm, keeping her from lunging at me. She seemed to calm down a bit. "And as for whether we tied you up for Capture the Flag? You're damn right we did! Just like we tied up Hakim and Neville and countless other boys in countless other tents, because we're everywhere!"

Hakim and Neville. They were counselors. The girls had captured counselors. This camp had officially gone to hell.

"But you found our headquarters," Down With Styrofoam said. "How?"

"I was in the middle of the *woods*," I said, my voice raspy. "The only reason I found your headquarters is because you brought me here."

"I knew we should've picked another place," Feminism said, more to herself than for my benefit. "The playing fields are too vulnerable to attack."

"I know how we can get him to talk," Clean Air said. "He has a huge crush on Poe. Pretty sure she can get anything out of him."

"I do not have a huge crush on Poe," I said.

"He so does," Feminism said. "It's pathetic. I'll go find her."

"No need to do that!" I said, but Feminism had already left. Poe was not going to get anything out of me. And not just because there was nothing to *get* out of me. I didn't have a crush on her. Anymore. But I also did not want her seeing me like this: tied up, weak, too skinny in all my shirtless glory, and quite possibly still tripping balls. I thought it'd passed, but then I realized the tent probably wasn't actually breathing.

"Well," Down With Styrofoam said. "We've got more boys to take down."

"And a flag to find," I said.

"Sure. Whatever," Down With Styrofoam said. "See ya around." She and Clean Air headed toward the tent opening.

"Wait!" I said. "You can't just leave me here. I'm so hungry! I could die!"

Down and Clean looked at me for a moment, considering. Then they both shrugged and stepped out of the tent.

I was alone and probably going to die of hunger. I prayed for someone from the boys' team to sneak in here and rescue me. Wasn't that someone's job? And then she appeared at the opening.

"Poe," I said. It came out more like a sigh, which I realized too late probably confirmed the rumor that I was crushing on her, but whatever, I was relieved to see someone.

"Hey, Gregor," she said. She sat down next to me. "So apparently I'm supposed to ask you for top secret info."

"I promise you I know nothing."

"That much is obvious," she said, laughing. "It's cool; I already know where your flag is. I saw it sticking out of Rights's pants. Which is totally cheating. And gross because it'll force one of us to go in there to get it. I can assure you that will not be pleasant for him."

"If you already know where it is, then why haven't you told the other girls?"

"Because we've been capturing *a lot* of you. And gender neutrality and equal rights aside, I kind of like seeing boys all tied up."

"You're not letting me go, are you?"

She shook her head, and I slumped back against my heaving pole.

"Listen," Poe said. She was distracted by something in her hand. A candy wrapper, one of those gum ones that had a funny joke. She was reading it, I could tell. Her eyes roved in a line, her lips upturned in amusement. It was good to know I was as interesting to her as a dumb joke on the side of a gum wrapper. I thought about asking her for the gum, actually. But, as usual, I was doing too much thinking and not enough doing, because she popped the pink cube into her mouth. "I'm sorry about the other night, in the woods. I shouldn't have teased you like that."

"Teased me?" I tried to laugh it off. The thought of us the other night was making me even more uncomfortable than I already was, tied up to a pole. "You didn't . . . It was . . . It's fine."

"It's just, when I know that someone likes me, I want to know just how much. You know what I mean?"

"Poe, rest assured that I do not like you."

She finally looked up from the wrapper, her brows knitting together.

"I mean, you're a great person, but I don't *like you* like you," I said. I couldn't even remember why I had liked her to begin with. She was pretty, but other than that, I could officially say that I was definitely no longer attracted to Poe. Also, she smoked, which was gross—not to say that people suffering from nicotine addiction were gross. "Anyway, let's just be honest and say everything we mean. It wouldn't have mattered whether or not I ever liked you because you're a lesbian."

"I'm bisexual."

"Of course you are," I said through gritted teeth. "Well, that explains you and Win."

"Me and Win?" Poe snorted. "We hang out because Win has a vested interest in my campaign."

I was still tripping, so even though this should have been totally clear to me at this point, my brain was still taking way too long to process things. I must have been staring at Poe blankly.

"Tell me you knew that Win—your own bunkmate— is gay."

I coughed. I did not know that. "Of course I knew that." It made sense that Win was gay. It completed the whole perfect

310

picture. "I'm sure he doesn't appreciate you outing him, though."

"Dude, Win is out and proud."

This was starting to get embarrassing. "You know what? It's fine. Like I said, I don't have a crush on you, so there's no need to keep talking about this."

She nodded, full-on staring at me. Her eyes were laser focused, bewitching. Her smile grew larger, and my cheeks must have been turning purple by now. She had the look of someone who was *very* in control. And here I was, shirtless, in a cape, and grinding against a pole. I thought maybe she was the type of girl who liked seeing me squirm. "You know what would be awesome right now, Poe? Setting me free."

"Nah, this is more fun."

"Psst!"

Poe and I turned toward the opening. "Ashley!" we both said at the same time.

Her hair was wild, and so were her eyes, and I was in love with her.

"Gregor!" she said, breathless. "I found you." She stepped inside, and I could tell by the way her eyebrows scrunched and her smile fell that she was instantly aware that this was a shady situation. She hurried to my side. "What's going on? Are you okay? Why are you all tied up? Who has won the most Oscars in acting?"

"Meryl Streep!"

"No! Katharine Hepburn! Quick, he needs air!"

It seemed she was always there to rescue me. I wouldn't have wanted it any other way.

"I'll untie him!" Poe said. Ashley held out her hand and I grabbed hold of it, letting her help me up.

"Ashley, wait, do you wanna hang out or something?" Poe said.

I'd never seen her so flustered.

"Not right now, Poe!" Ashley said. "We gotta get out of here."

I followed Ashley out of the tent.

31

Ashley and I ran.

Somehow, we were holding hands. Or I guess I should say we were still holding hands from when she rescued me. And as we traversed through the playing fields and headed back toward the woods where the two of us belonged, it was like we held on because we needed each other.

Holy shit, I was tripping balls.

That had to be the only explanation for the purple prose of my mind. And also the only explanation for why I saw at least a dozen boys running and five girls chasing after them, holding in their hands very large, blunt objects. One of the girls was holding what appeared to be a bone.

An actual please-don't-let-it-be-human bone.

"What kind of Capture the Flag game *is* this?" I asked Ashley, ahead of me. I was shouting to hear my own voice over the shouts and yelps and battle cries. "It's *Lord of the Flies* out here!"

Ashley turned to me while running. "I LOVE that movie!"

Campers were battling it out, right there on the grounds where we'd once peacefully sat for a sit-in. Ashley and I ran faster, in the opposite direction. We made it to the woods, and it seemed that within the trees we were safe, at least for now.

"Food," I said. It was all I could say at this point, heaving, hands on bended knees, my throat so dry.

"Let nature be your refrigerator, Gregor."

I was in love with Ashley Woodstone, but I seriously did not have time for this.

And yet.

I looked at the dirt all around me with the eyes of a man out of options. I was so hungry. I was desperate. "Screw it." I was on my hands and knees, scratching at the ground, loosening up the dirt like a dog sniffing out his long-buried treat. I dug at the dirt and then I put it in my mouth.

I was eating dirt.

How was this happening? How was I, Gregor Maravilla, crouched on all fours, the only clothing on my back a cape, stuffing genuine dirt into my mouth? I could hear Ashley laughing, but I was too ashamed to look at her. "Look at you!" she said in the tone of voice you use when you see a toddler using a pencil for the first time. "I knew you'd come around."

It actually wasn't half bad.

I was definitely still tripping balls if I was starting to enjoy dirt.

My face was probably smeared brown and crusty, but I was so hungry that I didn't care. I guess I should've just considered myself lucky that Ashley was probably the only girl in the world who wouldn't be grossed out by this display.

"I am so proud of you, Gregor Maravilla. You've really taken to dirt like a worm takes to dirt."

"Mphmgr."

"But don't get too stuffed. Nature has a whole supply of natural foods for us to try. Like these lovely flowers."

I stopped munching. Flowers sounded better than dirt. Ashley was by a small bush, picking the tiny purple things off its branches and popping them into her mouth like Skittles. "Whoa," she said.

"Are they good?" I asked.

She stood still, a curious expression on her face. "No," she said. Her eyes fluttered closed, and she placed her hand on a tree like she was about to lose her balance.

"Ashley?"

She leaned into the bark, slumped over it, and began to sink down, and I ran for her so fast that she didn't get a chance to fall all the way. I caught her in my arms, her face suddenly pale. "Ashley!"

"I don't—I don't think I should've eaten that," she said before passing out.

32

So many things had to go wrong to get us to this moment. Every counselor had to be tied up and utterly useless at their jobs. The camp infirmary had to be perpetually backed up, and Nurse Patrosian had to be completely unequipped to deal with this even if she wasn't already overwhelmed with life. Cell phones had to be banned. And Ashley had to regard nature's bounty as her own private all-you-can-eat buffet.

It made me angry. It made me mad, even as she lay unconscious in my arms. I was furious as I ran through the woods, one arm around her back, the other underneath her knees. I was stupidly, illogically angry at her. Even though she couldn't see it. She hadn't opened her eyes since she'd fainted.

"PIKA!" My voice was hollow through the trees, searching for him. "Pika is never too far," I said through haggard breaths. Ashley told me that herself when we were locked in the record store. Even if she told him to leave, he wouldn't go too far. "PIKA!"

Whenever someone gets poisoned in comics, it's always at the villain's hand, and he's got an antidote, and the superhero spends the entire issue thwarting the bad guy's evil plan, finding the antidote, and saving his love's life.

This was nothing like that.

I was angry at myself for being all Ashley had right now. I wasn't enough. Fuck, I was probably still high. The anger was just the tip of the iceberg. Below that I was terrified. My entire body was made of fear, operating off of it. I was sure the only reason I wasn't crumbling in it was the mission at hand. When she passed out I had to think fast, I had to take matters—and Ashley—into my own hands, and all I could think to do was run.

I couldn't explain the speed. Maybe it was that Ashley was so light. I'd never carried a girl before. Were they all this light? Her side knocked against my stomach anytime I stepped on an overgrown root wrong, but I did not stop.

There wasn't time to stop.

Why was Ashley so light? I snuck glances down at her whenever I wasn't trying to navigate through trees. Her lips had lost their pink color.

I couldn't figure out why she wasn't waking up. She was a scavenger. She lived off the land. Didn't she know what she was and wasn't supposed to eat? They were just flowers. Just pretty purple flowers. But then, this was just like Ashley. Even now she couldn't help but be dramatic. I wished someone would yell, "Cut!" I wished she'd wake up like this was just a take in a scene and she was only acting.

Irrationally, I wished she felt heavier. I needed her to feel more substantial than this. She was too light.

"Ashley, wake up," I demanded. It came out jagged and raw, stuck between the gusts of air crashing down my throat. "Come on."

I didn't know the woods as well as she did. She needed to wake up and tell me which way to go. Why couldn't I have spent more time in the woods with her?

"Ashley, talk to me. Who gave your favorite Oscar speech last year? I bet it was Meryl Streep. Chances are good it was her, right? She must be your favorite actress."

Ashley didn't answer. Her forehead was damp. I could feel my heartbeat in my face. I could feel the redness blossoming there, just below a layer of sweat. Why didn't I ever ask her who her favorite actress was? Why couldn't I do that one thing?

This was taking too long. "Please open your eyes. Please d—" My cape snagged on a low branch, choking me, forcing me to stop for too long. I forgot I had been wearing it, and the seconds that it was stealing from me enraged me. I tore the cape off with a grunt, struggling to hold Ashley up. This was so dumb. This was so stupid. I was no superhero. I wasn't going fast enough and Ashley wasn't waking up. I wasn't saving her.

"Hey, hey!" I needed to be loud so that she would hear me. I couldn't let her slip away. "You need to tell me how *Chasing Amy* ends. You can't leave me hanging." None of what I was saying mattered, but I needed to keep talking for her. She was too still. "Don't die on me, Ashley. Don't let go."

And then I saw him. I finally found him. Jimmy was still crying right where I'd left him. But when he saw the two of us he stopped. "I need help," I rasped. "We need your car."

33

The thing about origin stories—the thing I did not think about until now—was that most of them were tragic.

Spider-Man had to lose his uncle in order to realize his destiny. Batman lost his parents. Superman lost his entire planet.

At the start of the summer I was too focused on the idea that this camp was going to turn me into the person that I was meant to become, and what I didn't realize was that it wasn't my surroundings but the people in it that would shape me. Or one person in particular. And now all I was left with was who I would become if I lost her.

Death was too often the catalyst in the hero's life.

But then, I wasn't a hero. And I promised myself and whoever was up there listening that if anything happened to Ashley I would not learn a lesson from it. I would not learn a single thing.

So don't let her die.

I forced myself not to think about that.

It was the only thing I was thinking about.

The thought of losing Ashley enveloped me, wrapped itself around me so tightly that I sat frozen in the hospital waiting room seat. One of the nurses had come by earlier and offered me a paper gown since I was still without a shirt, so I sat there absolutely stock-still in my finest hospital wear, looking like I'd just tried to escape. I wasn't just scared—I was shocked by the magnitude of my fear.

I convinced myself that if I was still enough it meant that time could stop and I could still live inside the comfortable confines of the possibility that I'd brought Ashley to the hospital in time.

It felt like hours that I had not moved.

Jimmy, on the other hand, moved a lot. He hadn't stopped moving since he'd helped me lay Ashley down in the backseat of his hybrid. He was very animated in his concern, pacing the room, curling into a ball on the uncomfortable vinyl chairs, and digging worried fingers into his curly hair. But then, suddenly, Jimmy announced, "I think she'll be okay."

He was sitting opposite me, and a calm quality had come over him. "You know what I was just thinking about, Chil—Gregor? I was thinking about how I'd been crying in the woods when you found me. I was freaking out about the campers tearing each other to shreds. I was thinking of my stepdad. I mean, Robert. I mean, Mr. Drill. I was thinking about how much I was disappointing him with this whole fiasco. But then you came to find me with Ashley in your hands and I stepped up. I was able to help."

I wiped my nose with the back of my hand. "Congratulations?" I really wasn't sure what he wanted me to say.

"Don't you see, Gregor? I'd been worrying about so much. *Too* much. But when Ashley needed help I stopped worrying and focused all my energy on getting her here. I helped. I think everything happened the way it was supposed to happen. I was supposed to be in those woods, at exactly the right place for you to find me. You and me—we saved her life."

"We don't know that she—"

"Trust me, Gregor, she's going to be okay."

I watched him for a moment. I let myself believe in his new assured calmness, and I nodded.

I only realized the doctor had appeared by the look on Jimmy's face as his eyes gazed behind me. I jumped to my feet. "How is she?"

"Are you Ms. Woodstone's family?"

"I'm her friend," I said.

"I'm her head counselor."

"I'm sorry, I can only talk to family."

"Good luck with that, because *Ashley* doesn't even talk to her family," I said. I lowered my voice when I realized it was too high. I tried again. "Please . . ." I scanned the ID clipped to his breast pocket. ". . . Dr. Zaul. We brought her in. We just want to know if she's okay."

The doctor stayed silently grim, but after a moment he sighed and said, "Yes, she's okay." My body released all the tension I'd been storing and I was suddenly loose, weightless, feeling like I could take flight or pass out. "She was lucky you brought her in so quickly," Dr. Zaul went on. "And also that for some reason she had a large amount of charcoal in her system, which acted as a natural antidote, helping to neutralize the effects of the plant she ingested. Do either of you know why Ms. Woodstone would have ingested charcoal?"

If I had to guess? "Dessert," I said. "Can I see her?"

"I'm afraid not."

I waited until Dr. Zaul left before I turned to Jimmy and said, "I'm going to go see her."

Jimmy squeezed my shoulder. "I need to go clean up the mess at camp. Tell Ashley I'm glad she's okay."

I'd snuck into the counselors' office twice, so a hospital would be cake. And it was. No one thought twice about seeing a teenage boy in a hospital gown roaming the place. The tricky part was finding her room without asking for anybody's help. I surreptitiously searched every name next to every door. I was beginning to wonder if she was even on this floor, when her name popped out at me. *A. Woodstone. Room 3478.*

She was sleeping when I walked in, so I made myself as comfortable as I could in the chair next to her bed. I was dead tired, but there was no way I was going to sleep now. I grabbed the remote and turned on the TV in the upper corner of the room, flipping through the channels on mute. I stopped on a line of men and women dancing, dressed in highlander attire. The title of the show flashed onto the screen. *Village of Hoors.*

Three and a half episodes after I learned that Hoors, the lead character, was going to form a search party to look for his runaway wife, Ashley woke up.

"Gregor Maravilla." Her voice was a rasp but she had a smile on her face. Of course.

I moved my chair closer to her bed. "How are you feeling?"

"Better. What happened?"

"The doctor couldn't tell me too much, but you definitely ate a poisonous plant, and the only reason you're not dead is because apparently there was charcoal in your system."

She considered this, improbable as it was, and then nodded. "Makes sense."

"Ashley, you have to do something about your eating habits. A person can't subsist on a dirt-and-chia-seed diet."

"You worried about me, Gregor Maravilla?" she said, a coy tone to her voice, like she was needling me.

"Yeah. I am."

"Okay," she said, and I knew she was serious too. "The

charcoal may have helped, but I think the only reason I'm not dead is probably because of you."

I took a deep breath, weirdly uncomfortable with the magnitude of that. "It was Jimmy. He drove you here in his hybrid."

"Jimmy," Ashley said, her forehead creasing. "But he has to take care of camp."

She was in a hospital bed, having just dodged death, and she was worried about everyone else. My hand slinked up the side of the bed until it found hers. I squeezed it. "Don't worry about camp."

"Well, thank you."

"I didn't do anything."

"You need to stop selling yourself short, Gregor. Stop downplaying things and start recognizing them for what they are. You came to camp to save the world—"

"And it was a total bust."

"—and you *are* saving it," Ashley said. "You saved my life."

She squeezed my hand back.

"When Jimmy was talking to me in the waiting room he said something that I'm still thinking about. He was pretty overwhelmed with everything that was happening at camp. He was pretty down about it, thinking he hadn't done any good this summer and that he was just a big disappointment to his stepdad. And then when he was able to drive you over here he talked about it like him being in the woods at the exact place I needed him to be was fated. And like it didn't matter if the whole camp was just a failed experiment because at least he got to do some good by forgetting about everything else and focusing on one small thing. Which was getting you in his car and driving you here."

"Fate," Ashley said.

"That day that I snuck into Jimmy's office, when I found out that the only reason I was at this camp was because I'd been randomly selected, I was bummed. But maybe it wasn't random. Maybe I was meant to be here. To meet you."

Ashley smiled at me, and maybe it was the hospital setting, but it felt like medicine. The kind that tastes good and cures you instantly.

"Jimmy has a point, I think," I said. "I've been so caught up in making an impact on the world that I never stopped to see the impacts I'm making in the here and now. Even if they're small."

"You and Superman have that in common."

I narrowed my eyes at her. "What's that?"

"He always thought he could fix everything. It was his one flaw."

I let my head fall forward, and as soon as I did I could feel Ashley's fingers in my hair, smoothing the strands to the side. I could feel her trying to form the *S* again.

34

It was very early in the morning when I decided to walk back to camp. A walk would be good; I needed the time to think. I'd been waiting for this moment the entire summer, this clarity that I now felt. It took a trip to the hospital, my best friend almost dying, and a couple of weird conversations with my head counselor and a salamander, but I thought I finally understood what it actually meant to save the world.

It was only when I got back to camp that the reality of life—and war—came back to me. I didn't even have to step through the gates to realize the camp was now just the ruins of Color War. I looked up at the CAMP SAVE THE WORLD sign. Someone had knocked down the last two letters in CAMP and spray-painted the letters *N* and *T* so that CAMP SAVE THE WORLD now read CANT SAVE THE WORLD.

The irony was not lost on me.

*   *   *

Save for the morning song of the birds it was quiet all around, but not for lack of people. They were everywhere. Kids were sprawled on the ground, sleeping off their Capture the Flag hangovers. There were so many of them that I actually had to step over some on the way to my cabin. A few were stumbling awake with the pale-blue pallor of new zombies. Though, I guess the smeared, stale face paint of the boys' team was largely to blame for that. Some people were only half-dressed, wearing one sock, or in one particular boy's case, only one pant leg. Other kids bore the dazed and horrified expressions of PTSD. As terrible as my night was, I was beginning to suspect that it was just as horrible for the campers of Camp Save the World.

Win was in our cabin, sleeping in his own bed, but even he didn't look unscathed. He was on his stomach, his limbs splayed out like stiff planks off every side of the bed. He looked like he'd been dropped there from very high up.

"Win, wake up," I said, shaking his shoulder.

He opened his eyes slowly, squinting up at me. Shock and relief colored his face. "Gregor. You made it."

Were there people who hadn't made it? "Where's Rights?"

A solemn look fell over Win's face. "It's better we not think about it."

"Look, there's something I want to tell the whole camp. It's important. You think you can help me rally everyone together?"

He actually managed to laugh. "Bring the camp together? After what happened yesterday? Funny."

"Come on, you're the only person anyone will listen to. People love you."

"The camp is completely divided, Gregor. I don't know where you were last night, but you have no idea what went on here, man. You have *no* idea." His voice shook slightly, like it wasn't a Capture the Flag game he was reminiscing about but his time in battle. "The things they did to get our flag."

I sat on the side of his bed, surprised to hear him talk like this. The Win I knew was an eternal optimist. The purest kind of idealist. The Win I was looking at now, tangled in a flimsy sheet with all the light sucked out of his eyes, was someone I did not recognize.

"It couldn't have been that bad," I said, nudging him slightly. "I guarantee you your night couldn't have been worse than mine."

"It's not just what happened at Capture the Flag, even though I'll probably never get those images out of my head. It's everything. This camp has just left me so . . . disillusioned. When it was supposed to do the exact opposite."

"I know how you feel," I said. "I feel that way too."

"And I'm also kind of heartbroken? So I've got that to deal with."

I angled my body so I could face him better. "You? Got

your heart broken?" This was definitely a new side to Win. This whole summer I basically thought he'd been hooking up with Poe, but now that I knew he was gay, that theory was totally debunked. "Who?"

"I Like Paint."

"You mean Alec Pent?"

Win nodded.

Whoa. "I had no idea. I never saw you two hanging out together."

"Because I had a massive crush on him. I was totally awkward around him. You didn't notice?"

I shook my head.

"I don't know, the hair, the paintbrushes, the whole foreigner thing. And he was always covered in paint."

I flashed to the image of ILP stumbling into the picket sign competition, drenched in red paint. That probably was not what Win meant, though.

"I stayed away from him because it was torture getting too close. But when he left, that was a total blow. Unrequited love, I guess."

This was definitely a new side to him, but most shocking of all was learning that Win—perfect Win—was capable of having his heart broken. Clearly my idea of "perfect" was also misguided up to now.

"This camp has messed with a lot of us," I said. "And I

know that everything feels hopeless. But it's not too late to change things. There's something I need to do, and I need your help." I grabbed hold of his shoulders and looked him sternly in the eye. "Are you in?"

Some of the light that was missing before came back in his eyes and he sat up. Win nodded. "I'll do whatever you need."

Win and I spent most of the morning gathering whatever campers we could into the mess hall. By which I mean we spent most of the morning being ignored by campers and waiting for them to congregate at the mess hall, where they eventually headed anyway for breakfast. Not that there was much food around, save for cereal. The kitchen staff was MIA, as were the counselors. They had either abandoned ship or were recovering in their own quarters. But having no counselors around was not a new phenomenon at this camp. And anyway, we didn't need them right now. We needed to fix this ourselves.

With mostly all the campers there, I stood on top of a table. "Uh, everyone?"

Nobody turned to look my way, and I had to rely on Win to whistle to get everyone's attention. "Guys! Children has something to say!" He nodded at me to start talking. The campers were grumpy, and the expressions on their tired faces

331

told me they were not in the mood to hear me give a speech right now, but if I ever wanted to be a leader I would have to start somewhere. It was time to speak up.

"Hi, everyone," I began. "I wanted to talk to you about something important. I came to this camp hoping to do something great with my life and feeling pretty disappointed that I hadn't really done anything yet."

"Nobody cares about your cliché male ennui!" a girl shouted.

Harsh. But this was still going a lot smoother than I'd ever expected it to.

"I thought I hadn't accomplished anything!" I said, louder this time. "But then some friends told me something last night. I learned that, sometimes, saving the world means saving a bunch of *little* worlds."

I waited for this to hit them, hit them so hard that I could see the sucker punch of epiphany on their faces, but they only stared back at me blankly. I needed to hone my public speaking skills. I caught Jimmy's glance, though. He was standing by the entrance with his arms folded over his chest, but he nodded encouragingly at me.

"We all wanted to do great things at this camp. And we all had amazing causes. But instead, we chose to torture each other, sabotage everyone around us, and make enemies of each other when we should have been working together." I walked down the long table. "But there's still time to turn that around. Today I realized that if I want to do something as big as change the world, I need to start small. I need to start local. I need to focus on what's personally affecting me and the people that I care about."

"That's literally what some of us have been doing the whole time," Unity said.

"Because if we start small," I said, ignoring him, "it is totally possible to feed all the children one day!" The last step I took landed in someone's cereal bowl and I almost slipped off the table, but I recovered quickly and apologized to the girl whose breakfast I'd just ruined. I could see I was starting to lose them. (Even the ones whose breakfasts I wasn't stepping on.) A few people in the crowd looked at each other, sharing skeptical glances. I needed to get to the point fast.

"We've forgotten what it means to be real activists. We need to protest Robert Drill!" I shouted.

And then the groans started.

"You already tried protesting Drill and it ended very badly!" Down With Styrofoam said. "And anyway, why would we protest him? Why not just protest you?!"

This last statement was picking up more steam than my entire speech had. It seemed most campers agreed with Down With Styrofoam. This was definitely not going my way.

"Just hear me out!" I said, my voice rising to try to counteract the growing din of protest. "As I was saying, if we want to save the world, we need to start by saving this camp. Because I don't know if you've noticed, but this place looks like a wasteland. And you know why? It didn't just start at Color War. And it didn't just start when campers began getting thrown in the lake or when Alec Pent got blasted with paint or when Abstinence and Sex Positivity got locked in the sports shed together. It started when Robert Drill announced the internship!"

No comebacks. I had them. "As soon as this camp turned from being an inclusive and educational place for us into a cut-throat environment, we were all screwed! I mean, we all had names once! Feminism, you used to be Julie!"

Feminism nodded.

"And Men's Rights's real name is actually . . . Tomás!

"And Down With Styrofoam, you used to be . . ." She stared at me, angry, waiting, but I was drawing a blank. "I'm sure you had a name once!" I said. "Some of you know me as Feed the Children. Some of you even know me as Superman. But my name is GREGOR MARAVILLA!"

I paused, waiting for the inevitable cheering, but the silence was only punctuated when I stepped in another cereal bowl. Poe was staring up at me, droplets of milk spattered onto her face. I lifted my foot off her bowl and muttered a quick "Sorry." I tried to recover quickly. "What I'm trying to say, people, is what the hell are we all fighting for? An internship that we all knew from the beginning would probably go to Win Cassidy?"

Some of the kids nodded. Even Win nodded.

"That isn't fair! Because I know I didn't come here for an internship! I came here for you guys. I came to be part of a community of people who were as passionate about global consciousness as I was. I came here to fight for what I believe in, not to fight each other!"

Finally the cheers were staring to come. I had to admit that was a good line.

"We can still be a united camp. We can still show that we're worthy activists. We can show Robert Drill that we don't need his stinkin' internship!"

"Yeah!" the crowd yelled.

"I would still like that internship," I could hear Win say, but his voice was mostly drowned out.

"Let's take back our camp!"

35

We stood like sardines, every camper in camp crammed into the counselors' office—some of us spilling outside onto the wraparound porch—watching Jimmy's computer. We all squeezed together to try and fit our faces in the frame of the webcam. The only noise in the room came from the sound of elbows jabbing into soft stomachs and the bubbling ringing of the Skype call.

The ringing stopped and I involuntarily shushed everybody. It wasn't Mr. Drill's face that appeared on the screen. It was a woman's.

"Yes?" she said.

"Uh, hi," I said. "We're looking for Robert Drill."

"And who may I say is calling?"

"We're the campers of Camp Save the World."

The woman stared at us through her glasses. In the upper corner, inside the small square that reflected what was coming up on her screen, all I could make out were dozens of eyes. "One moment, please," she said.

We waited for a minute and then were transferred. I did not know you could transfer a Skype call, but then again, we were Skyping with a tech company. Robert Drill appeared before us on the screen, his face skeptically scowling.

"Who is this?" he said. "What's going on?"

"Hi, Mr. Drill, we're the campers of Camp Save the World," I said, slowly, tentatively, testing out how this would all work. "Uh, I'm Gregor Maravilla. You probably remember me from the press conference?"

Mr. Drill squinted and leaned forward. "Where is Jimmy?"

"I'm here, Dad!" Jimmy's voice came from the back of the room. "I mean, Robert. I mean, sir. The kids have something they want to say to you."

"Yes," I said. "It's important."

"Well, what is it that you want, young man? Are you out of food? Is the camp on fire?"

"No, nothing like that, sir. It's just that the other campers and I got together because we have an issue we wanted to discuss with you." I took a breath and went on. "We don't think it's fair for you to award the internship to just one person. By dangling it in front of us like a carrot, you turned the camp into a war zone. You ruined our summer."

"I see," Mr. Drill said. "I hereby rescind the internship prize. Now no one gets it. Is that it? I've got work to do."

I looked around. We were all a little stunned. "Uh, well, you don't have to resci—" But the Skype window went black. He'd hung up on us.

That didn't feel as triumphant as I would've liked. Kind of anticlimactic, actually.

"So now no one gets the internship?" Unity said. "Great going, Gregor. I was a shoo-in."

"No, you weren't," Win said. "I was. But we knew this was a possible outcome. And look on the bright side. Now we can enjoy the rest of the summer without worrying about competition or sabotage."

"But there's only one day of camp left," Unity said.

36

So we finally had our camp back. And it had only resulted in the loss of The Prize. It was a steep price to pay, but still, talking to Drill, fighting for what we believed in, and getting results felt kind of good. We achieved something, and we did it together. And that was something to celebrate. So the bonfire was perfect.

Jimmy decided that we should have another bonfire. Since the first one signaled the start of our demise, he figured this one could signal the start of something new. It was just like Camp Save the World to start with an end and end with a start, but I guess it kind of felt right. It was too bad it took us till the last night of camp to finally get our act together and truly be civil to each other, but at least we were finishing things right.

The bonfire finally resembled what it was always meant to: a picture of campers having fun. There were kids huddled together with marshmallows on long sticks, and others were roasting hot dogs and telling stories. Save the World With Song strummed a slow melody on his guitar, and a few kids lounged at his feet. Poe and Win sat together, talking, and it may have been the first time I'd watched them and not been hit with pangs of jealousy. I was also definitely not jealous when I spied Unity and World Peace, off in a shadowy corner beneath a tree, making out messily. I was happy for them. And I was happy for Feminism when Men's Rights sat next to her and she completely rebuffed him.

This was the good stuff, the kind of camp I'd always pictured.

Jimmy felt bad that Robert Drill had rescinded The Prize after five weeks of hard work. He said it would be a shame to have all the points on the scoreboard go to waste, so he decided to go through with the final competition anyway. The competition was called Fund-raising! Fund-raising, as Jimmy explained before the start of the bonfire, is an important part of activism, and vital if we ever planned to start our own grassroots revolts. For every dollar we managed to collect for our causes, Jimmy would award us one point. At the end of the bonfire he'd tally up the scoreboard and give the winning camper The Prize. Only this time, instead of a paid internship it would be a plastic trophy with the words "For Saving the World" written across the bottom in Magic Marker.

Nobody really cared about winning a plastic trophy, which explained the happy camaraderie. Not me, though. The trophy would look great in my room. I walked up to Rights, who still sat by himself, and smiled down at him. "I wanted to thank you."

"Why's that, Supe . . . Gregor?"

I took a fat envelope out of my pocket. "For your contribution to my Feed the Children fund. Your generous donations throughout the summer totaled just over five hundred dollars. Camp turned you into the best young philanthropist I've ever met, Tomás. You should be proud of that."

It hadn't exactly been fun every time Rights had thrown money at my face, or waking up to find it neatly placed under my pillow, but it had all been worth it. A lot of kids would go a little less hungry thanks to him. He didn't seem to appreciate the situation as much as I did, though. The muscles in his jaw flexed as he flashed me a begrudging smile. "It was my pleasure."

"If you'll excuse me, I have a trophy to pick up." Now that that was out of the way, there was someone else I needed to see.

Ashley was back at camp after her stint in the hospital, even though no one would've blamed her if she'd just decided to leave camp early. She was at the bonfire, holding in her hands a plate stacked with brownies, giving them out to any-one she saw. I couldn't tell what she was saying, but she must've been promising that the brownies were not made of dirt, because people were actually eating them. Pika was with her. After she'd woken up in the hospital she'd called him. And though Pika and I didn't have the best relationship, I was happy she'd brought him back. She needed her family right now. I caught his eye by mistake, and his glare was too powerful for me to look away from. He was already on his way toward me.

"Gregor."

It was still strange hearing him speak. "Pika."

"I heard about what you did for Ashley." He paused and stared me down, and I honestly didn't know whether he was going to thank me for saving Ashley or smash me for letting Ashley get poisoned. He kind of did both when he knocked the air out of me by wrapping me in a tight and sudden bear hug. "I'm thankful you were there for her when I couldn't be."

I tried to say something but, again, wind knocked out.

"I was wrong about you, Gregor. You are not a little shit after all."

All I could do was try to hug him back, though my arms did not go all the way around him. Pika let me go and I caught my breath, and when he walked away, Ashley was there, grinning at me. "My favorite people hugging is my favorite thing ever."

I smiled at her too.

"Enjoying the bonfire?" I asked her.

"Immensely. I can't believe this is the last day. I feel like there's still so much we didn't do."

"And so much we still don't know. Like who was responsible for the lake-throwings."

"It was the counselors," Ashley said simply.

I watched her face for signs that she was kidding, but she looked absolutely serious. "What?"

"I saw them every night when I went swimming. They usually had their hoods off before they made it into the woods."

Huh. That was weird. I guess the counselors wanted to get in on the mischief too. That or they hated us. "Wait, you went skinny-dipping every night?" I said. "So that means you went skinny-dipping with every camper who's ever been thrown in the lake?"

"So fun!" Ashley said breathlessly.

I tried to keep my smile from getting too big. Impossible. "You know, I never got your autograph this summer."

She beamed at me and started patting herself down, looking for something to write with, but I had it covered. I held up a Sharpie. I came prepared.

As was her custom, paper would not do for Ashley, so I presented her with my forearm. She wrapped her fingers around my wrist, and I wondered what her message would be. *You are special*, I thought. Or maybe *You light up my life*.

You're the cat's meow.

You're better than dirt—and that's something.

I took my arm back and read what she'd written.

I'm so glad I met you.

It was the first time she hadn't focused her message on the other person. The first time she'd used "I" instead of "you." A summer of firsts. I won't lie: It made me feel incredibly special (and like I was the light of her life, the cat's meow, better than dirt, etc.).

"This is probably going to sound so corny," I said. "But I used to think you were my kryptonite." I pushed my hair off to the side, shuffled my feet a bit. "I mean, I still think that. You're kind of . . . my ultimate weakness."

That smile. Bigger than ever, and matching mine. She was on her tiptoes in a second, and then her lips were on mine.

And when she pulled back, we were both surprised.

Neither of us tasted like dirt.

Hello, Mother, hello, Father, it's the last day of Camp Save the World.

I saved the world. I've got a trophy to prove it.

P.S. I am totally in love with Ashley Woodstone.

The end.

Thank you:

To Matt Ringler. I think every writer lacks some sense, and the editor's job is to make some sense. At the start of this process this story made about 2% sense. So thank you for making up the difference. You were right about everything. (Except the rival French camp. I still love that rival French camp.) And to the rest of the Scholastic team, who continue to make my publishing experience so magical: Jennifer Abbots, Yaffa Jaskoll, Alexis Lunsford, Alexis Lassiter, Jacquelyn Rubin, Jody Stigliano, Tracy van Straaten, Rachel Feld, Isa Caban, Vaishali Nayak, Emily Heddleson, Antonio Gonzalez, Lizette Serrano, Kerianne Okie, Alan Smagler, Lori Benton, and Ellie Berger.

To my agents, Jenny Bent and Gemma Cooper, who loved this story when I worried it was too ridiculous to be lovable. Your support was exactly what I needed.

To Rachel Petty, Kat McKenna, and everyone over in the UK.

To those who read first: Chaya Levinsohn, Esther Silberstein, Diana Gallagher, and Neely Stansell-Simpson.

To the indie booksellers who put books into people's hands, you are doing the good work! Forever indebted to you.

To my beautiful mother, Sonia, and sister, Yasmin. Ari, Maayan, Hadas, S. Akiva. Irina, Zinoviy. Mi Safta y todas mis lindas tias en Lima. V'ha Dodim sheli b'Aretz. And Alex. The sound of your laughter is what put pen to paper and fingertips to keyboard, and now there is a book! Hence: your fault. But long drives to Grumpy's, next to you, is still my favorite way to spend a Sunday.

And to the reader with a just cause and a passion—always keep fighting.

YOGURT IS ALIVE

ANTI-ROBOTICS

iStand
Against
Robots

RECYCLING

YES WE
CAN!

Save the World With Song

ZOMBIE ATTACK

MOMMY COULD
BE A ZOMBIE

DOWN WITH STYROFOAM

EAT DIRT

IT'S NATURAL!

SEAT BELT SAFETY

SEAT BELTS: A HU
FROM YOUR CAI

YOGURT IS ALIVE

ANTI-ROBOTICS

iStand
Against
Robots

RECYCLING

YES WE
CAN!

Save the World With Song

ZOMBIE ATTACK

MOMMY COULD
BE A ZOMBIE

DOWN WITH STYROFOAM

EAT DIRT

IT'S NATURAL!

SEAT BELT SAFETY

SEAT BELTS: A HU
FROM YOUR CAI